D1344982

Doggart and Fen

Attica

Jigsaw

JIGSAW

Garry Kilworth

www.atombooks.co.uk

First published in Great Britain in 2007 by Atom
This edition published in 2008 by Atom

Copyright © Garry Kilworth 2007

The moral right of the author has been asserted.

A CIP catalogue record for this book
is available from the British Library.

ISBN 978-1-904233-77-0

Papers used by Atom are natural, recyclable products made from
wood grown in sustainable forests and certified in accordance with
the rules of the Forest Stewardship Council.

Typeset in Tekton by M Rules
Printed and bound in Great Britain by
Mackays of Chatham Ltd, Chatham, Kent
Paper supplied by Hellefoss AS, Norway

Atom
An imprint of
Little, Brown Book Group
100 Victoria Embankment
London EC4Y 0DY

An Hachette Livre UK Company

www.atombooks.co.uk

This novel is for Rob, a fellow firegazer, who has often helped me find some of the shapes in the flames

Acknowledgements

Grateful thanks to my editors Tim Holman and Gabriella Nemeth whose suggestions and advice regarding this novel were invaluable.

Thanks also go to Robert Holdstock. Jigsaw owes its origins in part to the notion of a sequel to *The Ragthorn*, the prizewinning novella I wrote with my friend Rob, which was published in 1988. Rob's obsessions took him down his own paths, as did mine, and the sequel never happened. Rob agreed instantly to any use of those fragmentary thoughts we had, so many years ago, when I recently conceived the broader idea for *Jigsaw*.

'And fabulous beasts filled the earth, sea and sky, born during dark nights and days of blood, when the world was younger than earthquake or flood, and the moon was still an infant . . .'

Ribalus de Charnoc, AD 1411

Call me Max – everybody does.

Welcome to my blog. I travel a lot with my dad and I set this up so you can see what I'm up to. There's also another reason . . .

I have this big secret. Huge. I have lots of secrets of course, who doesn't? But this secret's special. It's time I told you, because stuff like this starts to fight inside you. It's like having a small animal trying to get out. I can't keep it in much longer. It's best I do it now in this way. It's going to get out anyway, somehow.

Here it is then, the whole story. I took it from the diary I kept in Jordan and on Krantu Island. You can believe me or not. I don't care. I know it's true.

29 April, Krantu Island

We were told by Ram that Krantu Island was formed by an underwater volcano. You can see it in the rocks: they're sort of jagged and sharp as chisels: they rip your knee open if you fall on them. Bits of volcano stick up in places, as weird pointed stacks which will probably look like the spires of drowned churches when the island gets covered by seawater. Dad says they remind him of Gothic towers.

Krantu is a good way off the coast of Sarawak, a Malaysian island. No one lives on Krantu anymore and it'll soon sink into the sea. Or the sea'll come up and cover it. I'm not quite sure which. Something to do with global warming maybe, but dad also said the reef is crumbling. A tsunami recently passed over the coral shelf and covered it with sand. Coral polyps are live creatures and I suppose they suffocated. Anyway, most of the reef itself is now dead. Dead stuff just rots away. Inside the reef, in the lagoon itself, some of the coral is still alive though.

When we first arrived we helped dad repair this massive fish-drying shed that the island people had left. There used to be fishermen on Krantu but they moved to somewhere else when this island was threatened. They left a village of sorts, though their huts aren't any good to live in. Mostly made of palm leaves, the walls and roofs have rotted and some have been blasted to bits by storms. There's also a sort of stockade made of thick bamboo poles, probably to keep out the wild hogs, but there are big gaps in it where clumps of the poles have fallen down.

We just moved into the village and made it our own. The fish-drying shed was to be dad's workshop. Dad and Rambuta, the Malaysian zoologist he'd picked up in Kuching on our way through Sarawak. Once they started work I knew we wouldn't see a lot of dad. He gets engrossed.

Repairing the fish-drying shed was fun though. I got to use some great tools. We sawed planks, nailed things together. It was fun somehow, to make a rotten old shed into something weatherproof. And when we had a break, we used to kick a ball around.

Rambutu is a terrific guy. He's a small man, very light on his feet. We have this open square of hard-packed dirt where we play football. Talk about twinkle-toes. Rambuta could give lessons to any top-class striker. His footwork's incredible. He's taught me and Hass some tricks I'd never have learned anywhere else. Dad got annoyed. He said he'd hired Rambuta because he had a p-h-d, not because he had magic feet.

You could see dad was impressed though. He even started playing himself. It was me and Rambuta against dad and Hass. I don't know why, but dad always seems to choose Hass over me. Sometimes it seems he doesn't like me much at all. My nan reckons it's because of mum, but that's not fair. I wasn't even there when mum died. Anyway, I try not to get jealous of Hass. Nan says it's not his fault either.

Whatever, dad was no footballer. Rambuta could take the ball away from him in an instant. It made dad mad as fire. He'd blunder across the pitch, trying to take it back again and end up tripping over his own feet.

We had a lot of fun. That was before the serious work started. Afterwards we hardly saw dad, and Rambuta only for lessons. They were busy making bamboo frameworks for something inside the fish-drying shed. They wouldn't say what. Not that I was that interested.

Hass and I went off and did our own thing in the rainforest, and in the lagoon.

1 May, Krantu Island

Trod on a spiny anemone and my foot puffed up like a balloon. Ram put some ointment on it which made it burn, but it went down again. Had to stay sat in one place till I could walk. Boring. Boring.

2 May, Krantu Island

This is just like when I went on digs. Dad is up to his eyeballs in work and hasn't any time to eat even. In fact it's worse. He never seems to come out of that fish-drying shed. As usual something strange is going on, but I don't dare ask what. Dad would just tell me to mind my own business and when I ask Ram he says, ~ It's not up to me to say anything to you, Max. That's something for your father.

So here we are, up to our ears in work and secrets, just like in Jordan, where I first met Hass. Even there, in the desert of Qumran, we were able to make our own fun, Hass and I. Maybe this is a good place to say what went on there, when dad went crazy over a new find.

My dad has spent most of his life in the deserts of Jordan and Syria, looking for old things: weapons and pots and stuff. Mum too, when she was alive. They both discovered some pretty mean artefacts. Most of them are in museums now, or in universities, or somewhere like that. I was quite proud of my parents, though I never said so. I just sort of bragged about them to kids at school, even when I was younger. I have this joke which came from me boasting about him. Some kid said his dad was a famous caver and had discovered a new cave in Brazil. I told him my dad was famous for finding ancient weapons.

~ What then? asked this kid. ~ What's he found?

I searched my brain for a name, but nothing would come – my head had gone empty, the way it does in moments like this.

~ Wouldn't you like to know, I said weakly.

~ Yes, I would, said the kid, folding his arms as other kids gathered round us. ~ You tell us just *one* rare weapon your famous dad found.

~ He found . . . I had just come from an RI lesson, and I grinned as I thought of it ~ . . . he found the axe of the apostles.

The other kids burst out laughing.

The axe of the apostles.

I still smile to myself about that now. I told dad at the time but he didn't see the joke then and now I think he's forgotten all about it.

I love the desert. Everything seems so clean and clear out there: the space between earth and the stars, the moonbeams amongst the rocks, even the very dust itself seems cleaner. And the sounds! Kids at my school back home who haven't been to the desert think it's a silent place. It isn't. Not at all. It's quiet, but in that quietness you can hear lizards rattling the gravel and birds turning over stones. There are creatures calling each other: scruffy pi-dogs, brown kites with ragged wings. Even the beetles make noises, clambering over the gravel. Some beetles are as big as your fist, with a back as hard as a bullet. These sounds aren't threatening, not to me anyway. They're kind of comforting, like hearing your parents moving downstairs when you wake from a bad dream, or the milkman coming in the early dawn. Good sounds.

~ When are you going to bed? asked my dad one night, looking up from his work as if only just noticing I was there. ~ It's past midnight.

~ I know. Just a few more pages.

~ All right. He went to his laptop computer, connected online through a satellite. ~ I'll send a few emails, but when I'm finished we really must pack.

My dad's an archaeologist. He says he's one of the lucky ones, who gets to do what he does best. This was his patch, the Middle East. Three years ago he was in Syria and found a load of old weapons that the British Museum went mad over. Then it was Jordan, a place called Qumran. There's lots of wadis — dry river beds — where there used to be towns back in ancient times. This dig was pretty boring so far as I was concerned. Only jars and agricultural tools. An adze. A thing for prising out roots of stubborn shrubs. Not much more. No swords or spearheads, like at the dig in Syria.

I kept reading, hoping dad would forget about me once he started studying the pottery again. But the yellow light of the bulb run by the generator was dimming and straining my eyes. The current needed turning up and if I asked him to do it, he would definitely give me marching orders. At that moment though, the flap opened and one of dad's Jordanian colleagues came in.

~ James, said Professor Ahmed, ~ we have a visitor.

Dad's eyebrows went up. ~ At this time of night? Then when he saw how serious Professor Ahmed's expression was, he said sharply, ~ What is it?

I knew straight away that he was thinking that it might be terrorists, or bandits, come to cause trouble.

6

Professor Ahmed must have caught the anxiety in dad's voice because he replied, ~ It's nothing bad, James — it's a goat-boy. He says he wants to see you.

~ Good lord! Doesn't he sleep?

Professor Ahmed shrugged and smiled. ~ He's a goatherd. He watches his goats.

~ Oh, yes. Yes of course. Bring him in then, though I can't think what . . . never mind, bring him in.

The professor lifted the flap higher and motioned with his arm, out into the night desert.

~ Taal hinna, he called to someone, meaning 'come here'.

A young Arab boy entered. He was about my age, maybe a bit older. He had a thin face with brown eyes set wide. Those eyes glanced at me and were a bit scathing, I thought, bloody cheek. His body wasn't broad, like mine, at the shoulders. It was sort of lean and whippy, especially about the wrists and ankles. There was white trail dust on his face and arms, and all the way up his legs from his bare feet. He needed a shower, but he didn't smell. It was clean desert dust. Not dirt.

When he'd run his eyes over this kid in the knee-length surfers and Arctic Monkeys T-shirt, he turned back to dad again.

You could see this was a kid who wouldn't take to being messed about. He had that sort of grown-up look of a boy twice his real age. I learned later that, not like me at all, he'd had some tough times and had had to grow up fast.

The boy was carrying a big urn which looked quite heavy. He put the pot on the ground and faced dad, at the same time as unwinding the ragged scarf he had on his head. At that moment someone called to Professor Ahmed that one of the camels was sick. I was pleased my Arabic was good enough to pick up the words. The professor grunted.

~ Excuse me, James.

~ Of course, said dad. ~ I'll deal with the lad.

~ Sir, said the goatherd in a hoarse whisper, once Ahmed had left the tent, ~ I bring you something very valuable. Very old.

~ You have remarkably good English for a watcher of goats, dad said to him. ~ Where did you learn?

The boy stiffened slightly. ~ My father was a teacher, he said, ~ in a school in Amman. He taught me well.

~ Indeed he did.

The kid seemed to think he needed to explain further.

~ My father was killed in an accident. I have no mother – she too died, when I was born. I was sent to my uncle, out here.

~ Your uncle owns herds of goats?

~ My uncle is a rich man with a big house, but he does not like me, so he sends me to a farm. I must work for the farmer.

~ I think I understand. Now, what have you brought me? This magnificent urn? It does indeed look quite valuable . . .

It seemed to me from his tone of voice that he was feeling sorry for this Jordanian boy. Me, I wondered whether this kid was just putting it on. Making up this sob story to get more money. Maybe the pot was worth something, maybe not, but dad was going to buy it from him anyway. Dad bent down and studied the pot, running his hand over it, tracing a pattern with a fingernail.

~ This design . . . he began, but the boy interrupted him.

~ Not the pot, sir – there is something inside.

Dad looked up at him quickly, studying his face in the sallow light of the lamp.

I stepped forward quickly, crickets buzzing in my ears.

~ A snake?' I cried. ~ Have you got a snake?

Why I yelled that, I don't know, but snakes had always been a thing with me. Local people, when they caught snakes, often put them in pots like this to carry them somewhere. It's not that I'm scared of snakes. I am a bit, the poisonous ones, but they excite me. It's the way they move in the sand, sliding along without any effort at all. It's the patterns on their backs and the way they shine in the sunlight.

The boy turned and looked at me again. There was utter contempt in his gaze.

~ A snake? he said. ~ Why would I bring a snake?

~ I dunno, I replied weakly, shrugging. Then rallying my own form of schoolboy contempt, ~ I give in. Why would you?

~ Don't be stupid, Max, dad said. ~ Have some common sense.

The two of them then ignored me, the boy saying to dad, ~ Please, sir, look in the urn. You will find skins. Goatskins, with writings on them. I found them in a cave in the mountains. There are twelve, sir. The writings look very, very old. Even I, a teacher's son, cannot read them.

Dad's eyes widened. I wasn't my father's son for nothing. I knew immediately what he was thinking. He'd told me time and time again that this was the area in which the Dead Sea Scrolls had been found. And other such writings. The story dad told me was this:

A bedu shepherd boy named Muhammad-the-Wolf (what a cool name! – what I'd give to have a name like that! – imagine your teacher calling that out in class) found the Dead Sea Scrolls in a cave after one of his flock went missing. The treasures were in sealed earthenware jars, a total of seven, wrapped in linen. There were other scrolls (more interesting I would think); one was called the War Scroll, on which there were lists of armies and weapons and battle plans. It said things like *'the sons of light fought a ferocious war with the sons of darkness'*. Really cool stuff like that. Like something out of a fantasy film.

Anyway, if you wanted to find ancient documents, this was the place to do it, and it seemed like history had repeated itself, as they say.

Dad reached inside the jar.

5 May, Krantu Island

Krantu Island is our tropical paradise, with lots of play and only a few hours each day of school work from Rambuta, thank you very much St Thomas Aquinas (Patron Saint of Education). Hass and I, we still wonder what's going on in that shed, but we've given up asking. Dad won't tell us and neither will Ram. We boys are forbidden to go anywhere near it and have been told that if we do we'll be sent back home to England straight away and our feet won't touch the ground.

That shed is a sort of dark temple into which my dad disappears each day. It's like, say, a demon's castle on top of a hill that you can't climb, or something at the bottom of a hell-deep chasm in a place no ropes are long enough to reach.

Not being allowed to look inside makes us desperate to look, but we know if we do the worst thing in the world will happen. We'll be banished from our island, never to return. I always thought banishment was a soft punishment, when I read about it in stories — much less terrible than death by execution — but now that I've found somewhere I really like, I've changed my mind.

I spat out my snorkel.

~ Did you see that stingray? I cried to Hass, coming up for air in the lagoon. ~ It was massive. Big as a coffee table.

We were snorkelling above the coral. There were hundreds of different types of fish in the crystal-clear water below us. Fish of all shapes and so many colours they dazzled you. The deadly ones were the most interesting. Lion fish with their poisonous spines; ugly warty stonefish with their kill-you-in-two-minutes dorsal spikes; sea snakes fifty times more venomous than a king cobra. They all swam through coral gardens that took your breath away. Brain coral, stagshead coral, fan coral — you name it, we had it here, all to ourselves.

~ What's that?

Hass was treading water, his face mask pushed up on to his forehead, his snorkel dangling.

He was pointing out over the reef.

I pushed up my mask and followed the finger. At first I could see nothing. The waves crashing on the reef were often a metre or more high and you had to wait for a lull. Then I saw it. A white sail on the horizon, dipping and rising through the troughs.

~ It's only a boat, I said. ~ Some kind of yacht.

~ It's coming this way.

~ Nah. Nobody's allowed to come here now. You heard what dad said. We're the only ones who've been given permission to stay here.

~ Maybe it's in trouble, Max? Or they're running short of water?

~ Who cares? Come on, have a look at this stingray. He's

settled between two rocks. You can see his eyes sticking up out of the sand . . .

Later though, when we walked back towards the camp inside the rainforest edge, we saw the boat again. It was moored inside the reef. The sail was down and I could see a tall man moving about the deck.

~ Dad won't be happy about this, I murmured to Hassan. ~ You wait.

Sure enough, he wasn't.

~ A *what*? he cried.

~ A yacht. A biggish one. 'Sout there now, in the lagoon.

Dad's hands went on his hips and he stared in the direction of the boat as if he could see through the rainforest trees.

~ Hass reckons they might be just taking on water, I suggested. ~ Didn't you, Hass?

Dad's face cleared a bit. ~ Ah, yes, that'll be it. Of course. Well done, Hassan. I was just about to march over there and make a fool of myself. Water. Yes, that'll be it.

But it wasn't it. Two hours later the tall man I had seen on the deck of the yacht appeared in the clearing. Dad was just coming out of the big shed and on seeing the man he slammed the double-doors shut with a *bang*. The man strode towards him with an outstretched hand, with what dad always called 'a company smile' on his face. The sort of smile bank managers and insurance men have when you first meet them.

~ Grant Porter, said the man in an American accent. ~ It seems we're to be neighbours for a while.

Dad ignored the hand.

~ This is private property, said dad. ~ You need permission to make a landfall here.

The smile instantly vanished.

~ Is that so? Well, it just so happens I *do* have permission.

Dad's hands went on his hips.

~ From whom, may I ask?

~ From the Malaysian government.

Dad said, ~ I was assured by the Office of Island Administration in Sarawak that we would not be disturbed here.

~ And my authority comes from Kuala Lumpur, the central government offices. It seems you only have local authority, whilst I have it from the top. What *do* you think about that, then?

Mr Porter's tone was very belligerent now. I knew something about Americans from the US expat kids who'd boarded at my school. When you first met them they almost always proffered the hand of friendship. But if it was rejected they turned really nasty. Dad had to watch himself; this Yank was twice as big as him. And dad was no good at fist fighting. He had a brain as big as a cathedral but even I could get the better of him in a rough-and-tumble these days.

However, Mr Porter turned out to be a gentleman. Like dad, he seemed to prefer words to fists.

~ Now see here, dad said, ~ I'm in the middle of a very – an important experiment here. I can't have strangers running about willy-nilly disturbing my concentration. You'll have to find another island. This one's about to disappear into the sea, in any case, so whatever it is that you've come here for you won't find it. It'll be gone soon.

Porter said, ~ It's precisely for that reason I *have* come here, and I have no intention of leaving for somewhere else. My papers state I have permission to remain here until I see fit to leave or six months have expired. How about *that* then?

With that the American stormed off, down the rainforest path, back towards the lagoon.

~ Bloody cheek! cried dad, kicking a lump of wood in anger. ~ Who the hell does he think he is?

Rambuta tried to calm things down.

~ James, he said, ~ if he has permission there's nothing we can do about it.

~ If he comes near this camp again, dad fumed, picking up the lump of wood, ~ I'll brain him.

Hassan then spoke up. ~ We must kill them, he said quietly. ~ It is the right thing to do. When your family is threatened . . .

My eyes opened wide. Hass was serious.

This reaction from his adopted son stopped dad in his tracks. It seemed he had gone too far. He was always talking about the differences in culture that mattered.

~ Hassan, he said, now in a calm tone, ~ I didn't mean what I said – about braining him. It's just an expression.

Hassan suddenly grinned and his eyes glistened with delight. ~ I had you both there.

I heaved a sigh of relief and punched my brother on the arm. Hass had been kidding. But dad didn't see the humour. He simply carried on with what he'd been saying.

~ If the man has permission from the authorities then there's nothing we can do about it. We must suffer in silence. But we needn't have anything to do with this intruder. I want you two boys to avoid him and anyone else from his yacht. Is he alone?

~ We didn't see anyone else, I answered.

~ So, he's most likely a lone yachtsman. Good. Avoid him. But Hassan – no violence. Do you understand? As your father, I forbid it.

Hassan nodded, widening his eyes at me and shrugging his shoulders. He wondered why dad took him seriously and where his joke had gone wrong. I explained later that it was very difficult to wake dad's sense of humour. It slept in a deep part of his brain. You had to hit him around the head with a joke like a wet fish to get it out of bed.

~ Come on, I said afterwards, ~ let's go and have another look at the yacht.

We raced along the path to the beach. It was a brief but brilliant red sunset. We were so often tossed such quick sunsets we now took them for granted. The white coral-sanded beach glistened in the soft warm evening air. Fiddler crabs dived down their holes as we leapt over a fallen coconut palm. Hermit crabs paraded the strand in their stolen homes. We raced along the edge of the surf to the point on the headland, there to stare out at the expensive-looking craft that swayed gently on the lagoon.

There was someone with Mr Porter. A woman was on deck with him, coiling ropes and fastening sheets. His wife or girlfriend, probably. She was about half his size and was plumpish and pleasant-looking. Like him she looked tanned and weathered by sea winds. Her hair was awry, probably stiff with salt. She had on the shortest white shorts I'd ever seen on anyone, and a man's shirt, the tails tied in a bow in the front.

When she straightened up she saw us watching her. There was a moment's hesitation, then she smiled and waved.

Without thinking, I waved back.

~ Traitor! whispered Hass.

~ Well, I said defensively, ~ it's only good manners.

~ They are our father's enemies.

~ Nah, I replied, ~ they're just unwelcome neighbours. Race you to the old log!

I ran off, along the beach to the massive white stranded driftwood log that had once been a massive brown living tree. Even on its side it rose over two metres from the sand: a waist that Moby Dick would have been jealous of. It was the skeleton of a giant tropical tree which had floated to our island. We could only get on top by climbing up through the sun-bleached network of branches and broken boughs of this pale ghost. This was our den, our meeting place, our parliament. From its highest point we could see far across the blue expanse of ocean.

A great lookout point.

A place to chill out.

As for Mr and Mrs Porter, I was embarrassed that we had been caught staring and embarrassed that I'd returned the wave. I always do that. I do things automatically. Yet when someone has a go at me I'm never quick enough to make a smart reply. It's sometimes years later when I think, I should have said such-and-such, *that* would've shut him up.

Why do I act quickly in some things, but can't do it when it matters? It's frustrating. I hate it. I wish I was clever.

6 May, Krantu Island

Told to stay in camp all day and study *Far From the Madding Crowd* by Tom Hardy. Dad said this wasn't punishment, but it felt like it. He said it was education and to stop us from running wild. Read the bit where Sergeant Troy dumps Bathsheba.

Sad, but if I'd got a girlfriend with a name like that I'd probably dump her too.

7 May, Krantu Island

Although the beach is our main playground, me and Hass spend a lot of time in the rainforest. In the middle of the island there are these ruins. Mum had told me Polynesians were in the Pacific, but Ram says these aren't Polynesian. He says Polynesia's further east than we are. Anyway, there's a sort of stone roof held up by four wooden pillars covered in carvings. Dad says not to go inside the temple because it was dangerous. The wooden pillars are rotten, he says. It's only a matter of time before the structure collapses.

We go in anyway. We dare each other to run under the temple. The one who's been dared then makes a dash while the one on the outside yells things like, ~ It's coming down. You're gonna die. You're gonna get crushed to death. You'll be squashed flat.

Alongside the temple is a raised platform. Rambuta told us this is an altar for human sacrifices. The black stains on it are old blood.

~ Most Sacred, Most Feared, was the way they viewed their dark gods. They would take the most handsome, the most exceptional youth or maiden, the most loved young person among them, and sacrifice them to their ancestors, to their past heroes and to their death-demanding deities, Rambuta told us. ~ It was a long time in the past of course. At least a hundred and fifty years ago.

17

A hundred and fifty years! That didn't sound so old.

~ Why the most loved? Hassan asked.

~ Because to sacrifice someone you don't care about is no sacrifice at all. It must be someone who means a lot to you.

I said, ~ Sounds a bit daft to me.

But I found myself shivering.

~ You have to remember, Rambuta said, ~ these people were very superstitious. They came here over thousands of miles of oceans in huge canoes. They had no charts, no instruments with which to navigate. Instead they used the stars, the colour of the sea, wild birds, the direction of the waves and other natural elements as their instruments. When they reached here, despite storm and tempest, despite hunger and thirst, they had to find some reason for their good fortune. They chose to believe the gods had guided them. Sacrifices were made to these gods, to show them how grateful the people were for giving them a fruitful island.

Dark gods! Yes, we could see that. We could sense them in a place like this.

A few days after the Porter yacht had arrived Hass and I were playing in the ruins. We'd become a little wild since we'd come to the island. We wore nothing but a pair of swimming trunks each. More often than not our bodies were filthy from falling on the forest floor. We carried assegais dad had brought back from South Africa. Assegais are Zulu weapons, with long blades and short handles, ~ Similar to the Roman short sword, dad told us, ~ they're not throwing spears, they're for stabbing.

Hass and I thought assegais were great for using in the rainforest. We were hunter-warriors and let everyone know it with our yells.

We chased wild bearded hogs with our assegais in the hope of killing one for supper. It was a futile hope. They were much too quick for us and we were scared of the boars. They were big. Big as St Bernard dogs. The long grey beards on their faces made them look like strange old men with small piercing eyes. Rambuta had told us they could bite through a seven-centimetre log their jaws were so strong.

~ They could bite right through your leg! said Hass, adding in his usual graphic fashion, ~ All they'd leave is a bloody stump.

That morning we had a taste of their temperament.

We found a boar grazing near the temple. The young boars were very quick, the sows even quicker. But this old boar looked like a slow lazy fellow. He lumbered when he walked. He breathed heavily, snorted a lot, and we knew the eyesight of these creatures was very poor. If you came at them from downwind they didn't know you were there until you were two or three metres from them.

~ We will do it this way, whispered Hass. ~ I will stun him first with my slingshot. Then we will rush in and finish him off.

~ Will that work? I asked doubtfully.

Hass stood tall. ~ I am a deadshot, he said. ~ I will strike him on the head and he will go down like a felled tree.

My heart was beating fast. ~ If you say so.

I imagined us carrying the carcass into camp, slung upside down on a long pole.

~ Wow, dad would say, ~ you boys made a kill, eh? Well done. We'll barbecue him for supper tonight. You get the choice pieces of meat, since you're the hunters . . .

Or something like that.

Hass fitted a stone into his sling. He whirled the sling

around his head. The humming noise made the hog look up. His tiny deep piggy eyes tried to penetrate the forest edge. Finally released, the stone went flying through the air. It struck the old devil cleanly on the brow. But he must have had a skull as strong and thick as a castle wall.

Instead of dropping to its knees the boar went mad.

It let out a terrible shriek that would have frozen a grown man to the spot.

Instantly it began to charge around the clearing in ever-increasing circles, looking for its attackers.

~ Run! cried Hass in fright.

I didn't need him to tell me anything. I ran, thrashing noises all around me.

Hass and I both flew off in different directions, hoping the boar would chase the other one.

I dropped my spear. I headed for the beach, thinking to jump into the water and swim. Blundering through the undergrowth I lost my sense of direction. In my fear I didn't stop to think. My legs wouldn't let me. My racing heart wouldn't let me. I became a victim of my own terror. Every vine, every rattan creeper, seemed intent on impeding me. They wrapped around my ankles. They whipped my face. I was scratched and scraped everywhere. Blood mingled with the dirt on my body. I scrambled through dense vegetation, not caring if I was torn.

At one point I fell and dived into the undergrowth. My face hit one of those carnivorous pitcher-plants chock-full of stagnant water. They always have this black raft of rotting flies floating on top. The foul gunge splashed up my nose, in my mouth, in my hair. I spat and rasped, horrified that I would get some deadly disease from the smelly sludge. Then I was up on my feet again, and running, running, running.

Finally I blundered out of the dark musty world beneath the canopy on to the sunlit beach with its dazzling sands.

I stood there, gulping down breath for a few moments, trying to get used to the brilliance. Bright blades of light were ricocheting off white foam and coral sands and piercing my eyes. It was almost painful to lift the lids. When my sight came back at last I was shocked to see someone sitting on our parliament log.

~ Hi! You need a wash. Oh my God, you're *covered* in blood. You've got scratches everywhere. Look at your hair! You're filthy. Did you fall in the mangrove swamp? You'd better go in the water or those cuts will go septic — the salt will sting like mad, but you need to wash that dirt off, boy. Go on! In you go.

The vision was misty, hazy. It was a girl. A girl in shorts and T-shirt. She was staring at me with an amused expression on her face.

My terror was gone, indignation in its place.

~ Eh? I said. I have always been good with words when it comes to the opposite sex. ~ What?

~ You're disgustingly filthy.

~ That's our log, I said. ~ We found it first.

Our log had been bleached by sun, salt and sea. Our fort. Our camp. Our laager. It was ours.

~ This old thing? She looked down but made no attempt to rise. ~ Why, it belongs to nature, not you.

She had a soft American accent which was almost musical.

~ Bugger nature, I said impolitely. ~ That's ours.

She patted the drift-tree, studying it.

21

~ What is it, your ship? Your galleon?

~ Never you mind.

My annoyance was starting to fade. I was suddenly aware of what I looked like. Here I was in just a pair of old swimming trunks. My hair was full of bits of twig. There were cuts and bruises all over me. I stank of rotting leaves and pig poo. I was dirty from head to foot and sweating like a donkey. I had decomposing flies sticking to my face.

On the other hand the girl looked like a Walt Disney princess. She had long blonde hair, blue eyes, a flawless skin, and she wouldn't need to wash for at least another three months. If she sat where she was, in the cool breeze, untouched by the rest of the world, she probably wouldn't need to bathe ever again.

~ You're staring, she said. ~ Oh, hello, another one.

Hassan had come tumbling out of the rainforest. He still had his spear in his hand. It must have seemed to the girl that Hass was hunting me. Hass didn't see her. He spoke breathlessly to me.

~ I nearly got . . . He pointed back into the green darkness, but stopped in mid-sentence on finally noticing the girl and asked, ~ Who's she?

~ She is the cat's mother, said the girl, ~ whereas my name is Georgia. You must be the boys of those two men who were rude to my father. We were very upset by that, you know. Your fathers should learn good social behaviour. Social grace is what separates man from the animalwheeeeaaaaaaaaahhhhh-hhhhhh . . .

Georgia squealed at the same time she jumped up on top of the drift-tree. She scrambled to the tallest end. We were swift in joining her. A snorting and angry bearded hog had come crashing from the rainforest hot on the trail of Hassan. It stood still for a moment. They didn't see very well, these pigs, but they had a terrific sense of smell. Our pursuer snorted and raged around the tree, gradually losing our scent in the dry sea breezes. Eventually it calmed down, sniffed for a while around the roots of our fortress, and then ambled back into the rainforest.

~ Thug! I called after it, making the other two laugh.

The ice broken, we decided to hang with Georgia. We started in on histories. Georgia was, as she had told us, the daughter of Mr and Mrs Porter. Her father was a jeweller and yachting was his hobby. He had taken a long vacation to attempt to find some black coral, to be used in making jewellery. Only dead black coral could be harvested, since it was illegal to kill coral of any kind. The Porters had learned that this island, Krantu, had some such coral. The family had brought scuba gear to investigate the possibility.

~ Why were your dads so rude to mine? she asked. ~ It makes it very awkward for all of us.

~ Dads? I questioned. ~ We have the same father – Hass is my adopted brother.

~ Oh, I naturally thought . . . and we knew she had in mind the darker-skinned Rambuta.

~ No, Hass said, ~ we're brothers.

~ How wonderful for you, she said politely.

~ Hass is a Muslim, I told her. ~ He comes from Jordan.

~ And Max is an Infidel, joked Hassan. ~ He comes from the land of Infidels.

~ So you're Hass and Max?

~ Yep, I said.

23

~ Hass is short for Hassan, said my brother, a bit stiffly, I thought. But then his name is more important to him than mine is to me.

She smiled. ~ And Max is short for . . . ?

~ You don't want to know, I replied. ~ It's a million times longer.

Amazingly, she got the joke straight away. ~ Oh, I get it – Maximilian – he was an emperor of Mexico, you know, in the nineteenth century.

We blinked.

There was silence for a bit, then Georgia said, ~ Was that a bit geeky?

~ Only a lot, I replied.

~ It doesn't matter, she said, making a face at me, ~ because I can swim better than either of you.

~ Who says so? cried Hass.

~ I do, she laughed. With that she leapt off the log and ran down to the lagoon. Within seconds she was doing the crawl better than I'd ever seen it done. Better, I had to say, than Hass or me could do it, though I'd never admit it to her. ~ I'm from California, she yelled back at us. ~ I can swim like a dolphin. How's that for a geek?

I wasn't sure girls could be geeks but we laughed at that. Then Hass and I went for a swim. The blood and dirt was getting a bit crusty and we washed it off. Once we'd been in the water, we were fit for anything. I slicked down my hair with my hand, hating the fact that when it dried it would bush up all curly and frizzy. We had both been toasted a bronze colour, Hass and me. The hairs on my legs and arms had bleached a golden colour. When we scratched our skins it left white salt marks. We made patterns like tattoos on our arms and legs. Dad said we were walking hieroglyphs. We were the kings of this small island and we knew it.

Back on the beach I bragged to this marvellous girl, ~ Yeah, we've been hunting wild boar. We're pretty good at it, usually, but that beggar was a big one.

~ I saw. She sat on the sand hugging her brown knees. ~ However, I should tell you I don't approve of killing defenceless wild creatures.

~ Defenceless? I echoed. ~ He could've bitten us in half . . .

We stayed the rest of the day, chatting to Georgia. She told us she came from San Francisco, in California. Her parents had allowed her to take time off school for this trip, but her mother was tutoring her in the lessons she was missing.

I said, ~ Rambuta's doing the same with us. He gives us lessons from six in the morning to eleven. The rest of the day's ours.

~ Six? That's early.

~ Not in the rainforest, it isn't. You sleep on the yacht. All you hear are the waves breaking on the reef. And it's always there, always the same. We get the noisiest birds and the cicadas and the animals. Some of the insects sound like buzz-saws — really, really loud. They all wake up when the sun hits them and they make sure we wake up too.

We were getting on well with her, both of us vying for her attention, until that mention of the rainforest.

~ My boyfriend, Bradley, has done a trek in the rainforest, in Thailand, she said. ~ Brad's been backpacking in the Amazon too.

Hass and I looked away. One of us out to sea. The other up

at the canopy. She had a boyfriend. This angel from the sea had a boyfriend called *Brad*.

~ Sounds like a surname, Bradley, I said. ~ Doesn't sound like a first name at all.

~ Well it is, she snapped, sensing the sneer in my tone. ~ I like it.

~ Good for you. Well, Hass — we need to get back. Cheers, Georgia. Come and chill anytime.

~ I will, she said.

Without waiting for a reply I ran up the beach. Hass followed me. He still had his assegai but I had dropped mine back at the temple. It was still light enough to fetch it, though the sun drops down like a brick at six sharp in these regions. There's no twilight at all, just a quick sunset. One minute it's daylight, the next minute it's black.

When we reached the temple the darkness had indeed come. Luckily there was a moon. We found our way through the glade. I caught the glint of my spear in the beams that slanted through the canopy. It was an eerie feeling, being in that temple glade at night. Hass didn't help things by whispering, ~ You can smell the evil in the air here.

~ Shuttup! I said, nervously, picking up my spear. ~ What are you, physic?

~ You mean something else.

~ Well, whatever I mean, I don't . . . I stopped in mid-sentence and peered at the temple.

It was gone.

At least the roof had gone.

We both crept forward warily. Indeed, the roof had fallen down at last. One of the pillars had been knocked aside. On closer inspection we could see a leg sticking out from under the massive stone. It had a trotter on the end of it. Squashed. That bearded hog boar had been flattened. It must have come back to graze and bumped against the pillar. Now it was just a splattered lump under that enormous roofing-stone.

~ Shall we take the leg back? asked Hassan quietly. ~ Or just let it rest?

~ Doomed. That old pig was destined to die today.

We left it where it lay. Let the ants feed on it. I had a giddy moment when I thought that could easily have been my leg sticking out from underneath that stone. I imagined Hassan taking my sandal back to dad and telling him that was all that was left of Max Sanders. Later I dreamed that dad tried to put me back together, like a jigsaw, in the fish-drying shed, starting with the sandal. *We need more pieces,* he called to Rambuta. *We need the other leg.* When Rambuta told him the other leg was as flat as a flounder, dad went into a rage. *Well, pump it up then, man. Pump it up. Do I have to do everything around here?*

13 May, Krantu Island

Schoolwork, but at least we got Ram going on another red herring. It wasn't long after meeting Rambuta that me and Hass learned he was interested in fables, legends, folk lore and all that stuff. Today we were doing the Ancient Egyptians and so I winked at Hass and then asked Ram where the sphinx had come from. Ram frowned and asked me what I meant.

~ I mean, did they invent it – the Egyptians?

~ That's one theory, but there is another, replied Ram.

He went on to explain that mythical creatures might have originated deep in our subconscious: perhaps we had a need for fabulous beasts to enrich our lives. Another theory was that mythical beasts actually did inhabit the Earth once upon a time, but had died or been wiped out.

~ Wouldn't we find the bones – like we do dinosaurs' bones? Hassan said.

Ram shrugged. ~ Perhaps their genetic makeup was so different from ours they had a different chemical base. Maybe not only their flesh rots but their bones crumble to dust.

~ Did someone say that? I asked.

We had him hooked. I knew that because his expression changed. He went into deep thought as he spoke. Hass nodded at me. Yes, we had Ram going on his favourite subject. It was as if we weren't there.

~ There is an ancient fable, Ram murmured, ~ which tells of a great creature similar to the musk-ox of today. A huge solitary beast with massive horns, big brown eyes and dreadlocks hanging from its back. Unique. One of one and all alone. It is said this creature gave birth to all the mythological creatures in the world – the gryphon, Pegasus, the basilisk – and all the rest. When this mother Beast died, so ended the birth of mythological creatures. They too died, there being only one of each. They crumbled to dust. They say also that this creature has the power of the phoenix, to rise again from the dead, one day to walk again on the earth . . .

Ram had a dreamy expression on his face. Whilst he was telling us this fantastic tale he stared out into the middle distance, as if remembering something in his childhood.

~ Where did you hear that story? asked Hass.

Ram suddenly seemed to wake up. He smiled at Hass and me.

~ Oh, I heard it a long time ago, from my grandfather, who heard it from his grandfather. And so on, and so on. It has been something of an obsession with me – well, perhaps obsession is the wrong word. I have written a paper on it, which your father read and that paper is partly responsible for me being here on Krantu, teaching you young mudfish about the Egyptians. Well, what have you learned, apart from how to divert me from my job of teaching?

We both grinned back at him, knowing we'd been sussed.

~ I thought as much. Well, that's enough of that – back to the Egyptians. Hassan, can you tell me the name of the largest pyramid . . . ?

14 May, Krantu Island

Even before the Porters had arrived Dad had decided to take a short rest from his labours, as he put it. He and Rambuta seemed to spend all their time in the fish-drying shed, doing whatever. We're still forbidden to go in, Hass and me. It's a bit like that time in Jordan, when dad was deciphering scrolls. The shed's out of bounds. What were they doing in there that was so secret? Of course we peeked through cracks in the shed walls, but it was very dim inside – just a 25-watt bulb, black with dead insects that had fried on the hot glass. You couldn't see much. I recognised those bamboo frames dad and Ram had made. They seem to be draping bits of cloth over them. Who knows what they're up to, these weird professors?

Hass and I, we find it pretty creepy when we think about it, but there are too many other things to distract us to think about it for too long. We heard dad and Ram arguing about which was best for their find, the Smithsonian or London's British Museum. But what find? The scrolls? Surely they'd been sent off somewhere long ago? Maybe it was something dad found *written* in the scrolls? Who knows?

One night dad said to Rambuta at supper, ~ I hope Porter realises that harvesting coral without a licence is a very serious offence.

Rambuta had been to the yacht, to speak with Mr Porter.

~ I am sure he has got a licence, father, said Hassan, who never called him 'dad' like me. ~ Mr Porter is a respected jeweller.

Dad's face narrowed. ~ What do you two know about it? he said, eyeing us both suspiciously. ~ You haven't been fraternising with the enemy, have you?

I said, ~ They're not the enemy, dad. They're just people.

~ They're interfering with my work. Do you boys realise how important this is? And how it's necessary to keep it a secret until I'm ready to reveal it to the world? Why do you think we're here on this remote island — for fun? He paused, before going on. ~ You stay away from the Porter yacht, you hear?

Hass and I looked at each other.

~ But dad, I suddenly blurted out. ~ There's this girl . . .

~ Girl?

Ram said, ~ There's a daughter on board the yacht, travelling with the parents.

Dad suddenly screwed his face up. I think he was trying not to laugh.

~ I see, he said. ~ A young maiden. A temptress.

30

~ She's not a temptress, I replied hotly. ~ She's a very nice person. She comes from San Francisco.

~ Oh well, dad said, openly grinning now, ~ that makes all the difference. For a moment there I thought she came from Sacramento, which wouldn't do at all, would it?

~ There's no need to get sarky.

Hass said in a sort of dreamy tone, ~ She is a very beautiful girl — and she spoke with us a long time.

~ You two — began dad, then he seemed to revise what he was about to say. ~ Okay, here's a ready-made companion for you. I grant that. But you must say *nothing* to her about my work.

~ Dad, I argued, ~ we don't *know* anything about your work.

~ What's this girl's name?

~ Georgia, we chorused, then glared at each other.

~ Say nothing to Georgia about what we're doing here. The project's going well, but I still don't trust that family. You understand? We nodded. ~ Good. Well, he said, ~ you two can be the first to see how our work is progressing. You can both go into the shed after supper. See the results of our progress. I expect you to be very impressed.

He went on a bit.

Dad always needed an admiring public. Professors are worse than actors for that kind of thing. He needed approval. Even if it's just us kids. Mum once called him an *egotist*. She said all men were little boys, but I think she only knew dad. She had loved him to bits of course — many people did — but he was pretty wrapped up in himself and what he was doing. If there had been other people here he wouldn't have bothered with Hass and me, but since there weren't, we were his audience.

We had to go into the shed and make the proper noises — *Oh, wow, that's really cool, dad. And what's that there? Really? Who'd have believed it was possible? This is a first, isn't it, dad? No one's ever done anything like it before, have they? I expect you'll get a knighthood for this, once the world knows you're a genius . . .*

All right, not as o.t.t. as that, but you get what I mean.

After supper Hass and I went to the shed. The generator was pounding away as usual, but there were only a couple of low-wattage bulbs to light the interior of the shed. Dad went in before us and seemed about to let us in with him when his arm came out in front of me.

~ No! he said sharply.

~ What?

~ You can't go in. He bustled us outside again, before we had a chance to get used to the dimness. ~ Away — off you go.

~ Dad . . . I started to protest, but on looking at his face I stopped in mid-sentence. He looked pinched and white. His eyes were almost starting out of his head. ~ Dad, what's the matter?

~ Nothing, nothing, he said quickly, but clearly he was upset. He looked shocked. ~ Fetch Rambuta to me — now!

We did as we were told, but instead of staying outside, we followed Ram into the shed. Dad almost screamed at us, telling us to get out. We left and Ram shut the door. Their voices were loud and urgent, but actually I couldn't understand what they were saying. Then I realised they were speaking in Latin. I had done a little Latin at school and recognised one or two verb endings, but the sense of the conversation was beyond me.

~ Hass, I said, ~ what do you think of all this?

Hassan shrugged. ~ Don't know, he replied. ~ Our father — well, he seemed to see something — in the shed.

~ Yeah, that's what I think. It was the way he stopped dead in front of us. You'd have thought he'd seen a ghost.

~ Perhaps he did. Perhaps he saw a ghost.

Dad finally stopped shouting. The shed door opened. He came out to us.

~ You boys — you must say *nothing* about this to — what's her name? Georgia? Nothing, you understand. If it should leave this island . . .

~ What?

~ Anything connected with my work. You must say nothing at all to anyone. Do I make myself clear?

We nodded dumbly. We knew next to nothing anyway. What did we know? That he and Ram spent hours every day locked in the fish-drying shed? That there was something going on in there that was deadly secret?

Just then I heard a thumping sound from the shed. Then a sort of snuffling. Finally, there was a sort of low moan, like the fog horn of a big ship, but not so loud, not so deep.

Dad glanced back at the shed with an anxious expression on his face.

~ What's that? I asked. ~ Is that an animal?

~ Go and play, dad ordered. ~ I — I have to be busy.

He strode back inside the shed, shutting the doors firmly behind him.

~ You're always busy! I yelled after him, my temper getting the better of me.

Hass said, ~ You must not speak to our father like that — respect, Max. More respect.

33

~ Respect buggery, I snarled, and stamped off towards the beach to get a cool dip in the sea.

As I walked down the forest path, I felt annoyed and cheated. Once more we were on the outside, like that time in Jordan, when dad had yelled at us for messing around with the scroll hides and then wouldn't let us go into his trailer again. Were they connected, that time and this? Who knew when you had a father like mine. He hardly ever spoke to me unless it was to tell me off about something. If it wasn't that it was 'Feed the goats' or 'Chop the firewood'. Nothing good.

Secrets, secrets. He loved his secrets.

Yet, when you found out what they were, they weren't all that. A few scrolls? So what? They're all over the place, in museums. What's so deadly hush-hush about old goatskins? Load of rubbish if you ask me. What's so important about scrolls, that you have to yell and bawl at people? Professors, they can make you sick at times. They're so flipping important – not.

~ Who does he think he is, I muttered, ~ ordering us about like that?

Hass came up behind me and said piously, ~ You should obey your father at all times.

~ Bugger off! Why?

~ Because he is your father.

~ He's not right all the time. Just because he's older. He doesn't know *everything*, either.

~ But still, he is your father. He must be obeyed. I am very angry with you, Max, for questioning his authority. You should not do this thing. By all means speak back to a mother, but never a father.

~ Bollocks, I said. ~ Anyway, that's sexist.

34

He shook his head. ~ Things are not the same in your country. Why do you not honour your fathers?

~ Because we don't. Not in the same way. I do what he tells me most of the time, but sometimes I think he makes too much of it. He – he respects me for telling him when he's wrong.

~ But he does not love you for it.

That bit into me like a fire ant. I felt my eyes fill with water.

~ What do you know about it?

~ I know what I see. Why would he take another son if he already has one he loves?

That hurt even more.

~ What? What are you saying? He took you in because he wanted to give you a home. He wanted to give you a family. Not because he didn't like me. He felt sorry for you – and – and you'd done him a big favour by bringing him the skin. You just shut up about him and me. You just mind your own business. My voice was hot with rage.

Hass turned away. ~ I'm sorry, Max. I did not mean to anger you. I thought you knew what I am telling you now. If it is a shock, I apologise.

~ It's not a shock. It's just not true.

~ If you say so.

I left him then and went down to the beach. Sitting on the coral sand, with the crabs busy all around me, I stared moodily out over the shining water. How dare he say dad didn't love me! Who did he think he was, coming into our family and making statements like that? He was just jealous because I was a real son and he was merely adopted.

Laughter came from out in the lagoon. I could see the Porter yacht moored about halfway from the beach to the reef. It was all lit up and rocking gently on the wavelets. Voices drifted to me on the night air.

I couldn't understand what was being said but the voices sounded happy. It was like eavesdropping on Tiny Tim's family around the Christmas dinner table. Sometimes I used to think the whole world was happy except me. I heard Georgia's voice, then a soft laugh cut short by the clatter of dishes. Then someone came up from below. Mr Porter. He stood tall on the deck staring out at the Pacific Ocean beyond the reef. There was the flare of a match, then later the smell of cigar smoke drifting across the lagoon. It was somehow comforting, the scent of that smoke.

I relaxed, hoping for a glimpse of Georgia. Would she go up on deck before going to bed? Would she look at the island before she went? Did she like me? Did she like me more than Hassan? Was there any chance she might be my girlfriend one day? These questions swam around my mind, as I sat there and dreamed the impossible.

~ I am sorry, Max.

~ Wha—? I nearly jumped out of my skin.

~ Max, it was wrong of me to say such things.

Hassan. Hassan had come down to join me.

~ Is nowhere private? I grumbled pompously. ~ I came here for a bit of peace and quiet.

~ Do you forgive me, Max?

Ungraciously I said, ~ I suppose so. If you like.

He sat down beside me. ~ You are looking at the yacht?

~ I was just — I wasn't looking anywhere in particular, I answered him, lying back and pointedly staring up at the bright stars in their southern constellations. Georgia's father called them the sky's jewellery. A star fell from the night's ear, dropping down to be lost under the edge of the world. ~ I was just gettin' some peace and quiet.

~ Ah, she is there, looking back at us.

~ What? I sat up quickly and stared at the yacht. All I could see was Mr Porter, his cigar end like a ruby ring on his hand. ~ Where is she?

Hass laughed. ~ Ha! I fool you.

~ You rat. You rotten . . . what did you do that for?

He nodded his head slowly. ~ I know why you come down here. It is to see her. I too come here on my own. Yesterday evening she came on to the boat deck. She was dressed in white things that floated on the wind. He sighed. ~ She looked like the daughter of the moon. She waved to me.

~ She did not! I punched him on the arm.

~ She did. He didn't punch me back so I knew it was true.

~ Well, she would've waved to me, if I've been here.

~ Perhaps.

~ No perhaps about it.

~ If you say so.

~ *There she is . . .*

We were both electrified. Georgia had come up on deck wearing a pair of shorts and T-shirt. She said something to her father. They both giggled. Then her mother came up and wrapped her arms around her daughter's neck from behind her, using Georgia's shoulder to rest her chin. They all continued to look out at sea, lost in their own familyness. It was a cosy scene I wanted to shatter for my own selfish reasons.

Look this way, I prayed. *Wave to me.*

God answered instead. Silver shards suddenly sprayed from

the shallows not three metres from us. My heart thumped. It startled the pair of us. They were there and gone, a shoal of small fish, probably being chased by a predator. The spell of the evening was broken.

~ We'd better get back, I said.

~ All right.

My feelings were still in turmoil. I was beginning to hate Hassan again. He was saying things about my dad and me. And he was after the girl I liked. Why was he with us anyway? He should be back in Jordan where he belonged. That's what I told myself. I simmered. At least, I did until we were on our way back through the rainforest. Then other feelings eclipsed my anger. It wasn't easy to stay mad when that musty darkness closed in around you. You start to think about other things. Things without names. Things without any proper shape.

We walked softly on the spongy ground. Spiders and beetles scattered. A wild pig snorted somewhere. At night it always felt the rainforest harboured twice as many secrets as it did during the day. *Most Sacred, Most Feared.* There were strange animal gods sharing our walk. Rambuta had talked of smelling the stink of ghosts. Ancestor spirits roamed the woods, he had told us, along with Jata, the red-faced crocodile with the body of a man. And Bujang Sembelih, the demon who jumped out of the bushes and cut the throats of night-time strollers. It wasn't easy to tell yourself you thought these stories were a load of rubbish. Not in the hot damp blackness. Not in the shuffling forest.

When we got back to camp I could hear dad saying fiercely to Rambuta, ~ I'll get rid of Porter, don't you worry about that . . .

15 May, Krantu Island

Rambuta, dad, Hass and I all went for a swim today. It was the first time I'd seen dad in trunks. Although his face and legs and arms were brown, his body was as white as flour. He only went in for a short while, then sat in the shade watching us larking about. Oh yes, and when we left camp to go to the beach I'd forgotten my towel and had to go back. I found Grant Porter in the camp. He looked at me a bit funny when we nearly bumped into each other.

~ Were you looking for me and Hass? I asked, thinking dad would have a fit if he saw him near the fish-drying shed.

~ Yes, yes. Have you seen Georgia anywhere?

~ No, I said. ~ Shall I help you look for her?

But he was already leaving the camp and he sort of waved a hand over his shoulder, saying, ~ No, don't worry, I'll find her. She's probably with her mother.

I decided not to tell dad.

17 May, Krantu Island

Dad doesn't like us seeing the Porters, but he's sort of absorbed and he doesn't know where we are half the time. I like them. They're interesting people. Georgia is the most interesting of course, because she's, well, beautiful. Not just beautiful. Brainy too. Hassan would tell you that. Anyone would. Georgia's, well, Georgia. Her being here helps me forget that there's something really quite scary about this place. Something's here, in the rain-forest. It's not just the wind in the leaves. It's not just the shadows. It's not just the dark temples and the giant monitor lizards that drop down from the trees on the path in front of you, when you're least expecting it. All those things worry me, but something else worries me more. There's something here that shouldn't be here. Don't ask me what. I don't know what it is or how it arrived. I hear it at night. I catch little movements in the trees.

It worries me a lot, but I can't talk to dad about it.

He's too busy. Even busier than he was in Jordan. I remember thinking at the time that nobody could work as long and hard as dad did then. But dad seemed happier in Jordan. I remember how his face lit up with pleasure that night when Hassan brought him the scrolls.

The scrolls Hassan had found were all my dad would wish them to be. They were covered in ancient script on one side, with sort of tattooed indigo symbols on the other. You could see how happy he was. He didn't say as much to me, but I could tell all right. I know my dad.

All that night he stayed up and studied the documents. And half of the next day, until he fell over, exhausted. Professor Ahmed and some helpers carried him to his bed in our tent. When he woke up he asked to see Hassan, the goatherd boy. Someone went off in a Land Rover and found him. They brought him back to our camp. Dad then asked Hassan to show him the place where he had found the scrolls. They went off together in the vehicle.

Dad didn't come back for two days. When he did, he had Hassan still with him. He said he had hired Hassan as extra help. Hassan didn't want to go back to the farmer his uncle had sent him to. He said he wanted to work for us, at the dig.

~ I can help your father with the writings, he told me.

I snorted. ~ You can't understand Aramaic.

He looked at me with anger in his eyes, then turned away, saying, ~ I can still help.

Later that day I felt a bit guilty about my bad manners. I went and found Hassan and said I was sorry. He grinned then and slapped my shoulder. ~ Who cares? he said. ~ Listen, I don't have to watch those stupid goats any more. That's all. I have a good job here, in the kitchen, and carrying things.

~ But we won't be here for ever, I warned him. ~ It's only for the summer – then we all have to go home.

His face fell a little, then brightened again.

~ Never mind. What is this summer?

~ You call it the Hot Season.

~ Oh, well, he said airily, ~ that lasts many weeks. Then comes the simoom and maybe you will not be able to go away.

The simoom was a hot, suffocating wind which was said to make men and animals go mad.

~ Oh, we'll go all right, don't you worry about that.

Hassan asked, ~ Which football team do you support?

~ The Tractor Boys, I told him.

He looked blank.

~ Ipswich, I confirmed.

~ Never heard of them, he said. ~ I, on the other hand, he was speaking loftily now, ~ support Manchester United.

I screwed my face up. ~ Surprise me.

~ What's that, Max?

~ Look, I've never met anyone outside Britain who supported any other team.

~ Manchester United is a very great team, Hassan said, puffing out his chest. ~ You should be proud of them.

41

~ Well I ain't. I might think about Arsenal, or even Liverpool, occasionally, but never Man U.

Now that we had talked I quite liked Hassan. He was just a boy like me, with the same enthusiasms. We had a volleyball net out on the sand close to the camp. Hassan soon became pretty good at the game — almost as good as me. In fact he could spike a ball better than me. He could jump higher than a gazelle. Sometimes he overhit, especially on his serve, but I have to say he picked the game up pretty quickly.

I taught him to play volleyball and he showed me the desert.

In the meantime, my dad worked on translating the messages on the goatskins. There were lots of interesting fragments, he said, as he gulped down his breakfast one day, but he wanted to get at the basic truth of the writings. He went over and over them, time and time again. But there was something missing, so he said. ~ It's not the language. I can translate that — it's finding the *meaning* behind the words. The hidden text. That's what's worrying me.

Anyone else would have stopped at just translating the Aramaic, but not my dad. He wanted to get at the truth.

How hard he worked, my dad.

~ Come, Hass said one day, ~ I will show you the cave where I found the jar of scrolls.

~ How far is it? I asked doubtfully. ~ I'm in enough trouble as it is, spilling that curry all over the clean washing.

~ Not far, really. We could run it in two hours.

~ My dad was there two days.

~ He stayed to do his investigations.

~ We'll get hell if we're not back by evening.

~ I can get there and back before nightfall, he said, which was a challenge if ever I heard one.

~ Well then, so can I.

We were wise enough to take a good supply of water. Hassan had been a goatboy out here and knew what he was doing. He also took his sling and I took my catapult. I'd always thought this sling business with shepherds and goatboys was just a bible story thing. But they still do it. Hass was brilliant with his sling. There weren't any lions to kill anymore, or bears or what-ever, but there were poisonous snakes. Dad had told us not to kill anything at all, but who knows what there was out there in the wilderness which might attack us? Hass could hit an empty drink can at twenty metres with that sling of his. I was dead jealous.

We jogged all the way to the dark hills, where there were out-crops and cliffs like at Petra, a city carved out of reddish stone.

The hills around us were sort of scary-looking. Jagged crags hung over sheer drops of crumbling rock. The caves were just holes in the rock face. They looked as if they'd been bur-rowed by a giant rat. Hass called it 'the empty place' and he was right: it was grim and dark and there was no life around. Wind stirred only dust. The shadows were so deep, black and cold you felt you might drown in them. I don't know how Hass slept in this place, when he had his herd of goats to look after. It gave me the creeps. Dad had told me it was an ancient burial ground.

~ Where's this cave then? I said, shivering. ~ They don't look safe.

~ No, no, Max – ours is a big cave. In that gully.

He led me to a place where there was a slope of scree

leading up to a massive cave. It was better than the others I'd seen, but I still didn't like the look of it.

~ It's dark in there — we haven't got a light, I argued, standing on the threshold. The blackness was not my only concern. I was worried about animals.

Hass lifted a big flat stone and underneath was a hole in which there were matches.

~ I left these here, he said. ~ We have to make a — what do you call it? — some burning sticks — out of brushwood.

~ You mean a torch, I said, looking around me doubtfully. ~ You sure this is going to work?

He was a little contemptuous. ~ Max, I have done this thing many, many times. Alone.

He had my undying admiration.

I made a couple of brushwood brands which Hassan lit with the matches. Then we entered the cave. It was really spooky. Shadows danced on the walls, making me nervous. The flames licked upwards revealing that the ceiling was covered in bats. I don't mind bats, but I don't like the mess they make. My sandals were gummed to the floor.

And there were scorpions too, scuttling on the walls. And hairy-legged camel spiders as big as soup plates. Things like that are all right out in the open but I don't like being trapped in a cave with them. They sort of have an advantage if you know what I mean. I kept whipping round, staring, in case they were sneaking up on me. The bats rustled whenever I made a jerky movement.

Hass grinned at me in the torchlight and I gave him a glare.

~ Well, you're used to it — I'm not.

When we got to the back of the cave Hass showed me where he found the jar.

~ There, on that shelf of rock, he said.

I was suddenly aware of the enormity of his good fortune. I stared at the spot, awestruck,

~ Wow, I wish it had been me.

~ You would never have come here alone, Max.

That was true.

There were signs that others had been in here. Hass said that was just dad and his workers. They'd made sure there were no more jars to be found on any of the other platforms of rock.

~ They look cut out, those shelves, I said. ~ What did they do that for?

~ To put dead bodies on, your father said.

I shuddered. ~ Where are the bodies now?

Hassan shrugged. ~ Someone took them away.

The torches were burning down to stubs.

~ We'd better get out now, I said.

We were just preparing to exit the main cavern when a piece of flaming brand burned my fingers. I let go of the torch with a yell that echoed throughout the cave, scaring the heck out of the bats. It fizzled out in the mess on the floor. Hass was ahead of me, round a corner, and the light was gone. I tripped, falling in filthy droppings.

~ Help! Hass! I cried, terrified. ~ Bring the light.

I didn't dare move. Just before I fell I had noticed a camel spider. It had been huge. I'd fallen right next to it.

Hass came back and stood over me.

~ What are you doing? You're covered in . . .

~ I know, I know, I said, looking around for the spider. ~ Just help me up, will you?

The monster spider had shuffled under a natural ledge at

the base of the cave wall. Hass's brand highlighted its eyes, which shone with a luminous brightness. But there was something else there. We both saw it at the same time as Hass leaned down to offer me his hand.

A carving. What I now know they call bas-relief. The shape of a bull chiselled out of the rock. The horns on the head of the bull curved out of the wall like ring handles. I grasped the bull by the horns and tugged. A section of the wall came free of the rock. It brought with it a lot of dust and grit. Something lay behind it. A piece of rolled-up animal skin.

~ Look at this, said Hassan, grabbing it. ~ Another scroll.

~ I found it! I cried, snatching it back. ~ Me!

When we took it back to dad he was at first pleased with us, for finding another scroll, then later he went potty with excitement.

~ This is the key scroll! he told us. ~ It unlocks the code.

We were pretty chuffed, Hass and I, with dad's delight. I felt so proud and pleased to be getting his attention. But of course it didn't last long. Dad soon went back into his shell. Once he'd got over the excitement he went back into the trailer and spent all his time with his scrolls and I began to wish we'd never found the key in the first place.

18 May, Krantu Island

We ran barefoot along the hot white beach to where the Porters' yacht was moored. Georgia was on the deck, waving to us. My heart thundered in my chest louder than the waves on the reef. Georgia! She is golden. Golden and beautiful. And bright. All things bright and beautiful. Fabulously golden. I love her desperately. We both do. Her favour is the biggest prize in the world. We fight a lot too.

The Porter yacht is long, sleek and white. A two-master. Grant Porter told us the deck's made of teak from Cambodia. He seems very proud of it. There are these lines and things that run everywhere, called stays and sheets. I always thought a sheet was a sail — and it could be that too I suppose — but it's also a bit of rope. Downstairs, or below decks as Georgia called it, the cabins are really cool. Four bunk beds and quite a lot of room, considering. A shower, a toilet that's called 'the heads' and a kitchen they call 'the galley'. There are things called 'bulkheads' too, but I never have found out what they are.

I started to run faster on the soft coral sand. Hassan knew what I was doing. With a spurt he came flying past me. We just had to race. We had to beat each other. That's the way it was. There had to be a winner. Georgia had to see who was best. One day she would need to choose.

When we were opposite the yacht, which was moored about fifty metres out, we dived in and swam. The lagoon was gloriously warm. I swam like fury. The race was still on. Hassan was a great runner but not so good in the water. He flailed his arms, having a lead on me he was desperate to keep. I lost sight of him in his own foam. Smooth and clean, that's how I'd been taught to swim. The Australian crawl. Like a shark cutting through the water.

I swear I touched the yacht first.

~ I did it. I beat you! cried Hassan. He looked up at Georgia for confirmation. ~ I beat him, didn't I?

~ You did not! I shouted, getting a mouthful of seawater for my trouble. ~ I touched first!

Georgia laughed, her golden face shining.

~ Oh, you boys! she said. ~ Come on, have something to drink.

She reached down and grabbed one of our hands in each of hers, to haul us up the side. The touch of those slim silken fingers! I thought my head would burst. But then we were on the red-hot deck. I hopped into some shade. Hassan lay down full length on the boards to get his breath back. He had tougher skin than me. Mrs Porter came up from below with a tray of drinks. She had a sunny smile which I loved. She had blonde hair which had turned almost white under the tropical sun. We were allowed to call her Lorraine, but not Lorry or anything like that. The Porters were not the kind of Americans who liked shortening their names. It was Georgia, Lorraine and Grant, nothing else.

~ Hi guys! Lorraine said, in that soft American accent. And then laughed at Hassan puffing away. ~ Good race?

~ I won — as usual, I said.

~ Did not, murmured Hass, still looking up at the sky.

We left it at that. Grant Porter came up from below then. He was a tall broad-shouldered man with tar-black hair and a huge black moustache. He stooped a little at the neck though. Georgia had told us her dad had hurt his back at college football — American football, not soccer — and it still pained him. You never heard him complain but I'd caught him wincing once or twice, when he sat down. Mr Porter had these hazel eyes that made you turn away after a second. They stared back at you like they were looking into your brain. Hass said Grant must

48

have stolen them from a wolf. Hass has seen wolves, or what they call wolves in Jordan, and he knew what he was talking about.

~ You freeloaders back again? Grant growled, but he was kidding. He liked us. He didn't like my dad and Rambuta, but he liked us boys. I guess it was because we were good company for his daughter. Without us Georgia would have been very, very lonely. Bored out of her brains, probably, since Grant's family and ours were the only people on the island. Anyway, Grant tolerated us, let us come to the yacht when we liked, and seemed to trust us. Or rather he trusted his daughter, which I suppose is a different thing.

~ Honey, Grant said to his wife, ~ I just had a warning on the ship-to-ship. There are pirates in the area we came through to get here. The guy said not to get too panicky — they were in one of the shipping lanes a good way from here — but it won't do any harm to keep a weather eye open. They're using a Chinese junk — a big black one.

~ Pirates? Georgia and I yelled both at once.

Grant laughed. ~ Don't get excited.

Hass sat up at last. I was glad. He was embarrassing himself, lying down on the deck like a dead fish. He saw my expression and made a face as if to say, up yours, brother. Then he gulped down the lemonade. Most of the time I liked my adopted brother. Other times I hated him. Georgia told us all brothers have the same sort of relationship, so it wasn't anything to do with the fact that we weren't real brothers.

I think we're better than real brothers.

But I didn't always think like that. There was a time I hated him.

After the summer in Jordan I was sent back to England, to my school in Suffolk. Hassan stayed with dad of course. Dad didn't say much to me when I left except to be 'diligent' at my studies and to get the best marks I could. I rolled my eyes at this, as if to say, well what else would I be doing. However, dad was too wrapped in this latest project of his to notice. There were dark rings around his eyes and his face still had that pasty look. Soon after, when I was back at school, he wrote to say he was doing a lot of travelling and wouldn't be able to see me for a while. I was a bit fed up about that, but I didn't say so.

Then one unusually warm April day dad finally arrived at nan's. He had Hassan with him. I was surprised to see Hassan and pleased, at first, to see both of them. Then dad dropped a bombshell, just like that, while we were having tea on the lawn.

~ Oh, by the way, Max, you'll be pleased to know I've adopted Hassan – you have now got a new brother. How's that?

Dad laughed as if he had just given me a computer for my birthday.

~ My what? I said, hardly able to take this in. Bits of uneaten sandwich dropped out of my mouth on to the lawn. I stared at Hassan, all dressed up in a suit now, looking like a little prince. ~ What, *him?*

Dad's jaw dropped and he looked at me angrily.

~ You like Hassan, he said.

I jumped up and shouted back, ~ What's that got to do with it? You didn't ask me. You didn't even ask.

I threw the remains of the sandwich at dad's chest, staining his shirt. ~ You just went ahead and did it, didn't you? Did you know, nan? No, you didn't. I can see by your face.

I turned back to dad to display my fury. ~ What if I don't want him as a brother? Have you thought about that? Maybe I don't want to be your son, either. I might as well not be. You don't do anything with me. I bet *he's* been all round the world with you, hasn't he? I just stay here and rot in school while your new son gets to go with you. Too bloody right –

I choked on my anger after that, unable to get any more words out.

~ You will apologise to your nan for that outburst . . .

Dad tried to lay into me, but I walked off. I was completely devastated. Inside I was boiling with rage, unhappiness, indignation and half-a-dozen other emotions. I felt I was going to explode, showering ugly feelings all over our garden picnic. I couldn't contain myself. How dare he! How dare he adopt another kid without asking me first. Would I have said yes? I don't know. Probably not. Hassan was a friend, not a brother. If I had wanted a brother I'd have asked for one, wouldn't I?

I heard nan hiss at dad, ~ You're wrong, James. Very, very wrong. How could you do such a thing?

Hassan followed me out of the gate at the bottom of the garden. There was a greengage orchard on the other side of the gate. I stood amongst the greengage trees and simmered. When Hassan caught up with me I eyed him with hate.

~ What do you want? I said venomously.

~ I am come to say I'm sorry, Max, said Hassan in a quiet voice. ~ I too would be unhappy if I was you.

I drew a deep breath. ~ It's not your fault. It's his.

~ But still, I am the cause.

~ Yes, you are.

We stood there, neither of us knowing what to do. After a while

51

nan came and indicated that Hassan should go back to dad. She sat on a seat under one of the trees, her hands in her lap.

~ Max . . . she said.

I blurted, ~ He should've asked me.

~ I know. I know that and you know that, but he . . . he's never been himself since your mother was killed. You know he blames himself for the accident. Somehow, perhaps you keep reminding him of what he thinks he did. You look a lot like your mother, Max.

~ That's not my fault, I said bitterly.

~ I know it isn't. And he's not a good father to you, not at the moment. I had hopes things will change — I still do have them. One day he'll see how badly he's been treating you and he'll be sorry for it.

~ It's just ordinary stuff, I argued. ~ It just comes naturally.

~ No, no it doesn't. For some people — people like your father — it's difficult, almost incomprehensible. He does certain things without thinking.

Mum had been killed in a car accident in Syria while they had both been on a dig. Dad was driving the jeep. No one knew for sure what happened exactly — dad said he couldn't remember anything about the accident itself — but the car left the road and went into a ravine. Dad had broken legs and concussion. Mum was killed outright. I was nine at the time. Even now I well up when I think about it. I was staying with nan — and granpa who was alive at the time — and they told me. They called me into the parlour and there were floods of tears from everybody.

~ He should've asked about Hass, I repeated lamely. I didn't know what else to say. ~ It wouldn't have taken much to ask.

Nan looked at me with dark eyes. ~ And would you have said yes?

52

~ I dunno that now, do I?

~ But you like Hassan?

~ He's okay. But as a *brother*? I shrugged. ~ It takes a long time to think over stuff like that. I mean, there's things like, now I'm not his only son. I'm just one of two. I've got to share my dad. That's a bit hard to take in. There's always just been me. And he hasn't said why he's done it. What about Hass's family? What did they say?

~ They agreed.

I snorted. ~ Who wouldn't? Dad's got pots of money.

I said this to dad, a bit later.

~ I suppose there's something in that. You asked why I did it. I can't tell you. I do things on impulse. I suppose I was grateful to him. Hassan has put me in the way of a discovery that any academic in the country — in the *world* — would give his right arm for.

He looked up again. ~ And believe it or not, I did give you a thought. I saw how well you two got on at the camp in Qumran. I thought when I told you, you would be delighted. You seemed to be such good friends . . .

He held up his right hand. ~ Now — now I realise that there's a big difference between having a friend and having a new brother. Your nan has explained that to me and believe it or not once things are put to me I can see them straight away. It's just that I don't see them at the time.

My eyes caught the red stain on his shirt that my black-currant jam sandwich had left. It looked a bit like blood. For some reason I turned my head away, not wanting to look at it. I was embarrassed, I guess.

Dad said stiffly, ~ Of course, you'll always be my *real* son, you know that.

~ Dad, I don't think you can say things like that. Not anymore.

At that moment Hassan came back. He stumbled through the tufted grasses of the orchard looking distressed.

~ I think I must go home, to Jordan. I am the cause of much trouble here. This is your father, Max. He is your son, sir. Here is a precious family. You have been very kind, but I must go home.

~ It's okay, Hass, I said.

~ No, no, you have spoken with your father now, but later you will have great resentment and we will fight.

~ Oh, we'll fight all right, I said. ~ Brothers always do. They fight like cat and dog. I know, I've seen brothers at school. They're worse than best friends for fighting. You an' me, we'll fight like mad.

Hass grinned at me. ~ You want me to stay?

~ Let's have a wrestling match to decide.

He knew I was kidding and he walked away, still smiling.

25 May, Krantu Island

Pretty boring week, really. Hass got impetigo on his neck and chin. Yellow weeping sores. Yuk! Hope he doesn't give it to me.

1 June, Krantu Island

Dad's very angry that the Porters refuse to leave but he can't do anything about it, so he just ignores them.

This doesn't bother Hass and me. We spend most of our time in the rainforest. In there it's at least green and calming, if not cool. It's noisy of course — rainforests are never quiet for long — but the sounds are sort of comforting. We hear them all the time. The rasping sawmill buzzing of insects, the clatter of hornbill beaks in the canopy. And out on the edge the cries of frigate birds and white-bellied sea eagles. To us these noises are like the sound of skylarks, or chickens in the back yard, or neighbourhood dogs barking. After a while you don't hear them. Your brain blocks them out.

There aren't any monkeys on the island. I don't know why. Maybe they took them away when they knew it was going to be flooded. Birds could fly away of course. But there are bearded hogs. I guess they don't care as much for pigs as they do monkeys. And there must have been dogs. There are always dogs where there're people. And rats. Plenty of rats. Dad calls them a special kind of rat. The 'ubiquitous rat'. I looked it up but when I first heard it I thought it meant an *evil* or *wicked* rat, or something like that. They certainly steal a good bit of our stores. The sugar and the chocolate powder, mostly.

~ What are we going to do, Max? asked Hass in a dispirited way. ~ About this situation — our father ignoring Mr Porter? How can we get them together so we can all be one big family? I would like for us all to sit around a table and talk and laugh together.

~ I dunno. We can't do anything, really. Once dad has set himself against someone, it's hard to change his mind.

Hass nodded. ~ It is like in my country, when two families are at war. There is only one way to stop them fighting each other.

~ And what's that?

~ If strangers come.

~ I don't understand.

He was patient with me.

~ What happens is this. For many years, sometimes centuries, two families have – what do you call it? – where neighbour fights neighbour?

~ A feud?

~ Yes, a blood feud. Then comes someone from outside, someone from another district, or even from another country. He causes trouble, steals land or insults someone's sister. Then the two families meet, feast, agree to join with each other against the stranger. This is the only way they get together, to drive out the stranger.

~ We haven't got any strangers. No one's going to come here, I pointed out. ~ We can't invent them.

~ Perhaps the pirates will come?

A chink of light came through the rainforest canopy.

~ Yeah, I agreed, thinking about it. ~ Sea-raiders.

Hass gave me one of his secret smiles. ~ We could say we have seen them.

I was shocked. ~ You mean lie? To dad?

~ And to Mr Porter. Hass stared at me frankly. ~ It is for the good.

My head was in a whirl and I went all hot. Not that I hadn't told fibs before. Show me a kid who says he hasn't and I'll show you a barefaced liar. But to make up a story? That's a bit different from saying yes when someone's asked, 'Have you eaten all your greens?' This was *inventing* a lie, right from scratch, which is a different thing altogether. If we were caught – well, it didn't bear thinking about. Dad would blame me of course. He always did, even when it was Hassan's fault.

56

~ Listen, I said, ~ if we get caught, you promise you'll say it was your idea?

~ All right, Hass replied uncertainly. ~ What shall we say then?

Once the blame had been sorted out I was all for it. I began to get excited as I thought the thing through.

~ We'll say we were at the empty end.

This is what we called the eastern tip of the island. The island was roughly the shape of a horned moon. The original village and the best mooring was to be found at the western tip. The eastern beaches were desolate, covered in flotsam and nature's debris.

~ We'll say we looked out to sea and saw that junk that attacked us. It wasn't heading towards the island, but was running along the horizon, as if it was sort of getting ready to pounce.

~ That sounds very believable, Max. You must be good at lying.

I bristled. ~ Not especially. I've just got a good imagination.

~ So, that's what we'll tell father.

And that's what we did.

~ Pirates? He was very sceptical. ~ How do you know?

~ Mr Porter said there were pirates in the area.

Dad snorted. ~ Him? He's a bloody pirate himself, stealing coral.

I glanced at Hassan, hoping to get help from him.

~ But father, he said, ~ we have to band together, to fight the pirates.

Dad did not seem to have heard this. His eyes had a glint to them I didn't like. He rubbed his hands together. ~ This has presented me with a good excuse to send for some policemen. I'll tell the government in Kuching that the island is being

57

threatened. The Sarawak authorities are well acquainted with sea-raiders. Dyak, Malay and Chinese sea-raiders have been terrorising these waters for hundreds of years now. The first white ruler, Rajah Brooke, was appointed as the country's monarch purely because he was able to control the pirates. Once the guards are here we'll put up a barbed wire fence and effectively isolate the Porters in the lagoon. We'll be like a fortress in here.

Our plan to get the two families together was not going well.

~ But dad, what if the guards find out what you're doing? They'll know your secret. What I think's best is we go and tell the Porters, and they move up here. Mr Porter could help you with the guarding. That sounds the best plan to me. How about you, Hass?

~ I think this is a very good plan, Max. Don't you think so, father?

Dad said, ~ I think Porter should leave now and avoid any conflict with pirates.

I said, ~ They might attack them at sea. You wouldn't want Mrs Porter and Georgia to fall into the hands of sea-raiders, would you, dad? I searched my mind for the appropriate phrase. ~ You'd be sacrificing them. You'd be an excessory.

~ Accessory, and no, I wouldn't. Dad's eyes narrowed. ~ You two are up to something. Are you sure you sighted the pirates?

I started to panic. ~ Well, we could've been mistaken. It might have been another boat – not a pirate junk. Maybe, I looked at Hass as I spoke, ~ maybe it wasn't a boat at all. Maybe it was just the shadow of a cloud on the ocean?

~ The shadow of a cloud on the ocean,' repeated dad flatly.

~ Could've been, now I come to think of it.

~ Or maybe it was a submarine? cried dad.

Hass said quickly, ~ This is possible, father — yes, it could have been a submarine.

~ A yellow one perhaps? continued dad. His face lit up with mock surprise. ~ Maybe it was the Beatles?

~ No, no, I think there were no beetles, Hassan stated gravely. ~ What would beetles do on a submarine?

~ He's being sarky, Hass, I said. My heart had flattened in my chest. ~ I think we'd better own up.

Dad nodded slowly. ~ I think that would be a good idea.

~ Well, I explained, ~ it was Hass's idea.

Hass spoke quickly and without any shame. ~ Oh, I think you are wrong, Max. I am sure you spoke of it first.

I knew it. Or I should have known it. And I didn't blame him. I'd have done the same. Hass was trying to save himself. What's one more lie on top of everything? Dad was much more likely to believe that I was responsible anyway.

I blurted, ~ We were worried about you and Mr Porter, being at loggerheads. We thought if we pretended we'd seen pirates . . .

Dad finished it for me. ~ You brought in common adversaries in order that Porter and I join forces against them? The pair of you conspired? At least Hass wasn't going to get away. ~ I think that's very bad — very bad. You lied to me, both of you.

~ That's about it, I agreed, feeling upset.

Hassan said, ~ Now you will beat us?

Dad looked shocked, but I said, ~ He doesn't do that kind of thing, Hass. He's never hit me, even when I burned down the store tent in Syria, that time when mum was still alive.

~ That's right, said dad, in a voice full of hurt. ~ But I am very, very disappointed in you both. Extremely disappointed. I'm not sure what to do with you. Send you back? I suppose that's not practical, but that's what I *feel* I should do. You obviously have too much free time on your hands. I shall get Rambuta to set you more school lessons. That won't be punishment enough, but it will have to do for now.

He turned away from us.

Hass and I retreated into our tent.

It was time for Hassan's prayers. He got out his mat, placed it so that he faced Mecca. The first time he did it he asked dad for a compass. I don't think he completely trusted us in those days. I left him to it and went to read a book.

Afterwards we went looking for reticulated pythons. We'd never seen any but Rambuta said there might be some on the island. We kept searching and hoping. Rambuta got excited about the white tropic birds that flew backwards, but we thought birds were pretty tame. We wanted something with a bit of danger about it. A giant python would do.

~ Father will not beat us? Hass said as we scoured the undergrowth with sticks. ~ Not even a little bit?

~ No – but we'll suffer, make no mistake about that.

~ How? If he does not strike us?

~ It's worse, I explained. ~ He'll keep giving you hurt looks all the time, like you've forgotten his birthday or something.

~ And that is all?

~ And his voice goes all stiff and cold when he's talking to you. You watch, he'll talk to Rambuta in a normal voice, then when you try to speak to him he'll turn to you with a puddin' face on and say, 'Did you say something, Hassan?' even though you know he's heard what you said the first time.

~ This does not seem too bad. My uncle would have beaten me. My uncle beats everyone, even his favourite goats. I think it will be all right, this new punishment.

~ There are uncles who do that everywhere, I agreed, then after a moment added, ~ They don't even have to be uncles.

But of course Hassan was wrong. He hated it when later dad treated him coldly. And he did the wrong thing. He tried to wheedle himself back into dad's good books. But that's the worst thing to do with dad, because it tells him he's winning. What you have to do is not care. You have to avoid speaking to him at all, stay out of his sight until he realises he hasn't seen you for a day or two, and when he does see you treat him as if you couldn't care less. Even when he starts to talk to you like a human being again, you have to remain distant and cold towards him, as if it's *him* who's being punished. Pretty soon he comes to believe it is and he tries everything to get things back to normal.

Sweltering days. Sultry nights. Evenings of moths and mosquitoes. Evenings with quick red-velvet sunsets. Mornings with crinkled edges. Afternoons of comics and books, of boredom. Rain. Rain coming down like heavy waterfalls from heaven. Rain gushing through bamboo pipes, filling the tanks, running off the eaves, shooting full and long out of broken gutters, turning the ground to mush underneath.

And after the swamping rain, plagues of frogs and snails, and wriggly things everywhere. Electric storms too. Not just one or two zig-zag flashes at a time. Not just a few rumbles and claps of thunder. Hundreds of savage electric forks, cracking across the sky all at once, lighting up the bowl of heaven, so fierce it makes you believe in dark alien gods. So loud you think the world has split in two. And afterwards the floor covered in fallen coconuts and leaves, broken branches, the odd dead animal caught without shelter, drowned or shattered.

It was during such a tropical storm I thought I heard that weird sound again: that hollow mooning note, like the horn of a ship lost in fog. It seemed to come from the direction of the fish-drying shed, though it was soon lost in the rumble and crash of thunder. The same sound I had heard once before, but this time much louder, much deeper somehow. It sounded like a beast in distress: an animal crazed by the violence of the wind and rain, the sharp cracking of lightning and the explosions of thunder that blew the bottom out of the sky.

It sent icewater trickling down my spine.

2 June, Krantu Island

I got up early after the storm. My heart was going faster than a machine gun. I had to see Georgia. Alone. I didn't want Hassan tagging along. This was a very private thing, this thing I wanted to do. Actually I didn't *want* to do it — I had to. There was something in me making me go and speak to her. I knew she'd be on the beach collecting shells after the storm. That's the best time to get freshly dead shells, when they've been tossed up on to the coral sands by the waves. One of the things I wanted to speak to her about was that weird sound I'd heard the night before. But that wasn't the only thing. There was something else.

It's not right to collect *live* shells from the ocean because you're destroying nature's bounty (dad says). The trouble is, once the molluscs inside the shells die, the colours and the sheen on the shell start to fade in the sun. You have to gather them before the sun's had a chance to get at them. So, as I say, it's best to collect them freshly dead after a storm, in the early morning, which is what Georgia would be doing.

I crept out of the tent, past the animal compound where we kept the two goats and the chickens we'd brought with us. Glancing back I made sure my brother was sleeping soundly. Then I made my way to the kitchen-hut to grab a bite of something. Not only was my heart running wild, my stomach was churning like mad. I didn't want a rumbling tummy while I tried to tell Georgia what I thought of her. Perish the thought.

Dad was in the hut, sitting at the stained wooden table. We gutted fish on that table but he had his papers spread over it. It was typical of him not to worry about things like that. He probably didn't even think about it.

He looked up from writing something as I came in. His hair was messed and he looked like death. There was a crusty look to his face and his eyes were the colour of red snapper fish. Had he been up all night? Probably. He probably hadn't been able to sleep. Since mum died he'd had trouble sleeping anyway.

~ Hello, son. Up early?

~ Yup.

I kept my answer short, hoping he was engrossed in what he was doing. I saw no reason to tell him anything he didn't have to know. I didn't get away with it though. He turned his full attention on me.

~ What's the occasion?

~ Uh, thought I'd go and look for shells.

~ Oh – yes, the storm. Good idea. Where's Hassan?

~ Uh, asleep. Look, dad, I sorta want to go on my own. Hass always see the best ones first . . .

~ Hawk-eye Hass, eh? Still, you should wait for him.

~ Look, dad, the sun's coming up.

He laid a sheet of paper carefully and precisely on top of the one underneath. His eyes had that faraway look in them that I was used to when he was obsessed with something. ~ If this doesn't make my reputation, nothing will. A chair somewhere, certainly. Somewhere important. Cambridge, I hope. It's not really my field, but is it anyone's field? A new field altogether? It's not zoology. Well, it is, but it's *ancient* zoology. Biological antiquity. Maybe I ought to think up my own definition for this type of study. Revitalised lifeforms?

I didn't understand what he was talking about. I crept away, leaving him to his dreams. I think all archaeologists are dreamers. Otherwise they wouldn't go looking for old bits of stuff in the ground, would they? When dad found something like a piece of pot, he didn't see it as it was, he saw it as it had been. He saw the whole pot, full of oil or corn or whatever. A lump of rusty old iron was a shining sword to him, clashing against shield in battle. I've seen him lost in some chunk of metal which no one could recognise. I've seen him lost for hours. He just sits there staring at a rotten lump of grot he's dug out of the ground. You can almost hear the wheels turning, very slowly, in his head. He gets excited about things other people would clear up with a brush and dustpan. If he wasn't a dreamer he wouldn't be able to do that, now would he?

But would you believe it, I was almost out of sight when dad suddenly came to the doorway of the kitchen hut and called out to me.

~ Have you fed and watered the livestock, Max?

Hell. This was our job, Hassan's and mine. But my brother would wake up any moment. I looked across the compound at the dirt-floored corral where the animals were kept. They were beginning to make a noise, as they always did when feeding time came round.

~ Can't Hass do it? He's the goatboy, after all.

I winced inwardly. Not good. I shouldn't have said that last bit.

I added quickly, ~ I fed them yesterday.

Better. Much better. And amazingly it was the truth.

~ Did you really do it yesterday?

~ Yes, dad.

~ All right, but don't call your brother a goatboy. He was forced into that work by his uncle. It's not as if it were his calling, Max. There was a thoughtful silence before my dad added, ~ Not that there's anything wrong with being a goatherd, of course. Not the noblest of professions, I grant you, but some good pastoral poetry has come from goatherds, shepherds and the like, and probably some very good philosophical ideas. It must give you time to think deeply, being out there alone in natural surroundings. And of course there were shepherds at the birth . . .

I left him wittering on and ran into the rainforest.

She was on the beach, head down. The sea strand was not as large as it had been when we'd first arrived. The water was creeping up towards the edge of the rainforest, having risen a little more each time we saw it again. This island was doomed. One day soon it would drown.

~ Hi.

65

Georgia jumped. ~ Oh!

~ Sorry, didn't mean to scare you.

~ You didn't.

People always say that, even though it's obviously untrue.

~ Yeah, I did.

~ Well, don't look so smug about it.

This wasn't going well. In my head last night it had gone much better.

~ Listen . . . I said.

~ What? Oh, look! she squealed, pointing to a pale shell with an orange pattern. ~ There's an Episcopal Mitre.

I knew my shells better than Georgia. ~ It's a Pontifical Mitre, actually.

~ Why do you English boys always say 'Actually'?

~ Why do you American girls always squeal?

~ British girls squeal too. Most girls squeal. It's what we do. Boys find it endearing. At least, most boys. You're obviously different.

This definitely wasn't going very well. The sun was hotting up. I was barefoot and soon I wouldn't be able to stand on the sand. Hassan could. His feet were as hard as brick. But Georgia and I had to seek shade every few seconds, once the beach was hot.

Behind us in the rainforest shades of dark green were growing paler under a fierce glare. Sea-green herds thundered along the reef, rearing, crashing down with white hooves. The lagoon was wrinkled with the overwash as the breezes pushed the ripples along. The brilliance of the white sand forced my eyelids into slits. I didn't have my sunglasses with me and soon I wouldn't be able to open my eyes at all.

~ Look, I said, ~ Georgia. I just wanted to say I like you.

She lifted her head. ~ Well, you're being pretty grumpy about it.

~ No, no – I mean – that is – see – I like you *a lot*. I really, really like you. You know.

She stopped what she was doing to stare at me.

~ Oh, that? she said. ~ I thought it would come round to this, sooner or later. First Hassan, now you.

I was nettled by her know-it-all attitude. I felt she was treating this far too casually. It was life or death, to me. Then I actually heard what she'd said.

~ What do you mean, Hassan?

~ He asked me to marry him.

~ He *what*?

~ He didn't mean now. He meant later, when we're of an age, I suppose.

The wind went completely out of my sails. ~ Bloody hell!

~ No need to swear.

~ Well, when did he do that – ask you?

~ Last night, in the storm.

So – he must have sneaked out of the back of the tent.

~ What were you two doing in a storm?

~ Getting wet. She grinned, showing her lovely white teeth. ~ C'mon Max, don't get heavy on me. I'm not marrying anyone. Not ever, if I have anything to do with it. It was just Hassan. You know he takes everything so seriously. Don't you be the same.

I turned away from her miserably.

~ You like him better than me, then?

~ I like you both.

But not in that special way. Not in the way everyone wants to be liked, when they're besotted with a girl. I didn't

67

want to use the word *love*. It sort of stuck in my throat. But I did love her. I was sick with it. It dominated every waking minute of my day. I dreamed it at night. I was a useless walking lump of miserable-happiness. I wanted her to be mine. Mine alone. Just me. I wanted her to think there was no one else in the world but Max Sanders. I wanted her to love me back, the way I loved her. If she didn't, I would just dribble away into a pool of misery.

~ Max, she said, ~ right now you're my best friend. Right now Hassan is my best friend too. You mustn't ask for more.

~ We're your *only* friends, I pointed out. ~ There isn't anyone else here.

~ But I know, and you should know, that if there were other kids here we would be special friends anyway. If you don't know that, you don't like me as much as you think you do.

Somewhere in there was girls' logic. It made me feel good, though I couldn't work out why. I mean, if there were other kids here, boys of my age, she would have a choice. At the moment there was no choice. Her statement couldn't be tested. But what she was saying was that if I didn't accept her feelings on the matter, I wasn't worthy of her.

Clearly this was all I was going to get. Good friendship. I wanted her to tell me no boy could hold a candle to me, but I wasn't going to get that, not yet. Maybe in a future letter, when she was angry with some boyfriend in America, but not now. Now we were 'best friends' and I would just have to dream about what might be, someday.

~ Okay, I said. ~ You're right.

~ I know it, she said, smiling, and she kissed me on the cheek. ~ You're a super guy, Max.

Now this was the sort of thing I wanted to hear.

A deep male voice, a deep hurt male voice interrupted my reverie.

~ You did not wake me, Max.

~ Hass! I cried. ~ I — I thought you wanted to sleep on. Anyway, it was your turn to feed the goats and chickens.

~ You steal some time with Georgia.

I got annoyed. ~ Just like you, yesterday.

He glanced at Georgia. He realised she had told me of their meeting. And seeing my expression, he knew she'd told me what he'd asked her. For a moment I thought he was going to call her a traitor. Wisely he kept his peace.

~ So you know.

~ Yeah — that's a bit dumb, Hass. Asking Georgia . . .

~ That's enough, Max. I told you that in confidence, interrupted Georgia. ~ No crowing. No mocking. Friends don't do that.

~ Brothers do.

~ Not while I'm here.

She meant it.

To relieve the tension I pushed Hass on to his backside. He rolled in the damp sand. It stuck to his brown body.

~ You want to wrestle? I asked.

~ I want to break your neck, Max, but I'll leave it until after lunch.

Later, I remembered I hadn't spoken to them about the creature in the fish-drying shed — if that's what it was.

3 June, Krantu Island

Hass's impetigo has burst out into pus so he wouldn't come with me to the yacht today. I went on my own. Georgia and I were on the deck, with Grant and Lorraine below. Georgia was reading poetry by some American woman called Dickinson. I sort of wandered around, looking at the brass and glass instruments on the bridge. There was a large telescope set up in a fixed position. I looked through it and saw dad, standing there. Weird. He could have been right in front of me, the telescope was so powerful. Then Ram came out of the fish-drying shed. I wanted to shout to them, but thought better of it. Anyway, it was too far to hear.

4 June, Krantu Island

~ We'll need to build a cage, dad was saying in a nervous voice. ~ I'll get on the satellite phone once that's done. We'll need a bigger boat than the one we came on, too. He glanced towards us as we came out of the rainforest.

Cage?

~ What cage, dad? What for?

Dad snapped, ~ Nothing to do with you, Max.

Rambuta looked at dad as if he disapproved of this remark, then he turned to us boys.

~ It's possible, he said, ~ that there's a rhinoceros on the island – a Borneo rhino. They're quite rare. We can't leave it to drown.

~ You're going to catch it?

This sounded exciting. ~ Can we help?

~ Perhaps, replied Ram. ~ When the time comes.

Later, Hassan said to me, ~ I do not think Rambuta was telling the truth, Max, about the rhinoceros.

I was surprised. ~ Why do you say that?

~ It was the way he looked.

~ What way?

~ I cannot say for certain, but he was lying.

Lying? That sounded even worse than 'not telling the truth'.

I didn't like Hass saying this. I respected Rambuta a lot. He was someone I looked up to. Why would he lie to us kids?

~ I don't think Ram tells lies — why would he?

Hass shook his head. ~ Something strange is happening, Max. They are holding secrets, those two.

I laughed. ~ My — *our* Dad is *always* full of secrets. He's paranoid. He thinks everyone's out to steal from him. You should know him by now, Hass. He's a walking box of secrets, him. You remember that time in Jordan, when he discovered the secret of the scrolls?

~ I remember, Hass said, nodding. ~ It was very strange . . .

Just a week before I was due to go back from Jordan to school in England, me and Hass were mucking around the camp. It was twilight over the desert sands. Dad was talking to Professor Ahmed in the trailer. Hass and I had earlier crept in the trailer which was air-conditioned during the day and heated at night. It was where dad kept his precious items and papers. There was a table in there where the scrolls were laid in a line. Dad had been trying to make some sense out of the indigo tattoos on the outer side of the hides, as well as deciphering the writings. I didn't think he was getting very far.

~ I have to pray, Hass suddenly told me. ~ What are you going to do?

He wasn't shy about his prayers, but I was. He did them five times a day. I must admit I was at a bit of a loss to know what to do with myself while he was at them. I could stand there like a twit and just watch, or I could busy myself with something else. It was best I simply went outside and waited until they were over.

~ I need a drink, I said. ~ I'll see you in a minute.

~ All right.

I left the trailer and made my way to the water truck. I wasn't really thirsty but you need to take in a lot of fluid in that climate. The nights had turned colder out in the desert but the days were still sweltering hot and we sweated a lot. I found the tin cup and filled it from the little brass tap on the water truck. Then I stared around me as I sipped.

Evening was coming in across the desert: bonfire night colours filled the big upturned bowl of the sky. There were some swirls of black cloud on the edge of the horizon, but they looked harmless enough. At first there was a soft hush: then one by one crickets began piping the sun down. When they were all playing together the noise was unbelievable. I could hear dad raising his voice above their chorus. He probably didn't even know he was doing it. Dad was often unconscious of what was going on around him and he simply reacted to certain things.

Some of the drivers and workers were also at their prayers. Their murmurings mingled with sounds made by the insects.

Just then a raptor bird shot over the tops of the tents as if he'd been fired from a crossbow. My heart raced a little faster on seeing him. He was a beautiful saker falcon. Any

72

sheikh would have given gold for a bird like that. Sakers make really wicked hunters. Professor Ahmed had one at home and had shown me photos of him. That's how I knew what I was looking at now.

In the gloaming the saker stooped down behind an outcrop of rocks and came up with a small mammal in its talons.

Suddenly Hassan was standing beside me.

~ Did you see that? I asked excitedly. ~ It dived and caught a mouse or something.

Hassan said nothing. He was looking scared.

~ Come — come and have a look at this, he said.

Staring at his pale face and shaking hands I didn't want to — not until I knew what it was. It frightened me just to look at him.

~ No thanks.

~ No, you *have* to, Max. Please.

~ What is it? Tell me what it is, first.

~ You have to see.

Although I didn't believe in ghosts or that sort of thing, I didn't want that belief to be shattered.

I held back, terrified of the unknown.

He said, ~ It's the scrolls.

The scrolls? Bits of skin with writing on them? What was scary about that? Immediately my nightmares flew away, into the darkness.

~ Oh, *them*, I said, relieved. ~ What about 'em?

He took my hand and led me back to the trailer. In the dim yellow light inside we approached the trestle table where the scrolls were laid out in a row. Dad had obviously been working on them and had got called away. Hassan went to the first scroll and motioned for me to go closer. I went and stood by him. He put the edges of the scrolls near to each other. What happened next made me jump backwards, my heart pounding.

~ Did you see that? I cried, unnecessarily.

~ It is what I was telling you. I was just looking at them.

~ You must have touched them.

~ Well, I suppose I did, Max — I saw that two of the skins looked like they fitted each other — you can see the jagged edges are the same? — so I pushed them together, just to see if they did fit. Then that's what happened.

At that moment dad came into the trailer. He stopped when he saw us and his face clouded over in anger.

~ What are you boys doing in my trailer? Haven't I told you this is out of bounds? Don't you ever listen to a word I say, Max? You're supposed to be a responsible boy now. How old are you?

Of course he yelled at me, rather than Hass.

~ Dad, I said excitedly. ~ Watch this.

I took another pair of scrolls.

~ Don't touch the scrolls without gloves on, he cried, horrified. ~ Haven't you learned anything? The sweat and dirt from your hands! They'll damage the skins. I have repeatedly told . . .

But I had already placed two skins with similar edges close to each other. As before they seemed to leap together and immediately join. It was like magic. One second they were two separate pieces the next they were a larger, single scroll. It was enough to make dad step back, pale with shock. The effect on him was worse than it had been on me.

Dad's face was like that time when he caught typhoid in Syria, all pasty-skinned and dark around the mouth. His eyes were wide too, with red veins in them. It seemed like he was going to yell some more. Hassan hung his head and murmured something about being 'very sorry'.

~ No, no, dad said. I could see he was shaking badly. ~ It's me who should say sorry, Hassan. I didn't mean to frighten you like that. I was shocked.

He took Hass by the shoulders in his two broad hands. ~ I want you to tell me something, though. What did you two see? Did you see the skins move? The scrolls? What did you see?

Dad's voice was full of urgency.

It was me that answered. ~ They moved on their own. They went together. They joined each other.

He stared back at the table with disbelief in his eyes. ~ Yes. Yes, they did.

He let go of Hass and then tried it himself, with the rest of the scrolls. Sometimes they joined, the edges melting into each other, sometimes they didn't move. Pretty soon he realised they were like jigsaw pieces. Where two edges fitted into each other, they would become one. It wasn't long before he had only two large pieces of skin on the tabletop, the twelve or so skins becoming just a pair.

~ I'm sorry I yelled at you two. It was unforgivable of me. Do you forgive me, Hassan? Max? He ran a hand through his greasy, unwashed hair. ~ I've . . . I'm not feeling too well.

~ I am sorry, sir, to disturb you, said Hass.

~ Listen, boys, he steered us to the doorway of the trailer. ~ I want you to forget what you've seen tonight. Put it out of your minds. And don't come in again without calling for permission. Dad looked at me. ~ Especially you, Max. You know how you chatter. Keep this to yourselves. Don't even tell Professor Ahmed. It's our secret. All right?

~ Not even him? I repeated, more out of surprise than anything else.

Dad's face hardened. ~ Max, I'm asking you to respect my rules. Do you understand? I mean it. I have — I need to concentrate on — on the deciphering. Stay out. In fact, stay out altogether. There's no need for you, either of you, to be in here again. If you want something — if you want to speak to me, call me outside the trailer. Am I understood?

We both nodded.

~ Good. We understand one another.

He turned on his heel and hurried back inside the trailer.

Hass said to me, ~ I have to go . . . and walked away, just when I needed someone to talk to about all this.

The darkness came. I wandered back and forth in the camp. Deliberately, I strolled near the trailer. Dad was still engrossed inside. He had a light, powered by the generator, and I could see his silhouette bent over the trestle table. Once or twice he straightened up and seemed to turn to look at the entrance to the trailer, almost as if he was afraid someone would burst in on him again. It was pretty eerie, the way his black shape kept bobbing up and down.

What was he doing in there? So the skins joined together. I supposed there had to be a scientific explanation he was looking for. Secrets? He didn't usually talk about secrets. In fact, the opposite. He usually wanted to tell everyone about his discoveries — show them his finds. And whatever it was, it was making him look ill. It was spooky. I wondered whether I actually *wanted* to know what it was all about. Maybe it was so ghoulish it would scare me to death.

I turned and stared out into the desert. There were dark

shapes out there too: pi-dogs rattling the stones. It was getting cold now, as it did out in the desert, even after a sweltering hot day. Sometimes there would be ice in the drinking water, but I wasn't thinking of that. I was thinking of what had happened in Dad's trailer, and wondering, wondering . . .

Later, just before we set sail for Krantu, Hassan told me that dad had gone off around the world, buying up other animal skin objects: an ancient Pawnee drum in America; a Tibetan banner supposedly once owned by the Dalai Lama; a tapestry that used to hang in a Kulmuck yurt; a Pushtun cloak and a Zulu war shield and some other stuff. Hass said it had something to do with the scrolls, but I don't know what.

5 July, Krantu Island

I woke in a sweat in the middle of the night.

I felt ill, so I went outside and was sick on the ground. Once I'd got it up, I felt better. But I still had a temperature. I could feel it. Hot. And swimmy. Things were a bit unreal around me.

There was a big round orange moon over the trees.

In the animal compound the chickens were scratching around. I heard a goat snuffle. From the rainforest came the snorting of a wild pig. We'd had trouble with the bearded hogs trying to get at the goats' food. They hung around the edges of camp during the night. Rambuta chased them off during the day. The other day dad killed one with his rifle and we had pork on the menu, though it was only me who ate it.

~ Don't feel so good, I told myself. ~ Bit woozy.

I took one of the big torches and went over to the water containers to get myself a drink.

Everyone else was asleep. Even dad, I supposed. He had to sleep sometime.

A huge insect the size of a humming-bird passed by my head as I sipped the cool water. I ducked instinctively. It had long dangly legs and buzzed. I was worried it was a hornet, but it flew too slowly for that.

~ Jurassic Park, I muttered to myself. ~ Prehistoric insects.

A noise came from the shed then. A shuffling sound.

Something — I didn't really understand what — something drew me towards the wooden building.

I could hear movement within. Hass and I were forbidden to go inside the shed without being invited.

Another sound, a bit fainter this time.

Had they already caught the rhino? That would be typical of dad, not letting us kids share in the excitement.

Crossing the yard, I reached the shed and opened the doors. I entered. But it was very dark in there. I still felt giddy, but the sick feeling had passed for the moment. The atmosphere was horrible. The stink of fish had never quite left the shed and added to this was the smell of a large enclosed mammal. Dung, and the pong of stale sweat.

I gagged and stepped back, tripping over a bunch of old tools left by the locals of the island: hoes, adzes, bits of rope, a spade, a rake. There was also a dirty pair of trainers minus laces and a small pile of rags. Bright blades of moonlight scythed into these from across the shed, coming through cracks in the walls.

There was a skylight in the roof which let in a bunch of

blunter moonbeams. There was a huge dark shape in there, though the light wasn't good enough to see what it was. It was on a platform partly veiled by old fishing nets. There was a metal barrier, like a hoop, which surrounded it. Studying it closely I could see the hoop was connected to a bank of car batteries standing in the corner of the shed. It was the sort of device farmers used to keep cattle in fields. It was probably there to keep out anyone who might get into the shed. Like me?

I lifted the big torch I had in my hand and switched it on.

I'm not sure what happened next. The bright beam of the torch was shining directly into a huge pair of eyes. They reflected light back at me, so brilliant it was like shining a torch in a mirror. I was blinded and confused. Then almost immediately a noise came from the creature: the sort of alarm call that might come from a frightened elephant. I switched off the torch, concerned that I'd scared the animal. In the darkness that followed there was stamping and a big crash. The next second I could see moonlight coming through a massive jagged hole in the back of the shed. Whatever had been caught in my torch beam had crashed through the flimsy wall of the shed and stampeded into the rainforest beyond it. It was all a bit too fast to take in.

I was absolutely horrified and worried silly.

My dad was going to kill me for this.

I suddenly felt very sick again and left the shed, staggering into the rainforest where I threw up all over some ferns. I was retching for several minutes before dad found me.

~ What's happened? asked dad sharply. ~ Did you make that noise?

~ No, I just got up — just this minute. I felt sick.

~ It's gone, Rambuta called out. ~ Broke out of the shed. There's a hole here.

Dad's face turned to stone in the moonlight. ~ Who's responsible for this? he snapped. ~ You, Max?

Hass was now up, sleepy-eyed, staring at me and dad.

It was always difficult to gauge dad's real mood, but when his voice became sharp-edged and cold you knew something was very wrong. He wasn't even angry. Worse than that, he was upset. I'd only really ever seen him like this once before, when mum died in the crash. I determined I wasn't going to own up. You wouldn't get a confession out of me with wild horses now. I could be as stubborn as my old man, sometimes. No way. No way. I had to spread the blame.

~ Me? I asked Hass. ~ Was it you who let the rhino out?

Dad glanced at Rambuta.

~ What? Hass seemed as horrified by dad's attitude as I was. ~ I have been asleep all night.

~ Me too, I cried. ~ I just woke up. I felt sick and woke up.

Then dad said, ~ One of you must have gone into the fish-drying shed. Max? You'd better tell me now.

Rambuta was instantly beside father. ~ James, he said quietly, ~ this will do no good. It's gone.

~ Someone must be punished, dad said, in a horrible matter-of-fact voice. ~ If I discover it was one of the Porters . . .

~ Assigning blame doesn't help, insisted Ram. ~ We must catch it again, if we can.

~ We will help, Hass offered. ~ Won't we, Max?

I was beginning to feel woozy again. All this aggro was making me feel hot.

~ Yes — I wanted to help catch the rhino in the first place.

~ Rhino? repeated dad.

Ram said quickly, ~ Yes, James — the rhino.

~ Rhino be damned, dad muttered, and walked away from us, presumably to cool off.

I heaved a sigh of relief. Thank goodness for Ram. He had saved me from certain death. I knew that inside dad was beside himself with anger and frustration. I think he was ready to flatten whoever had let the rhino out. What a fuss! What had they got the rhino for anyway? It wasn't our job to get it off the island. It was the Malaysian government, surely? I didn't get all this. Maybe Hass was right. Maybe Rambuta wasn't telling us the whole truth. Something was going on when dad got that heated.

~ I feel sick again, I said. I fell to my knees and promptly vomited on the ground. ~ It's my stomach . . .

Rambuta picked me up in his arms. He carried me to my tent and laid me on the bed. ~ I'll get you a drink of water, he said.

Then he was gone and dad was there.

~ Are you really sick? Is this a trick of some kind? You won't get out of anything by faking illness, Max.

My answer was to throw up once more, all over his feet.

Rambuta came back and said, ~ It must have been the pork. I did warn him about eating it.

Rambuta, like Hassan, didn't eat pork. My dad didn't like pork. I was the only one who ate it. Meat like that goes off very quickly in this climate. Even though we have a sort of fridge it's powered by a generator and isn't reliable.

~ Well, it's a good job he's sick, stated dad. ~ I'm sure it was Max who went in the shed. We'd better get that hole repaired as soon as possible.

81

I could hear all this from my camp cot. What a cheek! Why assume it was me? The Porters were surely a better bet.

9 July, Krantu Island

~ Oh, here's Georgia.

My voice rose a little when I said her name. I almost squeaked it out and then felt silly. But she hadn't heard. She was running along the shallows barefoot, listening to her iPod. Yesterday we'd had an argument about bands. She'd never heard of *Stagger* and I didn't go much for the ones she liked. I hoped she'd forgotten how heated it had become.

~ Hi guys! She pulled out her earpiece. She was wearing a T-shirt as usual, and white shorts. Her long lean brown arms and legs, her complexion, were all matchless. She was amazingly pretty. My heart began trampolining on my diaphragm. ~ What's happening?

~ Not much, I answered. ~ How's your mum and dad?

~ Same-ol', same-ol'.

By that I think she meant the war with my dad was still on.

Hass said, ~ I do not understand this expression. But Georgia didn't seem to have the energy or the inclination to explain.

~ Hey, she said, ~ did you hear that weird sound last night?

~ What weird sound? asked Hass.

~ It was like Jurassic Park.

~ A whale, probably, I said. ~ They come up for air and make these wailing noises.

I realised I'd accidentally made a terrible pun, but no one picked up on it.

82

Georgia shook her head. ~ Mom said it came from the rain-forest.

~ Could be one of the pigs, offered Hass.

~ No, said Georgia, ~ it wasn't like that.

~ It was probably from the sea, though. Sound carries. It does funny things, especially around the island. The other day I heard a gull and thought it was in our tent, but it was perched up on the roof of the fish-drying shed. You get these strange distortions, what with the wind and all.

Georgia said scornfully, ~ Where do you get this stuff from, Max?

~ I read a lot.

~ What, comics?

~ No, I said defensively. ~ Science books.

~ Boy's Own Science.

~ It is true, Hassan interrupted, coming to my aid. ~ Max does read a lot of books.

She let the subject of my reading material drop.

~ Well, I think there's something in the forest, she insisted. ~ So does my dad.

~ And? I questioned.

~ And nothing. We're not stupid enough to go and look for it, are we? We might find it. She laughed. ~ That's what happens in horror movies. The stupid ones go and look. They end up dead. Who wants a swim? I've got my swimsuit on underneath. Hey, I saw some manta rays last night. Three of them. They came under the yacht. We were just sitting, watching the sunset and they cruised under us, just below the surface of the lagoon. Big as quilts. I emailed Bradley about them this morning. He'll be amazed.

~ I expect *Bradley* has seen manta rays at Phuket. *Bradley* seems to have seen everything else worth seeing, I replied.

~ Don't get sniffy, Max. I told you Bradley was my boyfriend. I'm not going to not talk about him, you know.

Hassan looked at me behind her back and shook his head very slowly. He was warning me, saying, don't get into this, Max, or you'll regret it. I knew he was right but it was hard not to. I thought about asking whether *Bradley* had a Thai girlfriend as well as Georgia. Sort of sow the seeds of suspicion and hope they took root. However, I let it drop, sick though I was to hear that freak's name. I didn't know this guy but I hated his guts. I wished he'd get kidnapped or something.

We went for a swim, with Georgia chattering and Hass and me listening and offering the odd encouraging grunt.

Later, I told dad about Georgia mentioning the sound.

~ Oh, I shouldn't worry about sounds on a tropical island, he said, nodding. ~ There're all sorts of creatures here that could make such a sound.

~ But she said it was really loud.

~ So are the crickets — deafening sometimes.

That was true. They weren't like the crickets in Britain. They were so noisy sometimes you couldn't hear yourself think.

~ Maybe it was the rhino she heard?

I took a chance in mentioning the rhino, because dad was still sore about whoever left the shed doors open.

Dad gave me a sideways glance, then said, ~ Just keep look-ing as puzzled as she seems to be. And it wouldn't hurt to seem intrigued too. Rambuta and I tracked the, er, rhino today. Eventually we managed to find her, despite her — her ability to camouflage herself. We didn't exactly see her, but she leaves a definite trail, if you know what you're looking for. Fortunately Rambuta does. I must say, dad's voice rose a little, ~ she is a magnificent creature.

That night I think the rhino came back to the camp. I didn't tell dad about it, but I woke at about three. I heard something in the yard and thought it might be a pig. When I got out there though, I just heard something crashing through the forest. There was a big orange moon and I could see the treetops swaying across it as something moved them from below. I thought at the time that it had to be a big rhino, to do that. But why come back to the camp? Maybe the fish-drying shed had become a bit like home to the rhino and that's why she came back? It was a strange way to act, but I don't know a lot about wild animals.

The goats were all crowding in one part of their pen and they too were staring at the spot where the rhino had been. The way they were peering with frozen expressions freaked me out a bit. They weren't even chewing. Normally the goats took no notice of anyone or anything that did not look like food. But here they were, clustered together in a sort of nervous bunch, staring at the night forest with wide eyes. Were they frightened? They looked it. Maybe something as big as a rhino reminded them of animal predators, like lions or tigers? That was the only explanation I could think of for their behaviour.

That, or they'd seen a ghost.

In the morning Hass and I visited the yacht. Grant Porter seemed to be waiting for us. He offered us a drink of orange squash while Georgia's mom brushed her daughter's hair.

Georgia sat in a canvas chair with her back to us, staring out to sea. Her mother stood behind her and lifted the long silken hair, running the brush downwards through it, bringing a

85

sheen to the gold. I couldn't take my eyes off them, hypnotised by the slow deliberate strokes of the brush. Firm gentle strokes. A proud and loving mother's strokes.

It was a while before Mr Porter's voice broke through my fixation and he got my attention.

~ I said, I did some investigating yesterday.

~ What? Oh, sorry – Grant. He had told us to call him by his first name, but both Hass and I found it difficult. ~ What did you say?

~ If you could take your eyes off my daughter's back for one second, Max, you'd know what I'm saying.

Georgia called, ~ Is he looking at my back? Is my skin peeling or something?

~ It is a very nice back, Hass said. ~ It is a beautiful back.

~ I wasn't staring at Georgia's back, sir, I replied stiffly. ~ I was just – it was the brush – I dunno, I finished lamely.

Grant Porter smiled. ~ Well, whatever, he continued, ~ I'm trying to tell you I found flattened trails in the jungle. He always called it *the jungle*, never the rainforest. ~ There's something in there. An elephant, I think. What I want to know is, what's an elephant doing out on a small island?

~ Dad says it's a rhino, I suggested.

~ A rhinoceros? On an island this small?

Hass said, ~ They are native creatures to Borneo, Rambuta says. Perhaps someone brought one here, from the mainland. Someone once took camels all the way to Australia. I read about this. Now there are wild camel herds in the Outback. People take animals everywhere. Who can tell?

~ A rhino, though? muttered Grant. ~ What would they want to do that for?

Hass said, ~ Perhaps they thought they could train it — like an elephant — to move logs and things?

~ What's wrong with a tractor? Grant said.

Now this was one of Hassan's favourite topics. He could get very heated about this subject.

~ Machinery costs a lot of money, he said, almost wagging a finger in Grant's face. ~ People from poor countries cannot afford tractors and large machines. In my country the poor farmers use mules for all that kind of work. One day we will all have tractors, but until then we must use animals.

~ Okay, Grant said, giving in surprisingly easily. ~ It's a rhino — or an elephant. It doesn't matter which. I can't think what else it would be, anyway. Maybe we ought to tell the authorities — get them to come and look? We can't leave the poor creature to drown, once we leave. You know the island's due to be submerged.

The authorities rooting around in the rainforest? That would please dad — not.

Hass and I had a race back to camp. It was stupid of me to suggest it though, because he always won. He was faster on his feet than a gazelle. So it meant he entered the rainforest ten yards ahead of me. He was gone along the narrow path winding through the giant trees, with their buttress roots, before I'd even entered the undergrowth.

Just before I went in, I looked back, hoping to see Georgia one last time. In fact the yacht was cruising to a new spot and it left me looking out, over the reef, at the open sea. As I did so, I got a shock. I could see something out there on the horizon. I stopped and stared. It took me a few minutes to recognise it. I took off and followed Hassan. When I burst into the camp he was standing talking to dad about Grant Porter.

But my news was more urgent than his. My news was desperate.

~ The pirates are here, I cried. ~ Dad, dad, the pirates . . .

~ You've already played that joke, dad said, turning on me with a severe look on his face. ~ It's not funny, Max.

~ No, no, they're really here. A black junk. I saw it out on the ocean, to the south of the island.

~ You said that before.

I grabbed the sleeve of his shirt. ~ Come and see . . .

Dad followed me very reluctantly to the beach. Hassan came meekly behind him. When we got there though, the junk had gone. It was nowhere to be seen. It must have dipped down below the horizon again.

~ If we climb a palm tree, I blurted out, ~ we should be able to see it.

~ A palm tree? Dad was beginning to get that cold knifey sort of edge to his voice. ~ You think I'm going to climb a tree? Hassan, he turned to my brother, ~ did you see this boat?

Hass looked at me. I knew he was torn. His loyalties were pulled both ways. But we both knew he had to tell the truth.

~ I came to the camp first, he said. ~ Max was still on the beach.

~ Did-you-see-this-boat? dad said, deliberately.

Hass dipped his head. ~ No, father.

~ I'm not lying, dad, I cried. ~ I saw the pirates.

~ If you weren't lying, Max, then you must have been mistaken. He gave me one of his stiff looks. ~ It was probably some old cargo ship that's dipped down below the horizon. I'm giving you the benefit of the doubt, Max. Now, I don't want to hear another word about it. You understand?

~ But . . .

~ I mean it, Max.

I shut up. When dad's in one of his immovable moods, there really is no shifting him. He'd decided I was wrong. He still thought I was lying but was giving me a let out. Anyway, it was useless to keep harping on about the junk. He wasn't going to listen.

Hass left me alone. That was good. I had to think. I went back to my tent and lay on my back, looking at the ridge. There were spiders' webs there, with one or two balled-up spiders. They weren't big ones. We left them there to catch the mosquitoes. I was feeling really upset. What dad was suggesting was that I was having hallucinations. It's true that if you stare out to sea for too long, or across the desert, you can see mirages. In the desert they sort of appear out of the heat haze, in the wavy hot air that rises from the baking sands. On the ocean the white horses sort of mesmerise you until you see things in the spray.

Had I seen that seagoing junk? I thought I had. I was sure I had. But then the other day I thought I'd seen a tiger in the rainforest. It was the shadows probably, of a wild thicket, not a tiger. In the misty mysterious light of the rainforest, with its dusty sunbeams and pockets of humid heavy air, you see things that aren't there. Especially when you're on your own. And I was on my own on the beach.

Maybe it was an hallucination?

But it looked so real.

I decided that what I would do was to keep alert. Not *too* alert, because that's the sort of thing that brings on hallucinations, when you're looking *too* hard. Just sort of keep a wary eye on the horizon. If I saw it, I wouldn't tell dad. I'd get Hassan or Rambuta to look.

Three days later I saw the junk.

Hassan was with me on the beach.

~ Hass, Hass, look! Out there! I pointed eagerly. ~ There it is! The pirate ship.

Hassan stared. He shook his head.

~ I can see nothing, Max.

~ Look! There, you idiot. It's just dipping down below . . . uh, it's gone, I said in disgust.

Hassan was indignant. ~ I am not an idiot, Max.

~ Well, it was there, I cried, frustrated. ~ Why didn't you see it?

Hassan dug in his heels. ~ I saw nothing. I looked, but I saw nothing. Perhaps you are seeing ghosts, Max? Perhaps this is a ghost ship?

A ghost ship?

~ Don't be daft, Hass.

~ I don't understand that word.

~ Never mind.

Hassan went back to the camp in a huff. I stayed there. I climbed up on our log and the junk came back into view again. It was unusually calm that day so I could see quite a distance. There was a very slim dark line behind the junk. It was a little while before I realised what that line was. It was only when I looked at the cloud bank above it that I knew. Rambuta had told me that light green lagoons around coral islands reflect on the bottom of a cloud base above them. I could see that reflection now, on the underside of the clouds in the distance. What lay behind the junk was another island like ours. The sea-raiders — or whatever they were — were using that island as a base for their operations in this area. It was only a matter of time before they came to Krantu Island.

I asked myself, why didn't Hass see the junk?

I looked back at where we'd been standing. I'd been higher on the beach which sloped up to the rainforest than Hassan. I was also a little taller. Up here on the log the junk was easy to see. The higher you were, the further over the curving earth you could see. That made sense. Even centimetres made a big difference. Hassan had been too low to see the junk which was only just visible to me. It was not an hallucination. Nor was it a ghost. The pirate junk was out there!

I had to walk back to the camp through the rainforest on my own of course, since Hass had left me. These days I didn't much like lonely walks under the canopy. I had this horrible feeling I actually *wasn't* alone. Something had changed on the island since I'd had that bout of food poisoning. There was the sense of some presence in there. Not a ghost thing: more a feeling of being followed, or accompanied.

The light and the animals in there didn't help of course. It was always dim in the dense parts, with sudden splashes of sunlight in the small glades. Thick waxy fronds rustled against each other in the underdraughts. Birds, especially the hornbills, clattered around above in the canopy. Down below monitor lizards scuttled through fern and papery grass. Some of these guys were a metre long and they made a heck of a racket amongst the crispy plants. Once a big fat monitor dropped out of a tree right in front of me and thrashed away, leaving me having a serious heart attack. Small mammals darted back and forth.

And sometimes the insects stopped making a noise – just like that. Silence. And it leaves you thinking: what the heck? Why have they stopped? Has something frightened them? What? It had to be unusual to stop them making any noise at all.

And on the odd occasion, more often than you'd think, a tree would come down with a mighty crash to thump the ground so hard it vibrated like a drumskin. I once read that in the Amazon forests more people are killed by falling trees than anything else. I could believe that. Even on this smallish island they came down often. I reckon more people are killed by trees than are killed by sharks. People think trees are nice peaceful things that you ought to hug, but they're actually deadlier than poisonous snakes – except cobras I suppose which kill thousands of people in India every year – but anyway, I'm going on a bit, so I'll stop.

So here I was, following a narrow path covered with exposed interwoven roots, any one of which could be a deadly grey snake, back to the safety and sanity of our camp. I'd just been past some pools overhung with pitchers, the vampires of the plant world, when something happened with the freckled light. It was as if someone had folded the humid air in front of me, like a curtain. It stayed.

~ Wha—?

My heart hopped up into my mouth.

The cicadas fell into silence. Something was bothering them.

I stood stock still and began to shake.

~ Is that you, Hass? I called.

No answer. But for a few seconds I couldn't see the turning

in the pathway ahead. Something was blocking it, but whatever it was I couldn't get its shape. It sort of wavered there, like someone was shaking the curtain of air.

Then after a few seconds the path was clear again.

All of a sudden I was thinking of ghosts. Or evil spirits. Maybe the ancestors of the villagers didn't want us here? Could be they'd conjured up demons or something? I remembered the words on the ruined temple *Most Sacred, Most Feared*. We'd made fun of that. I wished we hadn't now. I'd have given anything not to have jeered at those words.

~ I don't like this! I yelled, making my trembling legs move forwards. ~ You bugger off.

Once my legs began to operate properly I ran all the way. Even then I thought someone was chasing me. But once out of the rainforest and back in camp I felt a bit foolish. I looked back. Nothing came out after me. Maybe I'd scared myself. I was quite capable of doing that. Especially when I was on my own. Hass waved to me from the tent, but I decided not to say anything. He might think I was crazy.

Instead, I went and found Rambuta.

~ Have we got any charts with us? I asked. ~ Any maps?

Rambuta looked around to make sure dad was nowhere in sight then said, ~ You should speak to Mr Grant. He'll have charts. Why do you want them?

Rambuta was not dad. I could speak to Rambuta without fear of him going into a lather.

~ I saw the junk again.

The Malaysian academic nodded.

~ The ghost ship.

I was startled. Then I realised Hass had been talking to him.

~ There's no such thing as ghosts, I said.

Rambuta stared me right in the eyes. ~ Of course there is, Max.

I was about to argue with him when I realised it was useless. Dad had told me it was simply a matter of different cultures. Ram's culture really believed in ghosts, mine mostly didn't, not in the light of day anyhow. I left him to his work without another word. I'd heard this before, when dad and Rambuta had been debating one evening about madness. Dad obviously believed insanity was all in the mind. Rambuta, however, had argued that outside forces were at work too.

~ Ancestor spirits, he'd said, ~ can turn you mad.

Dad had spoken to me later. I suppose he'd been worried that Rambuta's ideas might frighten me.

~ It's one of our many little differences, he'd told me. ~ Ancestors are very important to people in this region of the world. Even though they might be Muslims, or Christians, whatever, they still hold on to certain ancient ingrained beliefs. They believe the spirits of their dead fathers and grandfathers, mothers and grandmothers, watch over them in their daily lives. Mostly these spirits want to do them good, but one or two — a rogue uncle or a venomous great-aunt — might want to do them harm.

Dad had paused for a moment, then continued.

~ Rambuta is a very intelligent man. Well educated. He has a fine mind — superior in many ways to mine. You mustn't confuse this difference in culture with stupidity, Max. Rambuta's not silly for holding these beliefs. They're to do with his heart, not with his head. You might just as well call a man stupid for falling in love. You can't show love to someone. You can't hold it

94

in your hand and say, there it is, it's real. You can only say that you believe in love. There are those men who don't.

He'd stared into the distance, his eyes becoming moist for a moment. ~ I'm not one of them, mind.

I knew he was thinking of mum and I turned away, embarrassed.

When I got to the yacht I found the Porter family at lunch. Grant Porter, polite as ever to someone he thought deserved it, invited me to eat. It was sea-fare — biscuits made by Lorraine, with boiled seaweed and some fish caught in the lagoon by Grant with his spear gun.

The biscuits were good and I said so.

~ Biscuits? said Georgia. ~ Oh, you mean the cookies.

~ Yep, the cookies.

~ And where is the redoubtable Hassan today? asked Grant. ~ I thought you two were joined at the hip.

I tried pushing the seaweed to the edge of my plate, but caught Lorraine looking at me with disapproval so I ate a little.

~ Oh, we had a bit of a row, I replied. ~ I thought I'd seen this pirate ship and he didn't.

~ And Hassan thinks you're mistaken?

~ He won't back me up, with dad.

~ Well, if he didn't see it too, he can't say he did, or he'd be lying, wouldn't he?

~ Yes, but . . .

Grant said, ~ You can't expect him to tell untruths, Max.

I realised he was right. ~ No, I suppose not.

~ And you *could* have been wrong.

~ I dunno. You told me about the black junk. That's what I think I saw.

~ You *think* you saw?

~ Well, I said hotly, ~ people keep yabbering at me, telling me I'm seeing things.

~ You want to know what I think? Grant said. ~ I think we ought to keep an extra special watch. If you saw the junk, and it's still in the area, someone else is bound to see it soon. Thanks for the warning, Max. We'll keep a weather eye open from now on.

I had the feeling he was saying all this to make me feel good, but I didn't care. Someone was at least pretending they were on my side.

Grant stood up. ~ Come on, Max, let's go for a snorkel. I'll show you where some lion fish live. Don't touch them, they're poisonous to the touch, but they won't attack you or anything. Here, you can borrow Georgia's equipment.

~ Oh yuk, cried Georgia. ~ I don't want my snorkel back if it's been in some boy's mouth.

~ It won't hurt you, replied Grant. ~ Dip it in diluted bleach if you must, but I'm sure Max hasn't got a deadly disease. You haven't got a deadly illness, have you, Max?

~ Only foot-and-mouth, I said. ~ I dunno whether bleach is strong enough to get rid of foot-and-mouth disease. I rammed the snorkel in my gob.

Georgia wrinkled her nose. ~ You're disgusting.

My reply was to make a phlegmy sound into the snorkel.

~ Max Sanders, you're a moron, she said, flouncing to the back of the yacht.

~ Isn't that a bit non-pc? I said innocently to Grant. ~ Isn't that being unfair to morons?

~ Stop trying to goad my daughter, you'll only regret it, he grunted. ~ Come on, boy, let's get down amongst the fishes.

96

When I'd put on the mask and flippers Grant Porter took me down into the lagoon below.

With my head under water there was a sort of leaden silence at first. But then, after a bit, I could hear the live coral crackling. It felt like I was flying as I floated above that undersea scene. It was as if I was privileged, looking in on someone else's world. Everything went on below me just as if I wasn't there. Life and death. It was all happening beneath me.

The coral gardens were chock-full of brilliantly coloured reef fish. I started counting the different types and got up to thirty-seven before I gave up. We also saw some terrific coral, all colours of the spectrum. There was a lot of dead coral too, more than there was live, but still some had survived the tsunami.

We passed over a blue octopus, which again was deadly poisonous, like angels over a lone killer.

Finally Grant led me to a coral cave. Five lion fish swam in the entrance. They weren't very big, of course — lion fish aren't — but they were fascinating stripy fish covered in spines and lots of frilly bits around the fins. The lagoon was full of such grotesque and beautiful marine life. Once I even saw a lion's mane, the biggest jellyfish in the sea, which was the size of a house. There were also ugly beasts: big-mouthed thick-lipped groupers that stared at you. And stone fish, covered in lumps and warts and bits of growth, and a horrible slimy grey colour.

Mum used to reckon that during the six days when God created everything he had one comic Absurd Hour, just for fun, when he made all the grotesque and ridiculous creatures of the Earth, most of them fish.

There were sharks in the lagoon too. Mostly sand sharks and

reef sharks. Nothing too dangerous. I liked the idea of swimming with sharks. It made me feel like a warrior of the sea.

Once on deck again, Grant went below while I stayed and dried myself in the sun. Georgia and Lorraine had gone somewhere, either to the island or down below. I was left on deck alone.

I knew where Grant kept a few of his charts, in a watertight box aft. Going to the back of the yacht I opened the box and took out a roll of charts. The one I wanted — of this area of ocean — was right on top, being last used. I found Krantu Island. Then tracing a line south-east I found a second island, about twenty kilometres distant. Mangan Island.

This was it!

This was where the pirate junk was operating from.

Mangan Island!

My first thought was to rush back to dad and confront him with my find. But I changed my mind. It didn't matter what I said, he probably wouldn't listen. Once he'd made up his mind it took dynamite to shift it. I had to have positive proof.

The best thing to do, I decided, was to keep a wary eye out. Always to check the direction of this Mangan Island in the morning, at midday, and in the evening. Maybe check it five times a day, when Hass was at his prayers? Prayer times would make a good reminder.

Once the junk was clearly visible, I could then insist on dad or Rambuta coming to look and prove to them that it was here. But I had this awful feeling that they were going to attack us. I just hoped I could give the warning in time. I just hoped I wouldn't be caught napping. If I failed we were all doomed. There were too many pirates for us to contend with. They would wipe us out without a second thought.

17 July, Krantu Island

For some reason dad's banned us boys from going into the rainforest. We could use the wide path to the beach, but after that we were to stick to the shoreline. Dad said what with the wild animals and other things (what other things?) it might be dangerous in the rainforest proper. Hass and I hadn't gone in there much before but of course we did now we were banned. Well, it sort of lures you in when you know you're not supposed to be there. And we didn't go *deep* inside: just far enough to flout dad's rules. Well, only a bit deep.

In the middle of the island there's a sort of deep sunken glade, a valley if you like, about five kilometres long, with large pools of fresh water. It's a sort of rusty-coloured water, even deep brown in places. Not stuff we could drink or would even want to swim in. But the animals like it, of course. The valley is surrounded by craggy volcanic rock, which sticks up and forms the edge of a mossy bowl. Inside the bowl are mangrove swamps and areas of lush grass and once-cultivated banana orchards. This is where the animals mostly gather, so if you want to take photos and things, this is where you go to do it.

~ There it is, the one I was telling you about, I whispered to Hass. ~ Look, over there under that flame tree.

We were inside a den we'd built from staves and leaves. There was green gloom all around us. This part of the rainforest was dense with hardly any light getting through the canopy. We'd had to take off our sunglasses to see anything at all.

~ I see it, I see it, replied Hass excitedly. He had the camcorder so he got to shoot it. I took some stills with the digital. I guess we felt we were like two TV animal programme presenters.

~ Look, it's standing on its back legs, whispered Hass.

~ Don't make too much noise, I said nervously. ~ Look at the size of it . . .

It was a strange kind of massive rat-thing — as big as a housecat — with a really ugly face — and sort of horn-like ears. And its fur looked a bit like small feathers.

~ I'm not shouting, Max — it's you who's making the noise.

The hide was not much more than a bivouac. It rustled as Hass pressed his face to an opening which looked a bit like the opening of a letter box. The rat-thing paused in its actions.

We held our breath for a moment. Soon though, it was back to eating the durian fruit, which reeked worse than our cess pit. A durian's a bit like a spiky green rugby ball with pulpy insides. Rambuta loved durian. He said that though it smelled like a toilet it tasted like ambrosia. I couldn't stand the pong long enough to get the stuff close to my mouth.

Suddenly the creature stopped eating and went over to the nearest tree. There it rubbed its back and neck against the trunk. A few hairs came out. They were sort of blackish-grey. Then the beast went up on its hind legs and began raking the tree with its claws. My eyes widened as it stripped away bark. It came off in long thin shreds which looked like vermicelli. Maybe it wasn't a rat? Maybe it was some other sort of mammal? They were really, really sharp, those nails.

~ I wish I could send him to Barry Cox in the post, I told Hass.

~ Who's Barry Cox?

~ Boy who used to bully me at school.

~ What did he do that for? Bully you?

I shrugged. ~ Didn't like me, I guess. Or something. Maybe he thought I was a nerd because my dad's an archaeologist.

~ Are you a nerd?

I looked at him. ~ You've got a lot to learn, I said to him, ~ about Western kids. Nerds have buck teeth and thick glasses. They talk about one thing all the time.

~ What thing?

~ It doesn't matter, but it's usually something boring to everyone else, like aircraft numbers, Pokemon cards, or Peruvian spuds. I was particularly pleased with the last example. It probably made me a nerd, but I thought it was pretty clever. I'd read in a magazine that Peru has 200 different varieties of potato and it had impressed me for some reason. I probably *was* a geek. A funny-facts geek.

~ You should have challenged this Barry Cox to a boxing match, said Hass.

~ Are you kidding? I whispered, as the creature stopped ripping the tree to bits. ~ Barry Cox was built like a Sherman tank.

~ Our father says all bullies are cowards.

~ Our father has rocks in his head. He's an archaeologist. He reads too many comics.

~ But Max, it is we who read the comics.

~ Well, he must have read them as a kid then. Look, Barry Cox didn't *need* to be brave. He could have crushed me like a bug. Whether he was a coward or not didn't matter. I'm small and he's big. What d'ya think, I'm David and he's Goliath? Nuts.

~ Who are they?

~ Forget it. Look, it's eating roots now. It's digging them up with its claws. We'd better write this down when we get back.

It's all interesting stuff for our TV programme. I reckon this is unique.

Hass wrinkled his brow. ~ What does that mean?

~ It means it's very rare.

~ No it doesn't, murmured a female voice at the entrance to the bivouac. ~ It means they're *unique*. It means they are one of a kind. It means they're the only one in existence . . . what are you looking at, anyway?

Georgia shouldered her way into the hide. She peered at our subject and then poured scorn on what we were doing.

~ Uggghh! He's horrible, she said. ~ Haven't you got anything better to do than take photos of that thing? She wrinkled her nose. ~ And it smells sweaty in here. You two stink.

It was hot in the hide, but her voice had gone loud.

~ Now you've done it, Max, cried Hass, annoyed. ~ It's run away and I wanted to get a better shot of it.

I protested. ~ It wasn't my fault! It was madam here.

~ Don't talk about me like that, Max, Georgia said.

~ Look, Georgia . . .

I looked up to see her mouth was pinched, her eyes were wide and her nostrils had gone a fiery red. The fact was, we'd all been getting on each other's nerves a bit lately, cooped up here on a small island. It was inevitable. Hass irritated me. Dad annoyed me. And now I'd even started sniping at Georgia. I regretted it instantly. But with some girls you can't take it back. Georgia was one of those who took to heart attempts to score. I should have realised that before I opened my big trap.

~ I'm sorry, Georgia.

She said nastily, ~ You don't look it, Max.

~ You must not talk to my brother in that way, stated Hassan, still miffed. ~ This is not the place of girls.

Wow. Was *that* the wrong thing to say. Trouble was, Hass still had trouble with his use of English.

Georgia threw us a look of utter contempt.

~ Idiots! she muttered.

~ Georgia?

~ No. No, no, no. Not this time. Dugongs.

It had all got too heated over nothing. That was the trouble when you were thrown together too much. A bit like brothers and sisters. You didn't really mean half the things you said, but you said them anyway. And they were such *little* things, to my mind anyway.

She stormed off, thrashing through the undergrowth. I looked at Hassan and he shrugged. ~ What can you do?

~ She'll come round, I said lightly, wondering what a dugong was. She had used the word as if they were gross. ~ You see. She can't go for long without talking to us.

But I didn't really believe my own argument. She was really upset this time. No longer would she play our American-English-language word games:

'Pavement.'

'Sidewalk.'

'Conservatory.'

'Glasshouse.'

'Aubergine.'

'Egg-plant.'

'AluMIN-i-um.'

'A-LUMinum.'

I think she had finished with us for good. If she spent

months sailing with just her mom and dad, then she was used to being without us. We would crack long before she did. Hass and I were in deep trouble. It was going to be agony, seeing her from a distance, but not being permitted to speak to her. Girls can be rotten enough too sometimes.

Anyway, we pretended we didn't care, of course. We followed the rat-creature's tracks but it was . . . what? Sly? Not that, even. I'm sure I know the word for it. Oh yes, Jem Conner at school, his dad was a policeman who had named his house *Wily Copse*. I thought that was pretty cool, but that's the word I'm looking for — wily. It'd vanished into the rainforest.

19 July, Krantu Island

I dunno whether I dreamed some of this or not. Probably it was all a dream. Anyway, this is one of those that stick in your mind and later on you wonder whether it really happened or whether your head is mucking about with what's true and what's false. It takes on a sort of dream-type memory and probably gets mixed up with other things that might've happened but you sort of go with it, if you know what I mean. It all jigsaws together but probably the pieces don't quite fit each other.

It was early dawn in the camp. I got up. I was always getting up before the others. I sort of get thirsty early on. It was all very peaceful. The crickets had stopped for a bit and the birds hadn't woken up yet, since the light was still very murky. I thought about going down to the beach but dad had said we had to stick to the camp, especially at night.

Just then one of our goats started bleating like mad. It was the pregnant one dad had tied up outside the corral to stop it being butted by what he called the 'bully billies' — the male goats.

It was serpent-like and sinewy and it sort of slunk with its belly close to the ground. I could smell something which made me gag but I wasn't sure what. They say smell has the best memory of the senses but I don't think this stink had ever been in my nostrils before that moment.

The creature hadn't seen me. Its shiny eyes were mainly on the nanny goat. I kept as still as I could, though I was shaking a bit, terrified it would look my way. It crept forward, inch by inch, looking round every so often to make sure it wasn't being watched. Well it was, by me, but I was sort of partly hidden by the edge of a hut and I kept quiet.

You could tell this thing was sly and cunning and all that by the way it moved and turned its head. This head — I could make out the shape now as the dawn came — was long and thick like a huge log. Then when it got near to the goat the jaws opened and it was like a log splitting down the middle. There were rows of splinter teeth that glinted, even in the dullness of the day breaking. These teeth, they must have been as long as carving knives. Maybe bigger.

Then I almost swallowed my tongue in fright as the head shot forward and the jaws snapped up the nanny.

Her bleating stopped instantly. This beast from the rainforest had taken her whole into its long mouth. There was a crunch of thick bones and I got the idea it took only one bite to pulp the poor goat. She could have been a tiny sparrow in the mouth of a tiger. At first I could still see her legs sticking out from between the teeth of the monster. They jutted like matchsticks.

Then with a few quick movements of the mouth they were gone too, crunched up with the rest of the nanny.

I think I made a sound in the back of my throat because the monster's head turned my way. It seemed to stare at me for a short while and I got the horrible impression it was smiling. But that was probably just my imagination, seeing those teeth and everything. There was blood dripping from its thick lips and it wiped a huge tongue over them, lapping the blood back inside. Then it suddenly whipped its head away from my direction and stared at the goats inside the corral. I could almost hear it thinking *can I get another one?*, but a noise from a tent made it lift its head high. Then finally, with the sweat pouring down my back and chest, it turned and sort of trotted on its short legs back into the forest.

I was still sitting there trembling when the whole camp, the old village and everything, caught fire. *Whoomph!* — and it was blazing, just like that. But this is the part that I think was maybe a dream. Or it could be the sun had jumped up the dawn sky like it does and everything seemed to be ablaze at once. I dunno. I just have these mixed-up memories. You've got to remember I was scared to death. You can't think straight when you're that frightened. Shock, I think it is. I was shocked. But I do think the monster was real, and the way it ate the goat, just maybe I tagged the rest on because of what I found out later, about other things.

I do remember dad coming out of his fiery tent in his vest and pants, and yawning, stretching himself, his arms up in V. Then he saw the frayed end of the rope that had tethered the nanny. A puzzled look came on his face, before he looked across and saw me sitting there.

~ Max? he said. ~ Are you all right?

But my throat was still too clogged up to answer straight away.

21 July, Krantu Island

I bet there's never been a girl in the whole history of the world who said sorry first. I bet you could go all the way back into history till you reach Eve and not one of 'em has said, 'It was my fault,' before the boy owned up to it first. Well, I wasn't going to give in. Okay, I spent some time standing on the beach looking wistfully at the yacht, but that was as far as it went. I admit I missed going to the yacht. So did Hass. And whenever we were there, looking out over the lagoon, Georgia was always happy and laughing about something. I bet she did that on purpose to make us feel she didn't care. I don't think she *did* care.

~ I don't care, do you? I said to Hass, as we walked along the beach, Georgia's laugh tinkling across the water. ~ I couldn't care less.

~ Me neither, Hass replied. ~ Her silly laugh always annoyed me.

~ Me too. More of a girly giggle, if you ask me.

~ Not very attractive.

~ Anyway, I said, kicking an innocent hermit crab shell into the water, ~ what's that thing she said, a dugong?

~ I asked Rambuta. He told me it is a sea creature. He says sailors of long ago used to mistake them for mermaids.

~ Well, they can't be very ugly then. The way she said it sounded like we were as ugly as dugongs.

~ Yes, they are very ugly. Rambuta says.

I was a bit perplexed by this. ~ Well, what about the sailors thinking they were mermaids?

~ I too mentioned this fact to Rambuta, but he told me sailors in those times used to spend two years at sea and not meet a woman in all that time. It seems they must have forgotten what a female person looked like.

I kicked another shell. ~ I wish I could forget 'em, I growled. ~ They're not worth remembering.

25 July, Krantu Island

At last dad and Grant have started speaking to each other. I dunno what happened but I saw dad coming back from the yacht this afternoon. He looked a bit grim so I thought he'd been fighting with Grant. Then he told me he'd invited them all round to dinner. I don't suppose they're friends or anything, but at least they're speaking to each other. I suppose dad decided it wasn't worth it, keeping all this 'them and us' stuff going. I'm glad. I think it was pretty daft in the first place.

We had the meal together. It was all a bit stiff and formal. Dad and Grant discussed the rhino, but it was a funny sort of conversation. Dad and Rambuta, and maybe Hassan, were the only ones at the table who really believed in the rhino. They said they did, anyway. So everyone else sort of tiptoed when they talked, trying not to come out with accusations or calling anyone a liar outright. I don't know why, but Grant seemed so easily satisfied with dad's vague explanations. I know I wasn't. Something was going on and only dad and Rambuta knew what it was. I supposed I would be told sooner or later, but right at that moment I was more interested in getting back in Georgia's good books. Self-centred? Me?

Then Lorraine mentioned that sound we sometimes heard, like a ship's fog horn, and said no rhino ever made a noise like that. Dad gave no answer to her. He simply asked someone to pass the sweet potato. Grant gave his wife a significant look and Lorraine didn't mention it again.

When the Porters had gone, I tackled dad myself.

~ There's no rhino, is there, dad?

He wouldn't meet my eyes.

~ I can't tell you that, for the moment. You'll have to trust me. I'm your father, Max. I'm entitled to trust from a son.

I wasn't sure about that. He was a father but he was a professor too. It was the professor in him you couldn't trust.

I made the usual mistake and threatened him.

~ Shall I ask Ram?

He turned on me quickly. He looked livid.

~ You will not speak to Rambuta about such matters.

~ But . . .

~ No 'buts' Max. You and Hassan will have to — to await events. There is something you will eventually — what am I saying? You're a child. Children do as they're told.

~ Not these days, dad. And I'm not a little kid. I know stuff now. I'm not ten any more.

Now it was his turn to threaten.

~ Maybe it's time I sent you home. I should have done so ages ago.

We left it at that. I wasn't any wiser. But he hadn't won.

109

27 July, Krantu Island

Grant and dad went off together into the rainforest. I mean, what's that all about? Deadly enemies yesterday, best friends today? I don't think so. Hass says we mustn't interfere. What? No chance!

1 August, Krantu Island

We were sitting round the table eating dinner. The Porters weren't with us tonight. I had speared a giant red snapper fish in the lagoon and this was the main dish. Compliments had come and gone. I wanted them to continue with every mouthful, of course. I'd placed the spear gun where everyone could see it to sort of tweak their memories that it was me who'd caught the meal.

Rambuta especially was enjoying it, chomping away on the snapper and giving me nods and winks.

Hass just ate, of course. He couldn't care who caught the fish so long as he had something on his plate. Hass had a funny way of hunching over like a mouse and blotting out the world while he devoured his food. If you spoke to him he didn't answer. It was as if he was on another planet and there was nothing but silence all around him. Weird.

Maybe something had happened to Hass at some time which made him eat like that. Maybe he'd starved. When she was alive mum had always said that being hungry was not the same as being starved. ~ One is an irritable rash on your leg, the other is having no leg at all, she used to say. I used to think that was weird too, that saying, but I'm beginning to see what mum meant by it.

Dad's way of eating fascinated me too. His eating habits were, mum had once said, a product of his strict upbringing. Dad always ate like he was at a banquet for the queen. He sat bolt upright, his back as straight as a cathedral spire, and held his knife and fork with poised hands. He never rested them on the table. When they were not being used for cutting, or lifting the food to his mouth, they were perfectly level with the bottom of his ribcage. He didn't grip his cutlery, he held each utensil delicately between thumb and forefinger. My dad was nobility somewhere back.

~ Take your elbows off the table.

~ Who, me? I said, surprised.

~ Yes, said dad, ~ you, sir.

I did as I was told, just as a rat dashed out of the edge of the rainforest and grabbed a bit of food from under the table. No one saw it but me. We didn't worry too much about rats on the island. They're everywhere and nowhere. There was plenty to eat, for everyone – the rats, the frigate birds, the white-bellied sea eagles, the wild pigs. It was a paradise really, if you didn't mind eating the same thing a lot. We had fish pretty often and Rambuta knew a lot of stuff that grew on Krantu, like taro, yams, sweet potatoes and breadfruit.

I was fast learning things like that: names of root veg, fruits, nuts and all the different fish in the lagoon. Rambuta was able to teach Hass and me without actually seeming to. Dad would have sat us down and lectured us, but Rambuta sort of did it while we were walking around, just pointing things out and not testing us later like dad would have done, to see if we knew it.

Rambuta even made us a small outrigger canoe with a bedsheet sail which we used in the lagoon. He used some bamboo logs lashed together, for the hull, instead of a hollowed-out trunk because hacking out a log would have taken yonks. But it sailed with the two of us on board and that's all we wanted it to do.

He also taught us about the constellations, in case we ever got lost at sea.

~ I'll use Latin names, he said as we lay on our backs on the damp beach one clear night. ~ But I'm also going to tell you the local names.

Much more exciting. Secret information.

~ That there is *Sirius*, which we call 'Bird's Body'. Bright, eh? And over there the 'Path-Of-Three', or *Orion's Belt*. Now I'm pointing at 'Small Face', he gave a little laugh, ~ I've forgotten the Latin name for it. And over there is 'Double Man' and the 'Carrying Stick', *Alpha* and *Beta Centauri*. There the 'Sacred Timber', and up here the 'Adze' . . .

~ That's really cool, I said. ~ I'll never remember them all.

~ Yes, said Hass, ~ but that one really *is* like a stick. And that one an adze. The shape helps you remember.

~ You're right, clever clogs, I agreed, ~ it will help us to remember them. But what I find really strange is that people in this part of the world name the star constellations by their shapes, just the same as we do. I mean, they didn't know each other existed when they gave them their names, did they? People in the West and people in the East? I mean, one lot could have just named them something else, like 'Five-Stars-in-a-Bunch', or 'Three-stars-in-a-Row'.

Rambuta sat up and looked at me with approval. ~ Now that is a clever argument, Max. It shows original thinking. What you're

112

suggesting is that one group of people could very well have had a mathematical basis for naming their constellations, while the other group used shapes. Yet they both used the latter, which might be coincidence, or it might be the result of something deeply imbedded in the human psyche.

I felt good. Praise is wonderful. I felt very good.

After the meal that evening we sort of lazed around in the glow of lamps watching the moths batting the lampglass with their wings. I was bored. A huge flying fox flew across the moon, which got me thinking about my comics. Vampires and all that! Trouble was, I'd read all my comics a thousand times and Georgia didn't have anything worth reading. Her dad didn't approve of hero comics, which seemed daft to me, since most comic-book heroes were American. Superman, Spiderman, The Hulk, whatever. Georgia had some girly things which I wouldn't have looked at if you'd nailed me to a tree and pasted them to my eyes.

My boredom didn't last long though, because Grant came hurtling out of the rainforest and into the camp. He looked very agitated. He took dad aside and spoke to him for a very long time. Deadly serious stuff by the look on his face. Then he went off, back towards his yacht.

2 August, Krantu Island

Woke again in the night to the sound of that animal in the rainforest. Can't think what would make such a deep throaty note. Is it in pain? Is it in distress? Who knows? Nothing much else happened today. Hass went on the rampage with a flyswatter. We counted thirty dead.

3 August, Krantu Island

Too much schoolwork. Not even time for a swim. Dad's trying to keep us busy so he and Ram can do stuff in the rainforest. I think Grant went with them again. Where? I'd like to follow them, but Hass won't come and I can't face dad's anger on my own.

5 August, Krantu Island

~ Remember what I said, boys, dad warned me. ~ No going into the rainforest without an escort. Now I know you've sneaked in since I banned you – no more of that. I'm serious.

~ Why, what's in there? I asked.

~ This is not up for negotiation, Max. I'm giving you an order.

~ Yeah, but dad – there's this weird huge rat-thing that we found. We've got it on video . . .

Dad's face hardened even more. ~ No! he snapped. ~ Max, I shall be very, very angry if you disobey me in this.

~ Okay, okay. Whatever, I muttered.

~ This creature you saw. Did you recognise it?

~ No – it was really weird – like it had small feathers instead of fur, and it was as big as a cat – but the light was bad.

Dad looked thoughtful then he said to me, ~ Probably some Borneo mammal introduced by the locals. There're some very strange creatures in the Borneo rainforest. The pangolin might *look* as if it has feathers, but they're actually scales. That's about the same sort of size.

I was interested. ~ And the others – what other strange creatures?

~ Oh, you'll have to get Ram to tell you. He looked sort of sneaky for a minute, then added, ~ There's a leech that's half the size of your arm, of course.

~ Oh, *what?* No way, I yelled, shuddering. ~ You're kidding, dad.

~ Absolute truth. Suck your leg dry in a few minutes.

I'd experienced our local leeches, about the size of fishing maggots. They left you with a sockful of blood, even that small. You had to burn them off with a red-hot twig to get them to take their mouths out of your flesh. If you pulled them out they left their ends behind which rotted and gave you blood poisoning.

~ Yuk! I muttered.

~ Yes, well – I'll have a look at that video you took. Where is it? In your tent? All right. I can probably get Ram to identify it for you – he's the expert.

Later I spoke to my brother. ~ You told him, didn't you?

~ Max, I felt very guilty at disobeying our father, Hass confessed. ~ I'm sorry.

~ What about your loyalty to me? Your brother?

He looked suitably stricken at that. Now he was trapped between two duties: one to a father, the other to a brother. He looked so upset I had to let it go.

~ Well, never mind – I forgive you.

~ You do? His face brightened. ~ Thank you, Max.

~ Think nothing of it. You owe me, I said, immediately contradicting myself. ~ C'mon, let's go find Ram. He's promised to take us on a trek to the other end of the island. I only hope he doesn't show us that big leech, or I might throw up.

Rambuta was taking us fishing on the reef. At the far end

of the island the coral gardens were shallow. You could walk right across the lagoon knee deep to where the big ocean waves curled up and over you. You could see through them like green glass, before they crashed down on the outer reef. The fishing there was good. We noticed that as well as his rod, Ram carried a rifle. I thought that maybe he was worried about the bearded hogs. I asked him if he had loads of ammunition in his backpack.

Ram laughed. ~ No, not really. Just my sketchpad.

~ Sketchpad? repeated Hass.

~ Here — I'll show you.

He laid his rifle and rod carefully on a rock and took the pad out of his backpack. He showed us a drawing of a hornbill. It was pretty good. Then a bearded hog. And finally a flying fox.

There was no dragging either Hass or Ram away from the fishing, and I got fed up after a while. With the waves pounding the outer reef just a few yards away, booming under the coral shelf, my ears started to ring. And the salt sea-spray got into my eyes and made them sore. So I went back to the beach for a while. I took some fruit out of Rambuta's backpack and started to munch on it. Then I noticed the corner of his sketchbook sticking out of the pack. I got it and started to leaf through it, studying the animals and plants he'd drawn.

Halfway through the pad I came to something I recognised.

It was a drawing of that rat-thing Hass and me had photographed.

On the next page was a drawing of another strange-looking animal. ~ Must be a mutant, I said to myself. ~ Somethin' deformed at birth. You did get things like chickens with three legs. I was about to turn over the page when I saw Ram and Hass wading back to the beach on the coral shelf.

I returned the sketchpad to the backpack.

We caught a whole bunch of reef fish that day and walked proudly back along the beach to our end of the island. As we got nearer to the camp I said to Ram, ~ I know your secret.

He looked down at me, puzzled. ~ And what secret is that, Max?

~ I looked at your sketchbook, I said, and winked at Hass.

Rambuta went very pale and for the first time I saw a glint of anger in his eyes.

~ That was private property – personal to me, he said. ~ Do you usually peek at people's personal things, Max?

I was thoroughly taken aback. Ram had never been angry with us before now. I wanted to undo my meddling immediately.

~ I'm sorry, Ram. I shouldn't have.

~ No, he was almost shouting at me, ~ you shouldn't have.

~ I said I'm sorry.

He didn't answer me. He simply motioned with his arm that we were to go back to camp. Hass and I gathered up the fish we'd caught, while Rambuta picked up his rifle and went ahead.

The walk back to camp was miserable for me. Hass chattered to Rambuta, who gave him cursory answers, but nothing more was said to me. I wished I could undo what I'd done. Ram had never been angry with me before and it hurt a great deal. I tried to think what I'd really done wrong. I guess I knew. Looking in his sketchbook was like reading his diary or something. It was a private record. I hadn't known that though. I hadn't known how private his sketches were to him.

As soon as we got back, Ram spoke to dad. Dad looked across at me and I thought I was in for more trouble. But dad simply turned away and went back into one of the half-ruined huts we used as a storeroom.

Nothing was said at the meal. Hass seemed oblivious of the atmosphere around the table. I could feel it though, even if dad and Rambuta tried to act as if nothing had happened. Afterwards, while I was chopping some wood for the campfire, Ram came to me.

~ Max, I didn't meant to upset you, out there on the beach.

~ Yes you did, I replied. ~ You were angry.

He sighed. ~ It's the difference between our cultures — I'm a very private man, Max. Private property is precious to those who have not had it for very long.

I knew what he was getting at. ~ You weren't poor — your dad sold medicines.

~ We weren't rich, either. He was selling to people who had very little money for such things. If the community is poor, it doesn't matter what you do, you struggle for survival.

~ Okay, I said.

~ Can we be friends again? He stretched out his hand. I felt a little misty.

~ All right. I won't do it again, I promise.

~ Well, we all make mistakes. What — er — what did you see in the sketchbook?

~ Nothin' much. A couple of weird animals. On the first two pages. One of 'em I'd seen in the forest. That creature like a giant rat.

He looked sort of relieved. ~ Oh, that? And that's all? The one on the next page, the puppy-looking thing with wings? There are some strange beasts in the world. There's the dugong that Georgia mentioned . . .

~ She called me one, I recalled hotly.

Ram ignored this predictable outburst. ~ Then there's the molloch — the Australian thorny devil — that's really quite odd. And the aye-aye from Madagascar. And of course the ocean really throws up many, many horrifying shapes.

I told Ram I got the picture. There were weirdies everywhere.

Later, after we'd spent the traditional evening hour by the campfire, I went to bed. Hass stayed up a bit later. He was on kitchen chores. Dad came to me in the tent. He flipped back the flap and stayed outside.

~ You're letting all the mosquitoes in, I grumbled.

~ Max, I'm sorry you had that run-in with Ram. He's very sensitive about his property.

~ It's all right. We've made up.

~ I know — look, those drawings . . .

~ I don't know what all the fuss is about, I interrupted.

Dad looked at me and then said, ~ No, neither do I. He turned to leave the tent.

~ Can you let the flynet down now? The mozzies are swarming in.

~ Right.

He dropped the flynet and left me to my thoughts.

I said I didn't know what all the fuss was about, but that didn't mean I wasn't aware that something was up. Someone was holding something back. There were secrets to unravel. I wasn't quite sure what at the moment, but I was getting there. I lay there on my back for an hour after that, staring at the top of the tent.

I decided that tomorrow I would go and see the Porters. See what they thought about things. It was no good talking to Hass. He always took dad's side. I didn't mind that. I knew he was grateful to dad for rescuing him from goatherding, whatever. But you couldn't criticise dad in front of him. You got nowhere if you suggested that something sinister was going on.

7 August, Krantu Island

The next chance that I get I'm going to look where dad and Ram have been going. I followed them a little way into the rainforest, so I'm pretty sure I know where they headed. It's the valley in the middle of the island. The place where all the animals tend to gather. I can't believe all this secrecy is over a rhino. Why? It doesn't make sense. It's got to be something to do with the Qumran scrolls. I think I know what it is. Treasure! Got to be, hasn't it? The scrolls were a sort of treasure map which led dad to this island. He's been poring over them in the fish-drying shed, trying to work out just where it was buried. That's why the pirates are hanging round, waiting for us to leave with the booty.

Only one thing still bothers me. What was that animal that crashed through the wall of the fish-drying shed? Maybe it was a rhino, but nothing to do with what dad was doing. Maybe they were worried about it attacking them in the rainforest, so they trapped it and locked it up. It begins to make sense. They're all carrying rifles now, when they go off into the trees – dad, Ram and Grant. That's because they're scared the rhino will charge them, unawares. Now that it's been captured once they can't do it again because it's too wary.

Buried treasure! Time Hass and I went to have a look.

8 August, Krantu Island

Hass and I went to the yacht early next morning. The Porters were all up and about. As we swam out to the boat I could hear a lot of droning going on. That didn't sound good. Droning meant lessons. Sure enough Lorraine was propped in a canvas-backed chair with CAPTAIN'S MATE written on it. Georgia was sitting in a pool of curled rope on the deck. They both had their noses in small dusty-looking books. We emerged from the lagoon, dripping water over Grant's varnished deck. It dried almost as soon as it hit the hot planks.

~ Don't you have school work to do? asked Lorraine of us, looking up over her reading glasses.

Hass said, ~ We've done ours.

Georgia's mother shook her head. ~ We're comparing and contrasting Tennyson and Longfellow. Lorraine smiled. ~ Do you want to join us?

I shuddered. Surprisingly enough, much as I loved Georgia, and was thrilled to be in her company, the thought of a lesson on poetry didn't fill me with joy.

~ No thanks. We've done them.

Georgia sniffed. ~ You've read all the works of Alfred Lord Tennyson and Longfellow? Yeah, right.

~ Not me, Hass said, and promptly sat on the deck, his

arms back to support himself, and went into listening mode. ~ I do not know these people.

Grant looked at me. ~ Max. You want to come for a walk? he said.

This was a new one. Grant and me, going for a walk. Better than listening to poetry.

~ Yeah, okay, I agreed.

Grant went below and came up a few minutes later dressed in combat shirt, shorts and hat – and a rifle. The gun didn't surprise me. Since dad had revealed that there was a rhino loose in the forest all the adults carried weapons. We kids didn't of course (though not for want of asking), but we weren't allowed in the forest any more without being accompanied by an adult. The only thing we were allowed to do was use the wide clearway from the camp to the beach.

~ Okay, let's go, said Grant, lowering the inflatable dinghy. ~ I want you to show me where you saw that rat-like creature with feathers.

I was surprised. ~ You know about that?

~ I heard Georgia telling her mother about it – I wasn't supposed to hear.

~ She wasn't supposed to tell anybody.

~ Listen, Max, Grant said, looking me right in the eyes, ~ there are no secrets between a mother and a daughter. Remember that for the rest of your life. You tell one, the other one's going to know within the hour. Believe me, it never fails to amaze me how fast it works.

He rowed us to the shore. There was a light breeze blowing but apart from that the day was what my mum would have called a slightly mad day. (It was one of her jokes – she meant

122

balmy.) The waves were rearing out on the reef and the sky was as clear as blue plate.

~ Don't scratch, growled Grant, as he rowed.

My shorts and T-shirt were already dry by now, after the swim. They were all stiff and starchy with salt but I was used to that. Dad always made me wear a shirt if I was spending time in the water anyway, 'cause of sunburn. All the adults were hot on that. But though I was used to wearing sandpaper it still itched a lot and I scratched.

We beached the dinghy and I took Grant down a narrow path into the undergrowth, which closed around us like a moist-hot green blanket.

~ Where are we going? he asked.

~ The valley place, with all the pools.

He nodded, as if he'd guessed it.

I told him, ~ We can look for the treasure at the same time.

~ What treasure? Grant looked surprised now.

I said slyly, ~ Isn't that what dad's looking for? The scrolls and all that? They're a map in code, aren't they?

~ News to me, he muttered, hefting his rifle.

I said nervously, ~ You're not going to shoot anything?

~ Don't worry, Max — my daughter would never speak to me again if I did. I'm not even allowed to tread on a cockroach.

We entered the lacework of plants.

After we had walked some way along a narrow path towards the central valley, Grant said, ~ Rambuta showed you some drawings.

~ Well, I looked at them without permission.

~ What did you think?

I shrugged. ~ He's good at sketching.

~ No, what did you think about the creatures you saw?

I shrugged again. What was there to think about? What a fuss over a few sketches.

Grant seemed to drop this subject and started to talk about Rambuta himself. ~ Now that fellah Ram, he's no slouch. Mind you, you'd think he would miss his wife and family, wouldn't you? All this time here.

Grant was big on family and would find that slightly suspicious but I was just flabbergasted to learn that Rambuta had one.

~ He's married?

Grant looked at me. ~ Sure. Two kids. One's eight, the other's five – boy and a girl.

~ Heck, I didn't know that.

There was a shrug from Grant. ~ You have to ask – he's not the kind to offer it. Kinda private guy, Ram. I like that in a man. Civil, but private.

I tried to defend myself. ~ I learned other things from him. I was just about to tell him what other things when he interrupted me in mid-sentence. ~ Hey, Max, look at these. There were prints in the soft mossy floor. Big prints.

~ Looks like a big animal, I confirmed.

He unslung his rifle. ~ Let's check it out.

We began to follow the trail cautiously, but it soon gave out on harder ground. The trouble with the forest floor is that it's covered in roots. They stick up everywhere and form a great woven mat. It makes it difficult to walk on but also protects it from prints. It's only around the mangrove swamp areas that you find it soft and easy enough to leave a trail.

~ Damn, muttered Grant. ~ Maybe we can follow the broken foliage?

We tried that too, but in a lot of areas there were just these massive trees that went shooting up to the sky. They had trunks as thick as church towers and buttress roots taller than I was. They had parasites – these big dangly vines like ship ropes hanging down – but you couldn't tell whether they'd been walked through or not.

We got on to a narrow path. Grant was in front of me. The light shafted down on either side of us like bars of sunshine. There were butterflies and moths filling these beams. Suddenly Grant stopped dead and I ran into his back. He didn't complain. He simply spoke.

~ Mother of . . . holy crap, what the hell is that? he said in a hushed voice.

I looked around his arm.

There was this glittering lump of gold on the other side of the glade. Then I saw it was moving, stirring like some creature that had been curled up asleep. It began to unfold, open up, just like a flower blossoming quickly. When the sun caught it with a ray it dazzled me for a minute: a shining with a slickness to its fur and feathers. It had its back to us, sitting licking golden-syrupy threads from itself. It was small, about the size of a newly born pup. But it wasn't a dog. It was really, really quite weird – but beautiful to look at. A bit like the second sketch in Ram's book.

~ That's brilliant, I whispered. My body tingled as if there was electricity running through it. ~ Can we get closer? What is it?

I felt the shudder go through Grant. I looked at his face. It was full of revulsion. Clearly he did not think this animal was a wonder of nature. I think he thought it was hellish. I guess it was a bit freaky, but as Ram had told me, lots of creatures were.

125

~ That's disgusting, muttered Grant.

Not to me, though. I think this was a grown-up's reaction to something he hadn't seen before. It was kind of strange, I admit, with a body like a dog's and a long lizardy tail. There were things stuck to its sides as well, which looked out of place. And its head was too big for the rest of it. But I liked the golden colour and the way its fur shone.

I'd never heard of an animal like this, but then I'd never heard of a dugong, molloch or an aye-aye either.

~ Wow! I murmured, as the animal unfolded. ~ Look at that!

Grant raised his rifle, just instinct I think, and took aim. I don't know whether he actually intended to shoot the creature. Now when I think about it, I don't think so. His breath was coming out really quick, like he was scared or excited or something. Even if he had wanted to kill the animal he wasn't able to. It looked up, saw us, and slipped swiftly into the bushes. Gone in a twinkling. We were left wondering.

~ What in hell was that? Grant cried. ~ Max, did you recognise that one?

Why would I? I said that. ~ I've never seen one before. You should ask Ram.

~ I thought you could identify certain — creatures. I understood you'd seen all the drawings. Your father's remarkably tight-lipped about the spin-offs. Okay, he's talked about — about some things — tried to show me the big one, but she's too well camouflaged. But her children are easy to see, if you catch them out and about. You sure you don't know? Rambuta told me . . . well, never mind.

What was he jabbering about? ~ You mean Ram's drawings? They were freaks.

~ Crazy damn island, muttered Grant. He was very upset ~ Crazy, crazy. You saw it, Max? You're my witness. This is god-awful stuff. His hands were trembling. ~ Someone has to have some answers here. I've had enough of this. I want some straight answers or . . . he gabbled on and on ~ . . . I tell you, boy, your father needs a psychoanalyst. We all will, after this. Damn jungle's full of the creeps. My family could be in danger. When my family's in danger, boy they better watch out, because I get my dander up. Someone's got to do some talking, or I'll get real mad. You don't want to know me when I get mad, not where my family's concerned . . .

We went straight back after that. I had to walk quickly to keep up with this big hunched man with a rifle at the ready. Grant kept looking this way and that, as if expecting to see something fly out of the forest at him. Once or twice he twitched and almost blew some innocent bird to bits just for ruffling its wings. A wild pig ran across the path and almost gave both of us a heart attack but it was too quick for Grant, otherwise it would have been pork stew. He yelled after it, as if it had scared him on purpose.

All the way home I kept thinking about what we'd seen. It was mind-blowing.

We went straight into the camp. Dad was writing in one of his notepads, sitting at a table in the open. Grant blasted him from long range with that gravelly voice of his.

~ Sanders! There's one of those things in the jungle. I need to know what it was. Eh? I want some answers, *now*.

Dad looked up with a funny expression.

~ I've already . . .

~ No, not *that*. I know you told me about that.

127

He went on to describe the creature we'd seen.

Dad said, ~ Did you take Max with you?

Grant replied, ~ I did. How the hell else was I going to identify anything? You refused to do so. Rambuta is employed by you, so he won't help me either.

Dad's tone suddenly turned very bitter. ~ You should have thought of that before you came here to spy on me for the damned Krenshaw Institute.

My head came up quickly. Had I heard that word right? Spy? Grant was a spy? Yes, yes I had. I could see by their faces. Grant looked guilty. I was stunned. I looked at Grant, seeing him in a completely different light. Grant? Wow, dad wasn't as paranoid as we thought. Well, maybe he was, but this time he was right to be paranoid. Grant Porter was a spy for an institute. Archaeological espionage. What a sneak!

Grant was still furious and refused to go on the defensive.

~ Is my family in danger from those abominations? Because by heck, if they are, mister—

~ Don't be so dramatic, Porter, replied dad. ~ You can go any time you like. Pack up now and sail away. No one asked you and your family to stay here. No one invited you.

Rambuta had come out of a tent and now stood a little way off from the two men.

~ I'm calling the authorities, Grant warned. ~ I don't care if they send the whole Malaysian police force out there – maybe that's what's needed . . .

Ram spoke now quietly. ~ Mr Porter, he said, ~ you don't realise how important this is. Please. Can we talk? I'll tell you everything you need to know this time, I promise. All right, James?

My dad nodded. Grant went with Ram to a hut, where they started to talk in low voices. Grant still had a face that threatened thunder. When he left though, about an hour later, he looked a bit better. I'd like to know what Ram said but I didn't ask. He wouldn't tell me anyway.

9 August, Krantu Island

I'm trying to work all this out.

Dad comes here with some ancient scrolls to unravel a secret he's found in them. Some institute or other sends Grant Porter to find out what dad is doing here. There are pirates sailing around the islands, looking for something. There's a big animal somewhere which could have been the same big animal that broke out of the fish-drying shed. This island has one or two weird creatures wandering about.

Here's what I think.

The secret in the scrolls is a treasure – gold chalices, jewelled daggers, pearl necklaces – buried somewhere in the valley. Pirates in this part of the Pacific know there's treasure buried on one of the islands and somehow they've got wind that an Englishman knows where it is. The big lumbering beast is the rhino that Ram talked about. It was left here to deter people from looking for the treasure: a sort of guard, if you like. The two weird creatures are freaks of nature, nothing to do with the treasure. You get mutants and things on remote islands when nature goes wrong. Ram is interested in them because he's a zoologist and that's what zoologists do. Grant hates them because he's a jeweller and he likes beautiful stones and gold, not ugly 'abominations'.

That all seemed pretty tidy to me. I felt proud of myself.

10 August, Krantu Island

I looked from one to the other, first at Hass, then at Georgia. I had a spade in my hand and determination in my heart.

~ Come on, I said. ~ We need to find it first.

Georgia said, ~ You think there's treasure hidden in the valley?

~ What else could it be? I asked. ~ It's got to be something like that. Look, my — our dad has these scrolls that Hass found in a cave in the desert. Well, I found one, but that's beside the point. We found 'em. Dad spends months studying them. Then he buys some more with the same indigo markings on them, from all over the world. Next thing you know, we come to this island, with the scrolls and there's all this secrecy going on . . .

~ Hugger-mugger, said Georgia. ~ That's what Shakespeare called it.

~ Whatever, I replied, annoyed at being interrupted. ~ Anyway, if we can find scrolls when adults can't, we can find treasure. They're half-blind. They haven't got young eyes like us.

~ And what about these strange creatures?

~ That's just a smokescreen, I replied. ~ Definitely. A couple of weird creatures in the forest? You get weird things everywhere.

~ What, a rhino? said Hass.

130

~ Not the rhino – the rat-thing and the other thing. I've worked it out, see. Ram drew them because he's a zoologist.

~ You've already said that, she pointed out.

~ I'm just trying to make you understand. You know your dad's a spy. He was sent here to spy on my dad.

It still rankled a bit.

Now it was Georgia who became annoyed. ~ He wasn't sent. My mother and father have been planning this trip for years. It was my fault. I put dad's project on a website – about us planning to sail across the Pacific looking for black coral – and someone at the Krenshaw Institute saw it. They contacted dad and asked him to . . .

~ . . . spy on our dad.

~ Well, yes, but it wasn't as if they sent him specially. I didn't know about the spying. Even my mother didn't know. I heard dad telling her last night. You can hear everything on a boat – the bulkheads are very thin. He said the institute had heard the story of the manuscripts from a Professor Ahmed.

~ We know him! I looked at Hass. ~ He was our dad's colleague in Jordan. And they're not *manuscripts*, they're scrolls.

~ Yes, well, he told the Krenshaw Institute that your dad had found some manuscripts – or scrolls, whatever – and that he had leased an island just off Sarawak in Borneo. The institute deals in antiquities in the USA and they wanted to know what your dad was up to.

~ He's quite famous in some circles, I said, feeling quite proud of him. ~ He's found some very rare weapons in his time.

~ I don't know about that, replied Georgia. ~ I just know that dad said okay, he would do what he could. The other day he found out something and your dad had to spill the beans. You remember they went off together and after a long talk they came back. What they talked about, I don't know, but at least they're speaking now.

~ The treasure, I said. ~ Definitely the treasure.

~ One thing bothers me, said Georgia.

~ What's that?

~ People in New Testament times, coming all this way to bury a treasure. It doesn't make sense.

~ Ah, I thought about that, I said. ~ Ram says ancient Arab dhows were like the Viking longboats, or Chinese junks — they went all over the world, trading with other people. Look at the Silk Road. That goes all the way from Arabia into China. I think there was an Arab dhow full of treasure which got blown off course, like a lot of them were. It got wrecked and the crew were washed ashore here. They managed to rescue their gold and jewels and bury them. Then they built a raft out of bamboo and sailed to the mainland and finally got back to Arabia.

~ You made all that up!

~ Of course I did, I replied. ~ I know it didn't happen *exactly* like that — but something like it.

Hassan stood up. ~ Well, let's go and see if anyone's been digging anywhere in the valley then, he stated.

Georgia shrugged. ~ All right, I'm up for it — against my better judgement.

We set off with bottles of water. I led the way, first through the rainforest, then across the mangrove swamps. You have to be careful on the swamps because there could be quicksand. It's best to tread on knots of grass, if you've got good balance. Eventually we reached the edge of the valley, skirting outcrops

of jagged volcanic rock, and descending into the basin of vegetation which held the freshwater pools.

I was a little nervous because though I talked big, about the
treasure being there and everything, I wasn't as confident as I
sounded. Now I was nearing the valley my theory seemed a little
thin. What if we couldn't find any traces of digging? What if I
was completely wrong about everything? The other two would
have a field day. It isn't much fun being the target of the only
other two kids on a small island. You can't escape the sneers. I
can't just go out and make another friend. There aren't any. By
the time we stepped foot on valley moss, I was desperate for a
sign.

My keen eyes searched everywhere as I went, looking for
places where the surface had been disturbed. I was convinced
now that my dad was looking for something of great value. If I
could find it for him he would be pleased with me. I desperately
want his favour. It seemed to me that I've been a drag on him for
a long time. I want him to appreciate me, the way some dads do
their kids. I need him to notice me. It's as if I'm invisible most of
the time, except when I've done something wrong. The only time
he speaks to me is to tell me off for something. When we found
that key scroll for him in the desert cave he talked to me half
the night. I'd done it once, I could do it again, with Hass and
Georgia's help.

Deep in the valley, where the vegetation was at its thickest,
I was at screaming point. There was no evidence of any distur-
bance of the landscape. Georgia was out in front. Already she
was beginning to complain about a 'wild goose chase'. My heart
was sinking down towards my sandals. Pretty soon I'd be kicking
it along like a football.

Then all of a sudden Georgia stopped dead.

~ What? asked Hassan.

She put a finger to her lips.

~ Shush! Look!

I stared where she was pointing. Amazingly, there was a horse drinking from a pool.

A horse? So what. It's still only a horse.

We were near the biggest of the rusty-looking pools. Then the horse drew back from the water's edge. Except that it wasn't a horse. When it lifted its head I saw the most magnificent spiral horn protruding from its forehead. Then I saw how much more beautiful it was than a common horse. What an astounding, wonderful beast! Its coat had a sheen like no horse or zebra any of us had seen. When it turned its head our way you could see far-off lands in its eyes. Lands with castles and giants and other marvels. And its horn! Unblemished. Perfect. Ivory, with a blood-red tip. It took my breath away to see how gracefully the creature moved.

I felt a wave of heat go through my body, but at the same time I shivered. I think it was some sort of shock. This was supposed to be a creature of fiction, after all. My brain went into a spin as I tried to come to terms with this incredible sight. The unicorn wasn't the only strange creature drinking from that pool. There were others. But they were hazy figures as my mind grappled with the unbelievable. How could this be? Was it some kind of trick? Projections, or holograms? No, they looked too real. We could smell them. There were flies on the unicorn's flanks. It swished its tail to rid itself of them. These creatures were real.

~ How did they get here? I asked, when I could speak. ~ Who brought them?

~ Your father must have done, replied Georgia in a croaky voice.

Hass said, ~ Did he make them? Did our father make these creatures in the shed?

That didn't make sense. But did any of it make sense? Mythical beasts, alive and drinking from rainforest pools.

~ He's not a surgeon, I said scornfully, ~ he's an archaeologist. An idea struck me then, forcefully. ~ It's got something to do with the scrolls, I bet.

But that's as far as I could go. My imagination then failed me.

~ No wonder they wouldn't let us come out here, said Georgia. ~ And that giant rat we saw in the rainforest. That was one of them too. It had to be. And the beastie you saw with my dad, Max.

~ Ram's drawings! I cried, a little too loud.

The creatures around the pool were startled by my cry, their heads coming up quickly. They stared for a few minutes at where we were hidden, while we held our breath. Soon they settled down again. They were not wild beasts after all. They were what they were. Perhaps we had no need to hide, but I didn't want to test it. Nor did Georgia and Hass. This was unknown territory. There were no experts. We had to ditch everything we knew about ordinary animals and start again. We were as new to these wonders of supernature as they were to us.

Perhaps we could be friends?

~ But what about the treasure? I whispered, reluctant to let my idea go. ~ Do you think that's here too?

~ There's no treasure, said Georgia scornfully. ~ That's why your dad came to the valley — to photograph the unicorn.

~ And that — over there! whispered Hass.

We followed the pointing finger. Another fabulous beast had stopped drinking and was lying in the shade of a thorn bush. A huge golden lion. Yet as we watched, it unfolded a pair of eagle's wings attached to its flanks. It spread those wings as if drying them in the sun. A lion, yet even as I stared I could see differences between a normal king of the jungle and this beast. This one had the body of a goat and the tail of reptile. In one way it too was as beautiful as the unicorn — yet in another, it was terrifying. I didn't know whether to clap my hands or run for my life. A fabulous beast with claws and teeth that could rip you apart.

We sat down quietly, the three of us, to scour the glade with our eyes. We were terrified of course — at least, I was and I bet the other two were as well — but we couldn't draw ourselves away from that wonderful sight. I bet no one could've. We could have been scared out of our wits but we somehow knew this was that magical moment in our lives which we would remember for ever. Fear of death couldn't have dragged us from that place. Our whole existence on this planet of ours was pinned to this experience we were having and not one of us could leave it simply because we were scared. I wanted it to last for eternity. I kicked myself for bringing a spade instead of a camera. If I'd have had a camera with me I'd have been in half-a-dozen heavens at once.

How could we not be entranced? There were mythical creatures everywhere, lying, grazing, drinking, strolling through the trees. Many I couldn't recognise, but I did identify a gryphon, a sort of fox-like creature, a snake-thing with wings, a senmurv which I'd seen once in a comic strip, and one or two others that I might have guessed at. There was only one of each and they didn't seem to bother one another. The winged lion, which

136

Georgia said was a lammasu from ancient Assyria, which she'd seen carvings of in a museum, did snatch a bird from a bush. It ate the bird, chomping it down, beak, claws and feathers. So we guessed these mythological creatures weren't vegetarians. Or not all of them, anyway, though some must have been. The unicorn at least.

~ We'd better go, I whispered at last. ~ Before they see us.

Maybe they'd already seen us and didn't care? Anyway we crept away, into the rainforest, and made our way back to camp. We were all stunned by the wondrous nature of what we'd witnessed. Unnatural beasts, but creatures with tremendous power over your heart and mind. How had all these folklore beings come to be here? Dad couldn't have brought them. I'd seen what came out of the crates we carried with us and there were no live animals of any kind, let alone fabulous beasts. Yet there in that valley were some of the most wicked creatures ever seen. I just had to get a camera of some kind and record them.

My mind was spinning with amazement and wonder. Had these beings been here when we arrived? I decided not. Some magic had conjured them from the earth. The scrolls! I went back to the scrolls again. Not magic, surely? What then? How did we get from the scrolls to live beasts? I couldn't work it out. This indeed was the secret and why Grant had been so horrified. I could understand about Grant. He wasn't a man with a massive imagination. I liked him. I liked him a lot but mostly because he liked me and treated me as an adult. But you had to say he wasn't someone with a mind that flew in regions unknown.

~ Do we tell father? whispered Hass, as we came closer to the camp. ~ Do we tell him that we have seen these things?

137

~ No, replied Georgia. ~ Let's not.

~ Georgia's right, I murmured, chucking the spade behind a hut to collect later. ~ We'd better keep it to ourselves that we know. Let them tell *us* in their own good time . . .

However, as we rounded a broken section of the stockade we were confronted by a sight that made my jaw drop. There was dad, Ram and Grant, all armed to the teeth, apparently about to go on an expedition. Dad's face was like thunder when he saw me. The other adults looked pretty mad too, even Grant. Lorraine, standing behind the men, let out a screech of something like joy and agony, maybe tinged with anger. They descended on us and demanded to know where we'd been.

~ We were just about to come out as a search party, dad barked at us. ~ We thought you were lost — or worse.

~ We've been to see the creatures, I said, straight out, no messing. ~ The strange beasts.

~ Max! cried Georgia, in an admonishing tone.

I turned to her, saying, ~ Well, I had to.

It certainly had the desired effect. It took the wind out of all the adults.

Lorraine said, ~ You went to the valley?

~ Yes, replied Georgia, ~ and we saw them.

~ Did you see the mother Beast? asked dad, not denying anything.

Puzzled, I replied, ~ No. What's that?

~ It's the creature who gives birth to those mythological beings — not that any of us has seen her lately. I'll tell you about her one day, but now is too soon. You've had enough of a shock for one day. I suggest you get a hot drink . . .

But my dad doesn't know kids. We're better at taking in

things like this than they are. We can take shocks to the imagination better than they can. What is incredible to adults is just stretching the truth to us. Our eyes go just as round. Our mouths drop open just the same. But our minds are like deserts waiting to be filled with forests or cities. There's plenty of space there, ready for the most unbelievable facts or fiction. When I lay down that night I just let all this wash over me. I bathed in the incredible. I let it take hold of me and fill me with wonder.

Oh, what dreams I have had since seeing the unicorn!

11 August, Krantu Island

Grant Porter is in a fix, as he would call it. He wants to think dad is a nutter, but then that would make him one too. Two nutters on the same island? Poor old Grant. Georgia told me Grant was talking wildly about distorted science and stuff like that. I know he went into the rainforest armed with his rifle today, looking for I don't know what. Maybe he was hoping all the mythological beasts had gone away.

~ When I woke up this morning, I said to Georgia, ~ I had trouble believing about yesterday.

~ It feels like that, she agreed earnestly. ~ It's weird. I can't explain it. How could it be true? Yet there're those creatures out there.

~ I know. I feel like that too. My mind jumps backwards and forwards. I still can't get it, yet I know it's true.

~ What about Hass? she asked.

~ Oh, he believes everything. Gospel.

~ Must be nice to be so trusting, she said wistfully. ~ I wish I trusted things like that.

I said, ~ The other day in the rainforest, I found this slime all over a clearing. It was like it'd dropped from the sky.

~ And had it?

~ I dunno, do I? I don't think so. How could it?

~ It rains frogs in some places — they get taken up by wind or something and dropped later. What sort of slime was it?

~ Just slime, like gel only stickier.

~ I think my father wants to take us away now.

A bombshell. ~ Oh no, I cried, aghast. ~ He can't.

~ Well, he wants to.

12 August, Krantu Island

But the Porters didn't go in the end. I don't know why. Maybe Lorraine had something to do with it. They all came to the camp that evening and Grant said he wanted to talk to dad. They went off together and when they came back they looked like pals — or as close as you can get to pals with a bloke like my dad.

Dad was saying, ~ . . . we can study them at leisure, without interference from state or private institution. Don't you think that's a unique opportunity? A wonderful chance we've been given, to further the course of human knowledge?

Grant said, ~ Listen, you're talking about fame. I don't care about fame. I don't want it.

~ Just for one moment, dad said, ~ think — think of what's happening here. Think of the opportunity we've been given. We have marvellous creatures like the adaro, the basilisk, the unicorn. We have these exclusively to ourselves. And they're only really dangerous when you corner them. They get nervous and react violently when they feel trapped, like any wild creature. The mythical group are particularly sensitive to being enclosed — and I'm afraid that's how they must feel here, on this small island.

~ That makes sense, said Grant.

~ Well, whether it makes sense or not, it's what we've got. We can either study these creatures or we can call in the authorities. I've been videoing them and taking stills. You could do the same, from the yacht. You'd be reasonably safe out there . . .

Grant looked at his wife and Lorraine nodded.

~ Okay, said the Californian jeweller, after a period of silence during which he seemed to have done some deep thinking, ~ let's get the game plan on the table. We study these creatures — presumably since there's been nothing like them before in recent times everyone is an amateur here and has equal status, professor or not? Yes? In which case, we do some empirical research, combine notes and video footage at the end, and take our findings to the outside world together. Any credit will be shared equally amongst us, children included. Any money earned will be shared equally amongst us, married couples included. Is this acceptable to everyone around this table? If not, I call the authorities.

~ Are you issuing an ultimatum? dad asked.

~ If you want to call it that.

~ In that case, you leave me no choice, said dad. He let Grant have the ghost of a smile, ~ I accept.

Hassan and I gave out a little cheer. Georgia laughed and

clapped her hands. Rambuta smiled and rocked his head from side to side. Grant looked at his wife and shrugged, while she put an arm around his neck.

~ You're not such an old fuddy-duddy, are you? she said.

He looked a little shocked. ~ Why, is that how you both think of me?

~ Well, you are a little stiff and starchy, dad, said Georgia. ~ But we love you anyway.

~ Heck, I'm as loose and floppy as anybody, he complained. ~ I'm just a little – cautious, that's all.

At that moment a loud and frightening hiss came from the rainforest.

~ What's that? cried Lorraine. ~ Did you hear it?

~ Basilisk, murmured dad, jumping up. ~ The creatures have left the valley at last. That's a worrying development, I'll grant you. They're wandering free. I thought somehow this would happen in the end. Now, whatever you do don't look the basilisk in the eyes. I'll get my rifle . . .

13 August, Krantu Island

Dad didn't shoot the basilisk, of course. They're not like ordinary game anyway. You could be almost treading on one and you wouldn't see it. They're so well camouflaged. And the bit about looking a basilisk in the eye is only legend. What they say is, you'll shrivel up and die. No one's proved it yet, though.

Having said that, who wants to test it?

I had other things to think about too, apart from this

nightmare dad had created for us on Krantu. My worries were double the size of everyone else's, or so I thought anyway. The sea-raiders. Every day I watched the horizon for the pirates. But I never saw any more of the junk. I was beginning to think I had been seeing things. It's not hard to see mirages out at sea. Especially in the tropics where the heatwaves make funny patterns in the air. I didn't stop looking though. Just in case.

One day we three kids were wandering around just off the main path to the camp area when we came across a huge hide draped over the bushes. It took three of us to drag it back to camp. It was pretty heavy, being thick and big. It turned out to be a huge tattooed hide.

~ She's sloughed, said dad, looking towards the rainforest. ~ I wonder why?

~ Snakes do it because they outgrow their skins, said Rambuta. ~ Maybe she's just getting bigger.

~ Maybe. But why would she be growing bigger? She's already given birth to a manticore and lammasu. What's bigger than a lion?

~ Could be anything, said Rambuta. ~ An elephant creature?

~ Like?

~ I was thinking of a naga, a mixture of elephant and snake.

~ Well, whatever it is, I hope we don't meet it on a dark night, if that's the reason she's sloughing. Dad then turned his attention to the great hide, now spread over the yard. ~ He left us mystified as to what creature had shed its skin and refused to answer any questions.

Rambuta, Grant and dad built a frame over which they stretched the mighty hide with its strange symbols and patterns.

Even while they were doing this work a gryphon ran over a clearing in front of the camp. Grant was both fascinated and appalled. I don't think the jeweller was really ready for an adventure of this magnitude. Leaving California and yachting to Krantu was about as big as adventures got with him. To find that the island he had come to was magical was a bit too much for him. The gryphon didn't even look like entering our site but Grant was taking no chances. He picked up his rifle and for the next two hours stood guard. There was that dazed look about him which said *I don't really believe all this is happening and I don't really want to be here.*

Both Grant and Lorraine had gone through a terrible shock. Dad and Rambuta had had a much longer time to get used to the idea of 'marvellous beasts' as dad called them. Maybe he and Ram had been shocked by each little discovery which led to the big one, but they'd gone through it by slow degrees. Or slower.

The rest of us had had it dumped on us all of a sudden and the American adults had been hit hardest. Their whole world had been ordered before. They thought they knew all about the world and how to deal with things that came along. Now it had been turned upside-down and inside-out, and it had knocked the stuffing out of them. They were nervous, twitchy, jumpy, frightened of course, and they looked as if they had been suddenly trapped in the middle of a war. They walked around with grey lined faces and wild eyes. I bet Grant went to bed hoping that he would wake up and it would all be a big hoax.

Kids are different. Georgia said it was because things are happening to them all the time and because they haven't built up a huge bank of experiences. I think it's because we still have imaginations. Not so long ago I believed in Father Christmas. Not so long ago Georgia thought fairies were real. Hass still believes in ghosts. Our imaginations haven't turned to concrete, like with the adults. We'd still been stunned and we were still scared, but we got over things quicker.

And we kids chattered about things more.

Georgia said excitedly, ~ It was its face that I found weird.

~ Human face, Hassan said, nodding. ~ A winged lion with a human face. That is very unusual.

I scoffed. ~ Unusual? We need to teach you some more words in English.

~ Very beautiful though, Georgia continued. ~ A lovely amber-gold coat and a dark mane. And its wings! Did you get some footage of it, Hass?

Hassan nodded again, showing us the camcorder. ~ It is all on here, he said. ~ The world cannot doubt this proof.

~ You just watch, I said. ~ Dad says unless we take a lammasu home, alive and well, they'll do anything and everything they can to discredit him – us. He says there're a lot of sceptics out there, ready to attack anything out of the ordinary. I've seen stuff done on film that isn't true – people can make creatures out of odds and ends and make 'em look as real as anything.

~ Well, there are quite a few of us here, stated Georgia. ~ They'll see we can't all be lying.

~ They'll think it's a conspiracy – that's what dad says.

Anyway, Georgia was right about one thing. The lammasu

145

was beautiful. So was the other lion-creature, the manticore, which didn't have any wings but it had a tail that fired poisonous darts. Then there was the unicorn. The unicorn was a supreme mythological animal. It was gentle, yet it was strong. There was freedom in its eyes, mane and tail. It had been shaped by the wind. We loved the unicorn.

The adults accompanied us to see the unicorn drinking at the freshwater pools and we took loads of photos and video footage of it.

Naturally other mythological beings were constant subjects of conversation.

~ That naga thing you talked about, Georgia asked Rambuta, ~ what's it like?

Hass and I clustered closer. Rambuta had a way with words.

~ What you must realise, Rambuta began, sitting on our beach log with us, ~ is that though we give mythical creatures names, those names do not mean there are no variations in the shape of the creature itself. The naga of Cambodia might not be the naga of Scotland or Mexico. The naga has several forms. One of them is a curious mixture of an elephant and a water-serpent, another — as found on the temple carvings of Angkor Wat — is a seven-headed cobra-like creature. What you must know is the *power* of the naga, which is over water. It is a symbol of water — the rain, the river, the sea — which can mean to us all that is good, or all that is evil. We need water to drink, to wash with, to travel on — yet it can come in the form of flood or wave that destroys us with its force.

All the men on the island had now taken to carrying rifles with them wherever they went. It was as if they were expecting something not just accidentally dangerous, but really aggres-

sive. You could see it in the way their eyes were constantly looking, looking, looking. I'd asked dad about this but he hadn't
answered me, not properly.

~ Is the naga very savage? I asked Rambuta. ~ Do we need
to run like hell if we see it?

~ You need to stay away from it, certainly, Max. But I don't
think a naga will necessarily pursue you with an intention to
harm. We do not know. These creatures are outside our experience. There are things written about them, from ancient times,
but first-hand knowledge is non-existent. We must be very wary.
Treat all of these mythical animals as potentially dangerous –
that is the only way to proceed.

So it wasn't the naga they were scared of. What then?
Secrets. Secrets overlaid with secrets. You dig, get to one layer,
then another, then another, and you wonder when you'll get to
the bottom of this pile of secrets.

We kids stayed on the log when Rambuta left.

~ They're not telling us everything, I said. ~ They're still keeping something from us.

~ I think so too, Georgia agreed with me. ~ You can see
they're all nervous about something now.

Hass said, ~ Do you think it is the sea-raiders, Max? Can it
be that our father believes you now?

~ Nah. If it was, they'd post someone on the beach to
watch for boats.

~ Some of those mythical creatures are very dangerous,
Georgia said, throwing stones into the lagoon and making plop-
ping sounds. ~ You've only got to look the natural weapons
they've got – horns, poisonous darts, teeth.

~ Well, maybe it's them then. I didn't think it was, but I

147

wasn't going to argue away a whole day. ~ Hey, look at that, I pointed to the shallows, ~ a sand shark.

It was a very small fish, not much more than half a metre long, but the fact that it was a shark attracted us. We followed it along the beach as it cruised close to the shore, wondering if it was going to attack smaller fish. In the end it headed out towards the reef and we soon lost it in the rippling effect of the gentle waves. By that time it was coming on evening and the usual fabulous red sunset washed across the sky.

The Porters were practically living in our camp now so Georgia came back with Hass and me. There was a good fire going in the main yard. There was always a good fire going into the night now. The adults seemed comforted by it, though we didn't need the heat. When I asked why we always had a fire going in the dark hours dad said it kept away the mosquitoes and other bothersome insects.

We baked yams in the ashes that evening.

14 August, Krantu Island

It was twilight. I was walking across the quadrangle of my old boarding school. We'd been doing the Elegy that very afternoon with Mr Simmons. I felt like a ploughman plodding my weary way home. I could hear the sound of a cricket ball hitting a bat. The upper sixth were at the nets. Rain was threatening. Dark thunderclouds edged with a sort of lacy gold from the setting sun were looming overhead.

It was quite spooky on the quad, with no one else about. The school buildings, ancient as days, crowded around me. Some

Victorian brickie had put this place together with no other thought than to scare the pants off imaginative kids. The main building was four storeys high, with two wings and a main entrance. Windows, windows, everywhere. They shone in the evening light like the multiple eyes of a watching monster.

On the roof at the two corners and at the ends of the wings there were green cupolas of corroded copper supported by thin pillars. We kids called these the Devil's watchtowers, having the suspicion that masters would go up there to spy on us.

Gargoyles ran the whole length of the gutters. Ugly beasts they were, with demonic ears and gaping mouths. Black with grime, they watched a boy's every move. First Years knew the gargoyles were just waiting to drop to the ground and swallow late and lonely souls crossing the quad to supper. You ran under those beasts, you didn't walk. And they hated you. You could see it in their faces. Naked hate.

I ran too, even though I wasn't a First Year. It was too eerie, the quad before a storm. Lightning suddenly cracked in the distance. Someone in the nets yelled, 'Inside, lads!' That was my intention too. To get inside. Quickly. I could smell the rain sizzling across the arable Suffolk land, raising an earthy odour from the flint-flecked fields. A hawk dived swiftly over the bell tower, disappearing behind the chapel. Tombstones of old masters who'd died with their teaching-boots on were being splattered with large drops.

But I never made the brass-nailed doors. I never got out of the outdoors and into the indoors. Suddenly I found myself up there on the eaves of that horrible building, looking down. My head was an ugly head, my face hideous. I knew even though I couldn't see myself. I'd taken the place of one of the hanging gargoyles. I was all neck, and throat, and gaping mouth. My body was gutter and pipe and rooftile.

I'd become a mythical creature.

I looked down on the quad below. Two small boys were dashing for the main doors. I stared, my mouth agape. They almost made it. But the rain beat them. It came sweeping in as a torrent. It swished across the rooftop and then over the quadrangle. The two small boys were soaked in seconds. They disappeared inside.

I tried to call for help. But though my mouth was wide and my throat was open, no sound came out. Instead my gullet filled with water which came gushing up from my neck. I spewed it out in a fulsome flow. It shot forth from my mouth, spurting out into the space above the quad. I knew it had come from the gutters, collecting all the rain that fell on the roof. And it never stopped coming. Surge after surge gargled through my neck and into my throat. I gagged water, coughed water, vomited water out, out, out, into the void beyond the walls of the school.

Horrified and appalled by my fate, I struggled to break free of the building, to tear myself from the eaves.

I sat up, the sweat running from me like water.

Hass was fast asleep beside me. The rain was using the tent as a drum, beating on it. For a few moments I hardly knew where I was. Then I realised I'd been dreaming. I wasn't at school. I was on the island. Monsoon rains lashed down on the tent. Rivulets were forming at the entrance, creeping under the flaps. There was lightning, sheet lightning which lit the world, but no thunder. Just flashing skies and the constant battering rain.

Despite the storm I was too hot. The humidity was stifling me. I crawled to the entrance and out into the cool rain. There

I let it lash at me. It came so hard and fast it stung my skin. I stood up and began walking, trying to get rid of the dream state which had distressed me so much during sleep. Soon I was walking along one of the rainforest paths. In the forest the rain was louder. It struck broad waxy leaves with a noise like pebbles on wood. It hissed in the canopy above my head. It drove wet fists through the lighter foliage of the secondary layer.

I walked.

I walked.

Finally I entered a glade. It was pitch-black at first. Then a brilliant flash. Sheet lightning lit my path. We saw each other at the same time. Terror swept over me. Not two metres away, on its foul belly, was one of the nightmares that now ran wild in the island's undergrowth.

A beast with a jewelled brow: a forehead of glittering stones.

I knew what it was. I'd seen it once before. Rambuta had been with me then. He gave it a name.

Makara.

A makara has the head of a crocodile and the hindquarters of a pig. There's a small curved horn on its snout. It's an ugly creature. At least, I found it ugly. Rainwater was streaming from its head and its mouth was running red with blood. This one had just killed. Probably one of its own kind, one of its kin. These mythical creatures recognise no brother or sister from the same womb.

Dad had told us the problem was that they were confined to a small space – this little island. They should have been born on a continent where it would have been different. They'd have had plenty of space to roam, to get well away from each other, to avoid each other. But here they were like a swarm of scorpions trapped in a shoebox. They needed to be out wandering the landscape but were cramped, trapped, and probably out of their minds. They attacked each other whenever they met.

The makara turned towards me, sloshing through a muddy puddle on its short legs, its hideous jaws snapping.

Blackness again.

I stood in the dense rain, shivering now. I waited for those crocodile jaws to clamp on my legs. I anticipated the sharp teeth tearing the flesh from my calves. Horrible thing. A death's-head. It would pull me to the ground and, gripping me, thrash me against a tree.

A series of sheet-lightning flashes.

The beast had gone, leaving the carcass of its dead prey.

And its prey was ghastly.

Sickly pale it lay in the puddle, its back broken by the makara. I stared at it in disbelief. It was totally unexpected. I might not have known it was a mythical creature, but I could see it was sexless. Where its sexual organs should have been was a smooth rounded bump of nothing. A bald mound. It was neither male nor female, like all the other fabled creatures born to the Beast. Our Beast. She always produced just one of a kind, no more. It was probably because we were on a small island. There was room only for one fabulous creature of each kind.

They were always like this one, without the power to reproduce themselves.

And this was one of hers.

Looking at it, this dead thing on the ground, I was so shocked I could hardly breathe.

Stunned, I turned and ran from the place, leaving the evidence of a secret so terrible it threatened to turn me mad.

Somehow I found my way back to the tent. I crawled inside to find Hassan still asleep, snoring gently. The rain was still washing down. Wet, miserable and horrified by my find, I went to wake him. But I stopped myself in time. I spent the rest of the night curled up like a foetus on my bedsheets, wondering.

In the morning I couldn't contain myself. I went to dad. Dad was the only one I could tell about this. He would know what to do. Dad never panicked over strangenesses. He considered them, then gave his advice.

Dad listened to my story and then I took him to the dead mythical creature.

Something had been eating it, but most of it was still there. Dad brushed off the ants, put on some rubber gloves, and inspected it.

~ You're right, he said. I knew from the sound of his voice he was as shocked as me. We both looked at each other. He put a hand on my shoulder. ~ You will tell *no one*, he said. ~ No one, do you understand?

I nodded hard. ~ What — what shall we *do*?

~ For once in my life I don't know what *is* the best thing to do, he confessed. ~ Believe it or not, I don't know everything, Max. In fact, this one has me at a complete loss. For the moment I think it best we keep this between the two of us.

For some reason I got a thrill out of that. Dad and I, having a secret between us that no one else would guess.

~ Okay, dad. I won't tell.

~ Not until I'm sure what to do.

~ Okay.

~ Not Hassan, not Georgia, and certainly none of the adults.

~ I said I wouldn't.

He then realised I was close to tears.

~ Good, son, good, he said. Then he did something he'd never done before. He stepped forward and hugged me. A small wiry man, he folded me in his strong arms and held me for a few moments. ~ Don't worry, Max. It'll be all right. Just keep it to yourself. It's too big for you, I know. Much too big. It's too big for me. We just have to hold it. I know we can't forget it, but we mustn't let it out. Not yet. Maybe never.

~ I understand.

~ Of course you do. You're a boy with good sense. You realise what this would do to . . . well, we'll leave it there. When we get back you keep Rambuta busy while I take a shovel and bury this thing.

~ You're — you're not going to keep any of it?

~ I think it's best we put it out of the way altogether.

So that's what we did. I didn't *really* understand the need for such deadly secrecy. I *felt* it though. Some bit of me inside was utterly astonished by it. And I did as I was told. I haven't told anyone about the thing I found that night. Not until now.

20 August, Krantu Island

This morning after we'd eaten the last of the goats, a simurg — a huge, fabulous bird, came very close to camp.

Mostly, the mythical creatures didn't come near us humans. They bothered the real animals of the island and they fought each other, sometimes to the death, but there seemed to be something about people they didn't like. Rambuta said it was probably our body odour and dad agreed with him. Since we swam a heck of a lot and kept clean I didn't think we smelled at all. But Rambuta said he didn't mean the powerful armpit stale sweat that bothered us, but a sort of hidden human-being scent special to all of us Homo sapiens.

~ You can't smell it on yourself, or even on me, but animals can, dad explained. ~ It's a subtle scent completely our own. A dog can tell there's human around long before it sees one. True, these creatures are new to this age and can't have come across humans before now — but there's such a thing as genetic memory — memory carried by the genes. I don't think our new mythical creatures like the stink of mankind because deep in the recesses of their minds they remember those prehistoric hunters who killed their mother. We've got a bad track record when it comes to our fellow creatures. We tend to destroy them, sometimes without any provocation or good reason, often wiping out whole species without a second thought. It's no wonder the scent of man fills them with anxiety and fear.

It seemed true. When some or all of us went out, as an armed party, to explore the sixteen-kilometre-long island, we hardly saw any marvellous beasts. Just once in a while we caught a glimpse of one, but that was really as much as we got. It was a bit annoying, but at the same time, comforting. We wanted to photograph them, but we knew that many of them were very dangerous beasts. Some deadly. Dad reckoned a lot had been written about them which *wasn't* true, but I didn't want to put that to the test. Maybe a basilisk or cockatrice couldn't really kill you with a look from its eyes, but then who wants to be the first to find out?

It was Grant who suggested the fence first.

~ Okay, he said, ~ they're staying away, mostly – but that – what did you call it? – simurg? Heck, that thing nearly came into the camp this morning. It didn't seem to bother it that Georgia and Lorraine were here. We men had all been out fishing in the lagoon. ~ What happened to the *human smell* theory?

~ The women sometimes wear perfume, said Rambuta, ~ which might mask their underlying human odour.

~ Well, I say we repair the stockade. There are a few large gaps, but I think we can all set to and rebuild it. What do you reckon?

~ Good idea, murmured dad. ~ Can't do any harm at all and everyone can then sleep soundly in their beds.

Georgia said, ~ But that was a bird that came in. Won't they just fly over any palisade?

Palisade? She was always showing off with big words, was Georgia.

Dad said, ~ It is a most peculiar thing – a lot of the mythical creatures have wings – the gryphon, the phoenix, the simurg, the lammasu – but here on this island none of them seem to manage the power of flight. Rambuta has been writing a paper on it, haven't you, Ram?

~ That's not to say, Ram said, ~ that they won't develop it in the future. At the moment we haven't witnessed one in flight, but maybe it takes a little time for them to gather strength in their wings. Who knows? They're all very heavy creatures, unsuited for flight in the main. Perhaps they never flew. Or perhaps it's too difficult to fly in the rainforest. In the meantime, a fence would be good. Thanks for that, Mr Porter. We'll worry about flying creatures later, if it becomes necessary.

So we all set to that day, chopping down thick bamboo

groves and using the stoutest poles for the fence, or stockade as Grant called it. It was hot tiring work. The sweat rolled off our bodies and the insects had a great time drinking off my skin. I got splinters galore in my fingers. Plant dust got up my nose and I sneezed a lot. There were all sorts of creepy-crawlies and reptiles in the bamboo clumps which made us wary.

Hass was the first to tread on a snake which bit him, but it wasn't poisonous. It still hurt him though – he said it was like being bitten by a rat – and he bawled for a bit. I didn't blame him for that. Rambuta put some antiseptic on it and Hass calmed down. Then dad was bitten by a bright green one which was poisonous, but he said it wasn't deadly and the fangs hadn't penetrated the skin. ~ The fangs of this particular species of snake are far back in the throat, he told us, ~ it enables them to swallow rodents. He took some anti-venom serum anyway.

Lorraine complained that the work was destroying her nails.

What? Who cares about her flippin' nails?

She did, obviously. She gave up hacking bamboo to do the cooking.

Georgia didn't say anything about her nails which I thought was pretty good. But she got a big brown spider caught in her hair, which caused a good deal of fuss. It got tangled in the damp long blonde strands and got a bit frantic (I would've done the same if I was a spider) and tried to struggle itself loose. You could sympathise with it. It was like being caught in a fine golden net (she has angel's hair) but the more it wriggled the more it got stuck. In the end her mum had to cut it out with scissors, which finally brought on a few tears. Probably because she thought she'd been scalped, though it didn't look too bad to me.

Did you know, Rambuta told us as we battled away with the bamboo — which is wicked tough stuff to chop, I can tell you — did you know there are a thousand varieties of bamboo? No, we chorused, we didn't know. Tell us more. Well, he said, happy to be the bloke who had the knowledge, there are. Bamboo has a thousand uses too, from chess pieces, to kendo swords, to furniture, to drinking vessels. It is tough, it's light because of its hollow chambers, and it grows quickly. Sometimes it grows so fast you can see it shooting upwards. Well, would you believe it, we said, our muscles aching, our heads hammering.

Yes, he said, bamboo, like the coconut, has been saviour of small islanders. And here we were, using it to make a fortress to keep out mythical beasts. Another use, I yelled, interrupting him, that makes 1001! The others laughed but Rambuta looked at me sternly. You shouldn't joke about bamboo, he said gravely. It's too important to make fun of. So I tried to look as if I was sorry, though I didn't feel it at all. I felt clever.

It took us a few days to cut the bamboo and repair the fence but eventually it was done. We were quite proud of it.

~ I did that bit, I said, pointing to one section, ~ you can see my chop marks. I wanted to impress Georgia of course. ~ I've got a special way of using the parang.

A parang is a sort of curved machete the Malays use.

~ I've got a special way too, Hass piped in. ~ It's probably better than your way, Max, because I've been a goatherd.

~ What's that got to do with it? I cried. ~ Goatherds don't chop things.

~ Oh, they have to cut their own staves, he said, nodding at me. ~ You wouldn't understand, Max. A goatherd needs weapons to fight the wild animals that attack his goats. You know I'm an

158

expert with the slingshot . . . I ground my teeth but had to acknowledge this fact ~ . . . and am also a very good fighter with the staff.

Sadly, Georgia was impressed by all this bull.

~ Oh really, how exciting!

~ Hah! I said a bit pompously. ~ What wild animals? In Jordan? A few pi-dogs? A few desert kites? All the lions and bears have gone. You can't fool us, Hass.

~ There are still leopards in the hills, he replied darkly.

What? Were there? I didn't know enough to dispute this. Leopards? I suppose maybe there could have been a leopard or two. Georgia was looking at Hassan in awe.

~ You had to fight leopards?

~ Sometimes.

~ Give over, I said, grinning through gritted teeth, ~ you're just having us on, Hass.

~ No, brother, I am not, said my wonderful brother. ~ I have chased away leopards with my stave.

~ And you can use a slingshot? Georgia said. ~ Can I see?

~ Well, we've all got work to do now, said I, ~ there's still a lot to do around camp . . . But Hassan had gone to fetch his slingshot.

We got a fine display of marksmanship. He knocked a few cans off branches and broke a few bottles. I couldn't top it and I was smarting inside. But you can't show it, can you? Dad always told me women and Aussies don't like blokes who whinge. So I just kept saying what a brilliant shot he was and how I wished I could do it like that, and at the same time tried to change the subject to the latest bands. I knew more about bands than Hass and Georgia was into music. She wanted to be a singer someday.

Today though, she wasn't biting. She hung around Hass until it sickened me and I had to get out of their way. Sometimes it was like this: two ganged up on one. Anything I said was treated with disdain at the moment. They seemed to enjoy being nasty to me. Unhappy with them both, I went to my tent and wrote a letter to a girl I'd met in Wolverhampton when I visited an aunt last summer. She had a funny Brummy-type accent but I liked her. Her letters were bubbly and made me feel good, and she always put S.W.A.L.K. on the back of the envelope, where you seal the flap. (It means Sealed With A Loving Kiss.) At that moment in time I preferred her to Georgia.

Later Hassan came to the tent and I ignored him. He thought he could take up with me as usual, even though he'd been making fun of me with Georgia just a short while ago. He was hurt when I wouldn't answer him and he went out. But he came back again and started in at me, telling me I had bad manners and was being unbrotherly.

~ You should have thought of being brotherly, when you stuck up for Georgia against me, I said, aggrieved.

~ It was just a bit of fun, Max.

~ Well, try it from my end.

~ I'm sorry. Look, I am prepared to shake hands with my brother.

~ You might be, but I'm not.

~ Come and have a game of cricket — we'll get Rambuta.

Cricket? It seemed a bit tame considering what was happening in the rainforest around us. Mighty tame. But you couldn't sit around all day waiting for a sighting. We'd done that. We were stuck inside most of the time and I was getting fed up with doing nothing all day long. You couldn't stay excited twenty-four hours of every day. There comes a point when you want a bit of light relief from all the worry and fuss.

~ Oh, all right.

We had all the kit with us, including pads and gloves. Georgia came by and asked what we were doing.

~ You wouldn't understand, I told her haughtily.

~ Why, because I'm a *girl?* she snapped.

~ No, because you're American. Americans play rounders. This is cricket. It's not a game you learn in a few minutes. It takes years of study.

~ Yes, Hass agreed with me, ~ even Max doesn't know all the fielding positions.

I said quickly, ~ I know most of 'em.

~ What the hell is rounders? yelled Georgia, causing her dad, about fifty metres away, to yell back at her for swearing.

~ That's not swearing, she murmured, and let go a few horrendous ripe ones under her breath that would have curled her father's toes if he'd heard them. ~ That's swearing, she said with satisfaction.

~ Rounders? I think you call it baseball, Hassan told her.

She spun on her heel with a look of disgust on her face. I'd managed to prise her and Hassan apart with a neat bit of double-talk but I didn't feel as good about it as I should have. I felt mean. Still, it was done, and all's fair in war and war.

Later that night, just before going to sleep, I asked Hassan, ~ Have you really fought with leopards?

~ Yes, he replied sincerely.

I still didn't believe him.

21 August, Krantu Island

Girls, I hate them sometimes. Not Georgia though. What a boring day today. It rained from dawn till dusk.

22 August, Krantu Island

Our stockade works very well. Some of the bamboo staves are almost as thick as Greek pillars and dad has used steel wire to lash them together. It's strong enough to keep the mythical creatures at bay. Dad has started calling them scada which (he told us) is Old English for shadows. ~ You have to have some kind of short collective noun for them, he said. ~ Mythical creatures is such a mouthful. Trust my dad to come up with something as way out as Old English. You won't get him using common-or-garden ordinary English.

Anyway, everyone else picked up on it. Grant did ask what the plural of scada was and dad said ~ Scada is the plural, the singular is scadu, which made Grant a little sniffy for a while. He gets a mite irritated by dad's pontificating and you can't blame him really.

One or two of the scada tried to get into the compound. The unicorn charged the fence a couple of times and struck it with his shoulder. No real damage was done. And the girallon — a gorilla with four arms — tried to climb up and over it. Bamboo is smooth and shiny and the girallon can't get a good enough grip on the poles and keeps falling off.

So we feel pretty safe inside our stockade.

Funnily enough, now we are behind our tall fence the scada

wander right up to the village edge. It's as if they themselves feel protected from us now. Dad cut us viewing holes just a few centimetres square so that we can watch them. They come and go — not often together because they don't seem to like each other — but one by one. Some we never see. Others we see almost every day. So far as I know the ahuizoytl has stayed away. (Dad says because it's half-human half-monkey it's capable of being jealous of our fortress.) The unicorn comes all the time though and we've had a good chance to study it.

I bet most of you think the unicorn is just a horse with a single horn coming out of its forehead, don't you?

Well, you'd be wrong.

A live unicorn is one of the most wonderful creatures I've ever seen, and I've seen a few now, I can tell you. It's got the legs of a stag, the tail of a lion, the head and body of a horse. Its only horn is ivory at the base, turns to jet black in the middle and the tip shines with the redness of rubies. The unicorn's coat is white too, like the bottom of its horn, but its eyes are a deep blue — you can't look into them; they're so weirdly blue they give you a creepy feeling and you have to turn away.

Most mornings we get up and watch the unicorn prancing around the stockade. Georgia wants to put out a bucket of milk for it to drink (girls!) but dad says there was no reason to think it ate or drank at all. We never see it graze. He says we should leave it to its own devices because we might end up poisoning it to death. Georgia thinks that's silly but nevertheless she obeys dad's rule of not giving anything.

Anyway, the unicorn has come to be more like a pet than any of the other scada. I see the gryphon quite a lot and the grisly makara often skulks nearby in the shade of the bushes on the

edge of the rainforest but none of them have become so familiar as the unicorn.

~ I'd like to ride him, Georgia said, one day. ~ I'd like to climb
on his beautiful back and ride him through the forest.

~ Him? I questioned.

~ Her, it – who cares? I'd like to ride him.

Hass said, ~ It would be very difficult – a wild beast like that.
But I know what you mean, Georgia. It would be very exciting.

~ You could probably do it, Hass, she told him, ~ since you've
ridden Arab stallions.

~ And camels. Hass shrugged less modestly than he usually
did. ~ Perhaps I could ride the unicorn. It is true stallions are
the wildest of horses. I rode bareback, of course.

Of course, I thought, what else?

~ Well, this one's not even a horse, I interrupted. ~ It's a
scadu – and scada are unpredictable, so nobody should try it.
I felt my use of the singular and plural of Old English in one sen-
tence was an indication of who was the brightest star amongst
us.

Truth is, I'm jealous as hell. I can't compete with all this.

It seems both Hass and Georgia are good at riding horses.
Georgia rode often when she was in California, out in range
country or something. Hassan had ridden in the Sheikh of
Othman's races. Apparently lots of Arab boys where he was
brought up had ridden in the sheikh's races. Hass said it was a
way of earning money. All you had to do was stay on the horse
until the end of the race to earn ten dinars. What's more, Hass
had obviously impressed Georgia with the fact that he rode
stallions. Apparently most people ride only mares or geldings.
Geldings are doctored stallions, which takes a lot of the fight

out of them. If they're left as stallions they're very fierce and independent. Georgia says only really expert horsemen can manage a stallion.

~ I'm going to try before we leave here, said Georgia, waving at the unicorn. ~ It's such a beautiful horse.

~ It's not a bloody horse, I shouted at this idiot girl, ~ it's a weird bloody beast and it'll probably try to kill you. If you try I'll split on you. I will, Georgia. I don't care if it's grassing. If you try to get on that thing you'll get hurt.

Instead of getting mad as I expected she gave me a funny sort of smile and said, ~ Max is worried about me — how sweet.

So far as we know the rainforest is now full of scada.

A few days behind the fence though, and we've started to long for a bit of exercise and a swim. We miss our walks in the rainforest and we miss the beach and the lagoon. Inside the stockade we feel hemmed in and stifled. So we've begun going out again.

The walks in the forest have to be carried out under armed escort.

But getting to the beach is still a lot safer and easier.

The scada tend to stay amongst the bushes and trees where their camouflage works best. On the west side of the village, where we'd put the gate, there's a clear wide path to the shoreline. When we want a swim we dash along this path to what was left of the beach.

Oh, that water is glorious! It's just the right temperature. It cools you down but you can stay in it for over an hour and not get cold. Wrinkly, but not cold. Light green and as clear as bottle glass, it's the perfect playground for us kids. There's so much to see underneath the surface and when you get bored

165

with fish, sea plants and all the varieties of coral, you can hunt for beautiful seashells on the beach.

But we need to go to the lagoon for more than fun. Georgia's parents have to keep an eye on their yacht. The boat is now moored close to the shore in a channel and Grant visits it to get stores, use his computer and ship-to-shore radio, and generally make sure everything's all right on board. Thankfully (he said) there are no monkeys on the island because they're destructive creatures who'd climb over everything and steal anything that wasn't nailed down.

Grant hated monkeys for some reason.

~ Nasty little beasts, he said. ~ A mockery.

Grant was raised in the Bible Belt of the USA, so Georgia told us, and he didn't think much of Darwin's theory of evolution. Dad tried to argue with him once but got nowhere. You can't when someone's got an idea so stuck in his head it won't be shifted. Anyway, you can't tell him anything. He always knows it and what's more he knows it better.

Lorraine isn't like that. You can tell her something you think might be new to her and she'll squeal and say, ~ No! Who'da thunk it? and be really interested in what you're saying. She's really quite with it. Georgia told me her mum had been a 'lootenant in the army' and had fought on a Caribbean island called Grenada in 1983.

~ Not on her own of course, confessed Georgia. ~ She was just one American soldier in a regiment.

~ You don't have girls in regiments, I argued. ~ Some of them are doctors and nurses but . . .

~ We do. We have women in the army proper.

~ Did she carry a gun?

166

~ Army people aren't allowed to call it a gun. They have to call it a rifle. Anyway, officers don't have rifles, they have pistols.

Part of me thought this was pretty cool, and part of me thought it wasn't. I tried to imagine my own mum with a revolver or something and it didn't work in my head. Yet I knew Georgia wouldn't tell lies. So the other day, when we were on our own, I asked Lorraine, ~ Did you shoot people in the Caribbean?

She was cutting meat at the time and she carefully put down the knife before answering.

~ No, I never shot anyone in my life, Max.

~ But you had a forty-five or something? When you were in the army?

~ A thirty-eight, she said, with a little sideways smile. ~ Yes I did. But I never fired it in anger.

~ Did you see any fighting?

~ Yes, and it wasn't as exciting as you'd think, Max. It was real scary and afterwards — well, you get bad dreams. It's not something I want to talk about, do you mind? You see, I'm never sure of the rights and wrongs of these things. I joined the army because I lived in a small town and there was no work. The army sent me back to school and I made something of myself — became an officer. I was quite proud of myself and my friends and relations were proud of me too. But then suddenly it's not just a job with a nice uniform and a salary. You find you're in a war in some country you've only vaguely heard of and have got nothing against. By that time the army is your family and your family is telling you you've got to go there and do as you're told.

She went quiet for a little while, then she added, ~ If ever you think of joining the army, or navy or air force, Max, make sure it's what you *really* know you want to do.

~ But Georgia said you were a crackshot. You are a crackshot, right?

She thought she hadn't got through to me when I said that and she shook her head sadly before answering, ~ Yes. Yes, I was.

I was listening though and I knew what she was trying to tell me. She was telling me that you have to have soldiering in your blood — be a warrior born, something like that. Well, I wasn't anyway. I didn't want to join the armed forces. But I was still thinking about the pirates. If they attacked us Lorraine would be good to have on our side. We would need women who wouldn't scream and faint at the first sound of a shot. Lorraine wouldn't do that. She'd get her thirty-eight and start pumping bullets at the attackers, hitting one with every squeeze of the trigger.

~ How did you meet Grant? I asked her. I wasn't really interested but I wanted to sort of smooth things over a little because I could see my questions had ruffled her. ~ Was it romantic?

She smiled again; this time it was a sunny smile.

~ Romantic? Well, I fell in love afterwards so I thought it was romantic. It was on a streetcar. I'd left the army and was working for a company in San Francisco. I was just twenty-six and hadn't had a boyfriend for a year. Grant's car had broken down that day, otherwise he wouldn't have been commuting by public transport. He looked grouchy and upset so I made faces at him, to cheer him up. Not directly — I did it in the streetcar window — a reflection, but it just made him madder.

~ You made faces in the window at a strange man? He must've thought you were crazy.

~ You suppose? she laughed. ~ Anyway, we got off at the

same stop and I bought myself a coffee at my usual stall, but on impulse I bought one for him too. I told him, that's because I was so rude on the ride. And he asked me, what are you, ten years old? And I replied, yes, sometimes – and sometimes I'm much older. It all depends. Which made him look at me in that way he has when he's impressed by something. Anyway, he asked me what I was doing for lunch – and the rest is history.

~ You got married.

~ Yep. She started cutting the meat again. ~ I became Mrs Porter. I had another life mapped out for myself before I met Grant, but it didn't take long to revise it. Joseph-and-Mary, she laughed yet again, ~ my catch was a rich man! I didn't need to worry about money again. Grant is a very successful jeweller, you know. I was set for life.

~ And then Georgia was born.

Lorraine looked hard at me, then seemed to make a decision.

~ Well yes, Max – but not to me. Georgia is adopted.

~ Oh.

For a few moments I was a little taken aback by this news. Not because it mattered in the slightest to me or anyone else, but because I never guessed it. I'd always thought Georgia looked like Lorraine. They seemed so much like each other. But Georgia was adopted. So what? Her parents seemed to love her and no one had even spoken of it before now.

~ If you're wondering why we hadn't said anything, Max, it's probably because we don't think of it much. Georgia is fully aware. She has met her biological mother – the father is unknown – and she's happy with us, her family. A little frown appeared on Lorraine's brow. She stopped cutting the meat again. ~ You'd say she was happy, wouldn't you, Max?

169

~ Definitely, I replied without hesitation. ~ Why not?

~ Why not indeed. The frown disappeared.

Tentatively I asked, ~ Couldn't you and Grant . . .

~ Have children of our own? No.

That was all I was going to get and I was glad. I'd only asked because I thought it was expected of me. I honestly didn't want to hear any details.

So we left it at that.

23 August, Krantu Island

~ Hey, Hass — I've got some really weird news.

It was a hot afternoon. Hassan had gone to our tent and was having a nap. I knew I'd woken him up but I couldn't wait to tell him about Georgia.

~ What — what is it? His voice was thick with dreams.

~ It's Georgia.

He sat up and rubbed his eyes. ~ Is she all right, Max?

~ Yeah, she's fine. But guess what!

~ What?

~ She's adopted.

Hassan stared at me in the dimness of the tent.

~ Lorraine just told me, I continued, thinking he didn't believe me. ~ It's true.

Still he stared at me for a while, then finally he spoke.

~ Max. I already knew this thing.

Something flip-flopped in my stomach.

~ What? I said.

~ Georgia told me some time ago.

170

I felt a wrenching inside me.

~ Why would she just tell you – and not me?

~ Because I am adopted too, Max.

I felt shattered. Of course. Of course. So obvious.

~ Did – did she tell you not to tell me?

~ No, Hassan's face was very serious, ~ but she did not give me permission either. I decided it was in confidence. I am sorry, Max. You and Georgia would not think much of me if I had told you without permission from her, would you? It would have been dishonourable. I would have felt shame.

I was being torn apart inside. ~ I suppose.

At first my agony was because they had shared a secret. A secret I hadn't been allowed in on. That was bad enough, to think of them being brought closer by a shared secret. But worse thoughts were to come. It struck me a bit later that it wasn't just that they shared a secret, but they had something in common. Something I could never share. They were both adopted children. They were joined by a common history. It was an experience I couldn't know. It was probably something they could talk about between them for ever. I was on the outside. I couldn't get in. I felt so bad I even began to wish I was adopted myself, so that I wouldn't be on the outside. I would have something to say.

I felt rejected and miserable, remembering those times when they had cut me out, ganged up against me. I conveniently forgot those times when I had sided with Georgia against Hassan, and those times when Hass and I had teased Georgia. Such alliances always occur amongst threesomes. It's human nature, especially when people are cooped up and in each other's company all the time. But what I

171

remembered now was that they had once or twice whispered together, treated me like I had leprosy, found a song they both liked which I hated, laughed at me when I didn't know something which the pair of them decided even an idiot would know. Those horrible taunts.

I took the path to the beach and sat on the shore.

I suppose I'd been there for about an hour when I smelled Georgia's special brand of shampoo on the breeze.

She sat down beside me.

~ Max? What are you doing, down here by yourself?

~ I just heard something.

She sighed. ~ I know, mom told me. She thought it didn't matter to you.

~ It doesn't. I turned and said as fiercely as I could, ~ Of course it doesn't. Why should it? I couldn't care less.

~ Then why are you so upset?

I grabbed a handful of coral sand and threw it into the water.

~ I dunno.

~ Yes you do. What is it? Please Max, I shall lose patience and you know what I'm like when I fall out with you. We shall both hate it and there's all that awkwardness when one of us has to speak to the other one for the first time again,

~ It's always me.

~ What?

~ Who speaks first.

She showed me a gentle smile. ~ I suppose it is. I have a terrible pride, you know. We're Elizabeth and Darcy, you and me — you know, from *Pride and Prejudice*?

~ I know — I read books.

~ Have you read that one?

172

I smiled grimly at her, knowing this was sacrilege to her. ~ No, but I've seen the film.

She didn't react. Instead she asked again, ~ So, what is it?

~ It's you and Hass. There was a catch in my voice as I said it and it was one of the reasons why I hadn't blurted it out sooner. I knew I would get all emotional. ~ You and Hass are both adopted.

Georgia didn't say anything for a long while, then finally she murmured, ~ Ah, that's it. You're the odd one out.

~ I suppose. And you told him without telling me. My eyes felt hot. ~ You told him an' not me. Couldn't you trust me with it? You had a secret, you two together.

Her voice was soft and full of understanding when she spoke again.

~ Oh. Yes, I can see that now. I didn't before. That would have upset me too, if I'd been you. I'm sorry.

~ It's okay.

~ No it's not. You're still really upset.

~ I'll get over it. I was too choked up to say any more.

~ It's wasn't like that, Max — you know, hugger-mugger, a conspiracy against you — like in Shakespeare? It was just — well, Hassan was upset when my dad got confused about the relationships — you remember, he thought Rambuta was Hassan's father? So I said I knew what it was like, to be adopted and for people to get it all wrong sometimes. That was it. There wasn't any flood of feelings, with the two of us going, yeah, yeah, and this, and that, and sharing our past lives.

The sun was really bright at that moment, glancing off the water as sharp as a steel blade. It hurt my eyes. There's a period in the middle of the afternoon when it's almost

173

unbearably intense. If you're not wearing shades — and I wasn't — you have to close your eyes to slits, and even then the brilliance gets through. At such times it's best to get back in the shade of the rainforest, out of the white-hot searing sun, off the blinding-white coral sands, away from the foam-topped shining sea.

~ I have to go, I said, turning to get up but trying not to look at her. She was so beautiful sometimes it took my breath away. There was always the thought that I was just a kid and she was just a kid. Whatever we had it was only for now. It couldn't last for ever. Life would soon fling us apart, to different schools, different colleges maybe, different towns or cities in which we would have to work. This was what my dad called a childhood romance. Something to look back on in my old age but not something that was real and worthwhile. If that was so, I needed to have something really, really special to make the moment mine. Something that would stick in my memory until the day I died. But I had nothing really, except a few wonders and guesses. ~ I need to get back.

~ We both do, but not yet. Stay a bit longer.

~ Why?

~ Just because. Indulge me.

Normally this kind of talk would have me promising to stay until the end of eternity and longer. But today was different.

~ Okay, I said. ~ If you want me to.

~ Yes, I do.

We just sat there, me squinting at the sea, totally aware of Georgia's presence beside me. There didn't seem to be anything to say. I couldn't talk about films, books, or the things we normally talked about, because I felt so low. And Georgia said nothing either. It was a strange situation but somehow a little comforting to me. I was upset, but I knew I'd upset her too, now. I wondered how long we would go on sitting there, but finally Georgia's hand crept into mine. I didn't look down but I could feel her slim silky fingers. My stomach melted.

She said, ~ I know how it must seem to you, Max. That Hass and I are somehow bound by what we are, how we were brought up. That's not true, you know. I can't explain why, but it isn't. The truth is I love you both – for different reasons. You are two boys I'll never forget. But – and I'm only ever going to say this once, and never again because I would hope you wouldn't see the need to test me again – I love you best. Even better than Bradley, if you have to know. There, I've said it.

Then she kissed me quickly and lightly on my mouth and was gone, up the beach, before I could say anything.

There was a lingering taste of sea salt from her lips.

I could still smell her shampoo.

My heart was pounding ten times faster than the waves on the reef. Had she said it? Yes, she had. Elation surged through me. Suddenly I wanted to tell her things, and turned to see if I could catch her up, then just as suddenly I realised it wasn't necessary. She already knew. She was a girl. She could read boys' minds. All girls can. I didn't need to tell her. I was a little relieved at that, because I would have felt daft. I couldn't possibly have done it with the skill and ease that she had. I would have blurted it out and ruined every word. Probably destroying what she'd said in the process. I could be a real idiot when I wanted to be.

Instead I stood up and yelled in delight, picking up a piece of driftwood and hurling it end-over-end into the water.

I stayed on the beach until it was time for the darkness to fall. I wanted to nurse the bubbly feeling in my chest without people around. Have I said there's not much of a twilight time on Krantu? Because it's so close to the equator? Well, it's true. Night drops down like a black curtain. For about ten to fifteen minutes you get this stupendous sunset, usually all soft rosy reds. (There's a poem from a guy called Louis MacNeice which mum used to read to dad which has this line 'The sun going down in crimson suds . . .') Then the darkness thumps down.

Anyway, it was during the red-sudsy time that I saw it. A black vessel coming swiftly over the sea. A junk. Sea-raiders!

~ Dad! I yelled from the beach, then realised no one could hear me. I ran back along our wide track. ~ Dad! Dad! They're coming.

The gate to the compound is never locked, since scada aren't capable of opening a catch. There's a hole large enough to get a hand through and a catch on the other side. I slipped my hand through and opened the gate, remembering to close it behind me. Then I ran towards dad and Rambuta's tent.

~ Dad! The raiders.

Dad yelled something back from the outhouse toilet which was muffled by the walls rustling in the evening breeze.

(We had this palm-leafed hut we used. Dad had put a sign saying 'loo' on the door and when Grant first used it he told us he was going to the 'One-hundred'. We had a good laugh over that.)

When he came out dad looked furious.

~ What's all the yelling for, Max? he snapped.

Others had come out of their hidey-holes now and I was surrounded by everyone. I looked quickly at Georgia, then back at dad again.

~ The sea-raiders, I gasped. I didn't want to use the word *pirates* this time. It sounded too silly for the seriousness of the danger. ~ They're coming to get us.

Dad looked really stern. ~ Now we've talked about this prank, Max — it isn't funny.

~ No, really. Go and look. I pointed. ~ Go on, go and look if you don't believe me.

Dad folded his arms. ~ I went and looked the last time you yelled wolf and there was nothing there. This is the third time you've played this trick and I'm not going to fall for it again. You're really trying my patience, and the patience of everyone else here. Now pull yourself together, boy.

He started to turn away, and I yelled at him, ~ It's not a trick! I saw them, I tell you.

He swung round again to stare at me. ~ Look, son, I don't want to seem harsh. Maybe you *thought* you saw something. These sunsets often have so many colours in them it confuses the brain. Mirages. *Fata Morgana*. It's like being in the desert. You see things that aren't really there.

I couldn't get the words out; I was choking with annoyance. ~ I wasn't seeing hulluc — hullucy — hull . . .

~ Hallucinations, finished Georgia, for me.

~ Thank you, I said, grateful to her. ~ Yes, them.

Dad sighed. ~ People who see mirages obviously think that what they're seeing is real.

~ Please, dad, I pleaded. ~ Put a guard on the gate tonight?

Dad seemed suddenly aware that his shirt tail was hanging

177

out at the back and he tucked it in self-consciously. Then he turned his attention back to his annoying son.

~ You probably haven't noticed, Max, but there's a guard on the gate every night. Didn't you know Lorraine, Grant, Rambuta and myself share the night watch between us? You didn't think we'd let you kids go to sleep without someone remaining vigilant, did you?

~ Oh, I said.

As they all split up and walked away to their various chores and tents, I heard dad murmur to Rambuta, ~ What do you think? An extra watch tonight?

~ I saw them, I told Hass as we lay in bed. ~ You should back me up. You're supposed to be my brother.

~ But I didn't see them, Max, he quite reasonably pointed out. ~ If I had I would back you up, but I didn't.

~ No, well you'll bloody well see them soon enough when they cut your throat tonight, won't you.

I fell asleep a lot later, feeling used and misunderstood.

24 August, Krantu Island

Somewhere out there in the dark I heard a bang.

I sat bolt upright in bed.

Several more cracks followed, though fainter than the first. Gunfire!

~ Hass, I hissed, reaching over to shake him, ~ they're here.

His bed was empty. My hand was on a flat cotton sheet.

Where was everybody?

I soon found out. They were all outside. The adults were at the spy holes on the four sides of the compound. They were poking rifles through the stockade. Even as I was pulling on my shorts I could see Rambuta jerk back as he fired his rifle. Georgia and Hassan were crouched down behind a ring of steel oil drums. I ran to dad.

~ I told you! I was right, wasn't I? I cried, triumphantly, shivering a little with the shock of the moment.

~ Max, this is not a time to say I told you so, dad replied, looking harassed. ~ There's a torch — sorry, a flashlight — out there to your right, Grant, he yelled.

~ I see it. Grant fired and someone in the rainforest yelled.

~ If this isn't the time, then I don't know when is, I replied hotly. ~ If you'd listened to me you wouldn't have been caught napping.

~ We weren't caught napping, son. Lorraine saw their torches.

I couldn't let it drop. I'd been humiliated and I wanted an apology before everyone was killed. ~ Just say I was right. You can do that without looking away. Just tell me sorry Max, you were right and I was wrong. I told you three times. You just didn't listen.

~ Max, for heaven's sakes . . .

~ Dad — you're rubbish.

~ No, no, don't say that. Okay, okay, you were right and we were wrong . . . His rifle kicked as he squeezed the trigger.

~ No, not we. No one else called me a liar. Just you.

~ Just me, he snarled, through gritted teeth. ~ I was wrong. There, I've said it. Now get with Georgia and Hassan behind those oil drums — keep well back out of danger. Some of their weapons are capable of piercing the bamboo. They can go right through this stuff.

As if to underline these words a bullet crashed through the bamboo just above dad's head, leaving a huge splintered hole.

~ Rambuta, Lorraine, Grant – second line of defence, dad cried, backing away from the perimeter. ~ Behind the drums.

I dashed ahead of them.

When they'd built the stockade the adults had also arranged some old oil drums in a circle then filled them with sand. They formed a very strong central tower in the bailey of our castle. The outer walls might be breached, but the attackers would then still have to cross a deadly stretch of ground to reach our well-defended round tower of steel. Bullets might be able to go through our bamboo wall, but they certainly couldn't penetrate oil drums packed with coral sand.

~ We are coming to get you! cried a thickly accented voice from outside the stockade. ~ You might as well let us in. You can't escape us. We are all around you. Why not surrender, sirs, to a superior force? We can be lenient and kind if we are not put to a great trouble.

~ Come and get us! yelled Grant, without consulting anyone. ~ We're waiting for you!

No one argued. In fact, dad said, ~ Shoot anything that moves.

I knew what all this meant. If there was any chance that by surrendering we'd get out alive, Grant, dad, and the other two adults would have taken it. I guessed then that the adults knew if the raiders got to us we would be massacred. It was obvious. I didn't say anything to Georgia and Hass, but we were all shaking in the tight space. There wasn't any reason to talk, really. So we didn't.

For a while it seemed to me that bullets were being fired all over the place. It was wild. The raiders didn't seem to care much whether they hit anything on purpose or by accident. They were just letting off their guns in our general direction. Bits of tree bark and leaves were flying everywhere. Pigs were squealing in the bush. Our goats were going berserk in their corral. It was pure mayhem.

After a while I began to hope the pirates would run out of ammunition. If only they would. But I guess they knew how much they'd brought with them and as Grant said, bullets are cheap. You can buy them by the crateload anywhere. No one says, ~ Are you a pirate? Well, you can't purchase ammunition if you are.

In America you can get them at chain stores for a few cents, so I saw in a film.

Our guys just shot when they saw something, or thought they had a good chance of hitting one of the enemy. We hadn't brought an unlimited supply of ammo with us like the pirates seemed to have. None of us guessed we would be in a big battle.

After a while it did quieten down for a little.

It was very dark. We couldn't see much, but then neither could the raiders. As soon as one of them switched on a torch they stood a chance of being shot. You didn't even need to see a person. You could just shoot at the light. And when they lit a fire under the wall to burn a section away, they showed us exactly where they were coming through.

Dad, Rambuta, Lorraine and Grant just lined up their weapons on the flames and poured shots through the gap. The raiders were actually more at a disadvantage than we were, since we knew the island and the immediate surrounds of the compound. The raiders were stumbling around in the blackness out there, not knowing which way led where.

Sure enough, after they were unsuccessful in burning down the bamboo stockade, they seemed to retire into the rainforest. For a time they kept up a stream of insults, whistles and taunts, telling us that they were going to gut us like fishes and chop us to pieces. One of them kept asking us if we could hear him sharpening his knife on a whetstone.

~ It's for you, he called. ~ I will stroke your throats with it very slowly and watch the blood run out like a river.

~ Graphic buggers, aren't they? muttered dad. ~ Take no notice, kids, they won't get in here.

But we weren't as daft as that. I knew that once daylight came the raiders would no longer be at a disadvantage. And I think the other two also knew. It was clear the raiders would storm the place and drag us off to carry out all those horrible threats. We didn't stand a chance really. But none of us said anything. It wouldn't have been right to let the adults know we were scared silly. It wasn't fair to worry them.

Later in the night it seemed the raiders tried to start a forest fire — several of them, in fact. We saw the flames and the burning somewhere out there deep in the rainforest. But a tropical forest is nearly always damp through and through and it would need a lot of heat to get a real blaze going. Many of the plants had thick succulent leaves and soft squashy stems. And there's moisture trapped in the dense undergrowth. No fire could catch hold without using engine fuel to start it.

There were lots of yells, cries and shouts coming from the forest, but Lorraine said they were probably trying to scare us again. Some of them too might have been jungle noises. It's difficult to tell the difference between a parrot screech and a human scream.

Morning came.

We waited fearfully for an attack. There were provisions in our little round tower. The adults had put water and food in there, just in case. Not that they had expected pirates. It had been set up in case we were attacked by the scada. Dad had always felt that the danger from the scada was minimal, but when Grant came into the camp things changed a bit. He had persuaded the others to err on the side of caution.

Good old Grant.

No one came all day.

Towards the evening the unicorn made a brief appearance. We kids cheered, thinking it was a good sign. But though dad was all for going out and looking around, Grant and Rambuta were against it.

Rambuta said, ~ It's an old trick, to keep quiet and let the enemy think you've gone. They're probably still out there, waiting for us to show our heads above the parapet.

Dad saw the sense in this argument.

~ Well, we've got provisions for three days — no sense in rushing things.

Grant had put a pack of playing cards in the provisions so those who weren't on sentry duty sat and played various games.

Then night came and put a stop to the cards. But at least we could go out in the dark to go to the toilet. The women went first, then the men, all in a bunch. It was grotso, having to do it close to someone with a gun. Grant said it was more satanic than sanitary, which made us all giggle.

I wanted desperately to talk with Georgia, but we were in a tight space. Even a whisper could be overheard. So I had to contain my impatience. She'd told me she would never say those words again but it's funny, once you've heard them you want to hear them over and over. I think the word I'm looking for is assurance. You need assurance. Knowing Georgia I didn't think I was going to get it though. When she said something, she meant it, which was good in one way but it did mean I was going to have to keep my trap shut. Maybe our time within the oil drums was good for me. Since I *couldn't* speak to her, I didn't, and that probably saved me from making an idiot of myself.

Something continues to disturb the parrots and parakeets — they've been shrieking like crazy all night.

When I finally fell asleep I dreamed about that dead creature I had found in the forest. The one dad told me not to talk about to anyone. My mind keeps going back to it, over and over again. It is a secret that makes me feel uncomfortable in my own skin. It makes me feel a trespasser on this planet we call Earth. That dead thing changed everything, all I've ever learned about myself. I'm not as I was, but as I am, which is something quite different, something strange.

25 August, Krantu Island

Two of the men, dad and Grant, left the compound this morning.

We stayed inside the oil drum tower with Rambuta and Lorraine. I was fascinated by Lorraine. As well as carrying a rifle she wore a pistol on her hip. What a mum! Not that she approved of violence (she told us) but in a dire emergency it was sometimes necessary. In fact she said she thought the world would be better off without weapons, especially handguns. An American archaeologist friend of dad's always said that if you buy a handgun the most likely person to be shot with it is yourself or a member of your family. I've never forgotten that.

While dad and Grant were away we played cards again, but everyone was fretting. We didn't talk about it but we kept looking in the direction of the hole in the compound wall through which the two men had disappeared. Everyone was worried about them. At about eleven o'clock we heard a loud crack and all jumped up together. The cards went flying every whichway.

But it was just a tree coming down.

We heard the crash and thrash of the branches as they tore earthwards through the foliage of neighbouring trees. Then the thump of the trunk meeting the forest floor. Then finally the silence again, except for the sound of the birds and cicadas. Those giant trees – some of 'em hundreds of metres high and with the girth of a castle tower – they make a dickens of a row and a wallop when they finally fall to the ground. The whole world shudders.

Afterwards we didn't bother to collect the cards – everyone had had enough.

Instead Hass entertained us with his pets. He had a praying mantis that he'd trained like you would train a dog. It would stand up on its hind legs and box Hass's two fingers. And he also had a pet chit-chat which could walk up a vertical mirror. He fed them both flies. I had to admit Hass was good with creatures of the wild. I suppose when he was a goatboy he'd had to keep himself amused. You could get pretty bored watching goats all day long and (yeah, yeah) chasing leopards.

When we got tired of the mantis and the gecko we just chilled out, fed up to the back teeth yet worried too.

It was midday before the two men came back.

Lorraine looked very relieved to see her husband. You could see the anxious expression drain from her face. She waved like a schoolgirl as if she was greeting someone she hadn't seen for years. Rambuta let out a sigh that must have had the crabs on the beach wondering. We kids were much more dignified. We just nodded at each other. Natch, said those nods, we knew they'd come back all right.

~ Are you all okay? Lorraine called, as her man approached.

~ I'm fine. I'm here, aren't I? Don't fuss, woman, said Grant. But he tried to smile at her to soften the rebuke. I think he was embarrassed in front of dad. Then for some reason he put on his sunglasses, even though the camp was in the shade.

I was looking hard at dad. I knew him better than anyone there and he looked shaken to me. His face was pale and his eyes kept flicking this way and that. He kept licking his lips too, in a nervous sort of way. It takes a lot to get to my dad. He's not easily upset.

In his time dad has been abducted by religious fanatics, taken hostage by the fierce tribesmen in the Yemen, lost in various deserts, and attacked by wild animals. It takes something pretty drastic to shake up my dad. But something clearly had.

Grant's attempts at hiding his jumpiness were also a bit weak. He continually took off his sunglasses and cleaned them. They must have been the cleanest pair of aviator shades in the whole of the Pacific.

~ Did you see the raiders? I asked. ~ Were they there?

Grant and dad exchanged funny looks.

~ Ah – the junk's gone, said Grant. ~ Lorraine, could I speak with you a minute . . . ?

~ Hey, none of that, cried Georgia. ~ If there's something wrong we're entitled to know too.

~ Well, dad intervened, ~ it's not necessarily something wrong.

~ Whatever, I said. ~ We should know.

~ Let's eat first, replied dad in a weary voice. ~ I'm bushed and I'm starving too. You don't need to stay inside the drums any more. We can make our usual meal out at the kitchen. Georgia, Hassan – can you collect some breadfruit? Or is it breadfruits? I'm never sure. Max, can you help Rambuta with the dried fish? We'll have *baccalá*.

~ What the flippin' heck's that? I asked irritably.

I was peeved that I had to help Rambuta while Hass and Georgia went off together. They'd have to stay in sight of course, but I still didn't want someone else going off with my girlfriend, especially my brother.

~ I haven't got time to explain it now, muttered dad, but Rambuta informed me, ~ It's an Italian dish – salted cod. We haven't got any cod, but red snapper will do.

~ Whatever, I said in a tired voice, which wasn't really fair on Rambuta. It wasn't his fault he had to put up with me.

So we all set to at our tasks. Lorraine and Grant went off in a huddle, clearly allowed a bit of breathing space together. They whispered a lot and I could hear Lorraine's sharp intakes of breath. I hoped they weren't cheating and they were actually going to tell us kids everything they knew.

When we finally got round to the meal it was a funny affair.

187

It was eaten in silence. Finally it was Georgia who blurted out, ~ Tell us what happened.

Dad said, ~ Grant, do you want to . . . ? but Grant waved a hand indicating that dad should tell it. So he did.

~ What we found, he croaked, then paused to take a sip of palm wine to clear the frog out of his dry throat, ~ what we found were some charred remains — a lot of them, in fact. Burned bodies. All over the forest. Some dozen or so. What we don't know is whether it was the result of an accidental fire, or perhaps started on purpose.

~ What does that mean, father? asked Hass.

Despite indicating that dad should tell the story, Grant broke in here.

~ We were attacked by raiders, as you know, but something happened. Some of those men were horribly disfigured by fire. There's evidence of a big forest blaze. You know the jungle won't catch light on its own. I can only assume a raider must have used boat fuel to start it off. He glanced nervously around the table.

I asked, ~ Are they still there, then?

Dad said, ~ We don't know. The junk has gone and we assume the rest of the men with it. The thing is, we should think about leaving. We can't stay here. The raiders — those who got away — are now sure of our location. We have to leave fairly soon. After supper I'll send an email to the mainland.

Georgia said, ~ Why don't we all go now? We can cram together on our yacht, eh, dad? she asked Grant. ~ It's not that far to Sarawak.

~ Fact is, replied Grant, ~ they've ransacked the yacht. Stripped it clean. All my navigation instruments gone. Everything.

~ My clothes? cried Georgia.

We all stared at her.

She jutted out her jaw defensively. ~ Well, that's not so shocking – clothes are important to me.

~ You've got your iPod, I pointed out.

Georgia's next look withered me.

Grant continued. ~ When I say they took everything, I mean it. Stores, sail, fuel for the engine, even the stock of toilet paper rolls. Every damn thing that wasn't nailed down, and some things that were. My black coral samples . . . he gestured hopelessly with his hands again and we sighed in sympathy for him, while Lorraine patted his shoulder in a 'there, there' way. ~ Anyway, self-pity doesn't help. What I'm trying to say is, the yacht's no good to us as it is.

~ I'll get that email off, said dad, rising. ~ You guys help with the clearing up. He pointed to us kids, then he went towards the fish-drying shed. He came back shortly afterwards, his face as white as the belly of a stingray.

~ Bullet holes, he said, ~ in the fuel cans.

Grant dropped the kettle he was holding. ~ What do you mean?

~ I mean some of those shots the raiders fired at us hit my fuel cans. We're lucky they didn't go up. Punctured them. We have no fuel for the generators. It all drained away. Dad looked angry. ~ Two damn good generators and nothing to run them with.

~ None in the generators themselves? asked Grant.

~ The night before the raiders came I ran them empty, doing some late-night work if you remember.

No one remembered, but it didn't matter. There wasn't any fuel for the generators and that was that. We had no means of

189

providing electricity. We couldn't run dad's laptop computer. We couldn't use the radio transmitter. Dad called us all together for a council meeting.

~ Well, you know the facts — what do you think we should do? Everyone's got a say here, even the kids. Any ideas are welcome. To my mind there are only two alternatives. One, we stay until help arrives, hoping the raiders don't return in the meantime. Two, we fashion a makeshift sail for the yacht and trust to God we find land soon.

~ We don't need to trust to God, I interrupted. ~ Well, maybe we do need to do that too, but we've got Rambuta.

~ Explain, said Grant, looking at the Malay academic.

Rambuta said, ~ I think what Max is trying to tell you is that I'm an expert navigator in the old ways. My ancestors used to sail these waters without charts or equipment of any kind, using the stars, wave patterns, sightings of sea and land birds, cloud formations — that kind of thing. He's right. I do have knowledge of them. But I've never used them in earnest — never had the need to use them in a practical sense.

~ In other words, said Lorraine, ~ you're a complete beginner.

Rambuta shrugged. ~ I have the theory, never put into practice.

~ Personally, Lorraine then added, ~ I think we should settle down here. We have food and water on hand. Okay, we're surrounded by strange beasts and there's the possibility of the pirates coming back, but what chance would we stand if they attacked us on the water?

Grant said, ~ That's true. We could never outrun them with a home-made sail and we'd have a hell of time defending ourselves on the open water.

~ Here, Lorraine continued, ~ we have the stockade which we've already defended quite successfully. We won't – excuse me, Rambuta, I don't mean to doubt your skills but you did say you'd never proved them – we won't get lost. I say we wait till someone realises we're missing and they come and look for us.

Dad said, ~ That might be quite a time.

~ Well, we've been here quite a while already and, pirates apart, I like the place, said Lorraine.

Georgia said, ~ I want to go. I can't stay here. Brad will be wondering why he hasn't heard from me. She looked close to tears. ~ He'll – he'll find someone else.

Grant muttered, ~ Never liked the boy anyway.

~ You don't have to, daddy – he's my boyfriend. I love him, cried Georgia. ~ And Brad loves me.

~ Honey, said Lorraine, ~ if he can't wait a little while . . .

Georgia was almost choking on her tears now. ~ It won't *be* a little while. It might be ages and ages. Mr Sanders said so. Brad's only human. If he doesn't get an email from me he'll think I'm mad at him for something and – and he'll go out with some-one else.

Good riddance to Bradley, I thought, but was wise enough to keep my peace. I was feeling a bit peeved with Georgia. Only a couple of days ago she had said I was the best. How come Bradley was suddenly the most important person in the world? Girls! You couldn't work them out if you had a machine to do it. The machine would explode.

~ Fact is, dad said gently, ~ there's more at stake than worrying about how it will affect people at home, Georgia. All our lives are on the line here. Brad will have to take care of him-self. Your mother's right. If he doesn't bother to find out what's happened to you, he isn't worth it. Could be he'll be our saviour. Raise the alarm. Get the authorities thinking about why they haven't heard from us.

Bradley the hero. That's all I needed.

~ Or he might just go out with the first girl he sees, I murmured, unfortunately loudly enough for everyone to hear. ~ I mean, from what I've heard . . .

Georgia's eyes opened wide. ~ Max Sanders, you're an idiot, she shouted at me.

~ A vote, said Rambuta. ~ Hands up for staying.

I stuck my hand up.

Hassan said, ~ I will vote with my father.

~ Creep, I muttered in his ear, but I was secretly pleased with him when dad stuck up his hand.

In fact everyone but Georgia put up their hands. She jumped up saying we were all morons and stamped off to her tent. We could hear her sobbing in there for ages afterwards. I felt really guilty and asked Lorraine to apologise to her for me, for making that remark. Lorraine smiled at me.

~ Don't worry, Max. She isn't crying for Bradley.

~ It sounds like it, I said, jealous to the core. ~ Listen to her! She must love him to bits, to cry like that.

~ That's just her getting rid of a few emotions.

~ Like what?

~ Oh, anger, fear, frustration. Lots of things. It's the way we women do it sometimes. Bradley? She hardly knows him, really. They only met briefly, and Grant's right — he's a bit of a — well, his father's rich and basically Bradley's a spoiled brat. A very good tennis player. A very good student. Georgia was impressed by those attributes. But as a person — who knows what he's like? He has charm and he has confidence, but I would have thought that when it comes to it, Georgia will go for someone kind and thoughtful rather than accomplished. Anyway, you're all far too young for that stuff. Just be happy being friends. She looked into the middle distance, remembering something. ~ But I do know what it's like to be a teenager. You get your emotions in a tangle. When you get to my age and look back on it – well, I shan't spoil it for you.

~ I'm lousy at tennis, I said, biting my lip. ~ I suppose I could practise.

She laughed at me. ~ Not here, you can't.

At that moment a human scream came from the rainforest. It stunned the whole camp into silence. Even Georgia stopped sobbing.

No one wanted to stay in camp after that horrible scream.

~ There's someone out there, dad said. ~ We ought to go and find him.

~ Sounded like a woman to me, Grant said. ~ That scream.

~ Well, whoever it is, Lorraine added, ~ it seems they're in trouble.

~ Rambuta should stay with the kids, said dad, ~ while we . . .

~ I'm not staying here, I shouted.

~ Nor me, cried Georgia.

~ We should do as our fathers tell us, Hass said piously.

~ Shut up, Hass, Georgia and I chorused.

~ We should all go out together, Rambuta announced. ~ I'm not happy always being the baby-sitter.

~ We're not babies . . . Georgia began to argue, then like me she realised Rambuta was on our side and her voice trailed away.

193

There followed loads of arguing which eventually dad and Grant lost. Rambuta pointed out that if anything happened to the adults as a group the 'children' would be left to fend for themselves. It was unlikely but it could happen. In which case the kids would need to have full knowledge of what was happening on the island to survive.

~ That's true, Lorraine said. ~ The kids need to know.

So, in the end, we all went out. Each adult carried a weapon. I was a bit peeved that we weren't allowed to. Not real ones. Dad let us have parangs but he said there wasn't a hope in hell of letting us carry rifles or shotguns.

We set off in line formation with dad at the front and Grant at the rear, we kids and the other two adults in the middle. It had rained in the night so the forest was dripping. It always smelled damp but after the rain the smell was thick and heavy with moisture.

Insect-eating pitcher-plants lined a lot of the paths through the forest, brimming with water after the rain and trembling with the weight. High overhead the canopy formed from the giant trees blocked out a lot of the light, but rattan and other climbers used the trunks to get to their tops. You never put your hand on anything in the forest. There were dangerous insects and reptiles, it was true, but the reason was the plants. Many of them had vicious thorns, centimetres long some of them, which could rip your skin open easy as pie. And a few had poisons.

So we stuck to the paths, splashing through rusty-brown pools of water and tripping over the thousands of roots that criss-crossed the trodden ground. At one point we came across the immature gryphon. It sat in the middle of the path looking grey and papery. It rustled its wings when it saw us, lifted its grisly head, and made a noise like a panther. We stopped and stared at it. Eventually it let us have the path, slinking off into the undergrowth followed by the muzzles of four rifles.

Every so often dad or Grant shouted, ~ Anyone there?

Sometimes they would be answered by mocking cries from birds or animals or even scada, and we listened hard to hear a human voice amongst them.

At one point a soldier ant almost the size of a mouse bit my ankle and I yelped, startling everyone.

Finally we came to a burned area in the rainforest where two black things were hunched on the ground. I knew they were burned corpses. They looked like charcoal. The only white bits were the teeth which seemed to be fixed in a grin. Lorraine ushered us past and into the forest beyond but not before I'd seen dad turn a corpse over with the muzzle of his rifle. It was like one of those lava victims at Pompeii which I saw on a school visit to Naples. Ghastly was the word our housemaster had used then, and ghastly was the word that popped into my head as I stared at that crispy corpse in the forest.

~ Nothing we can do for those poor beggars, muttered dad, pushing ahead.

Grant said, ~ Maybe bury them later?

We walked on with our own thoughts.

At about noon we came across a clearing and we saw signs of the large scadu. There was a trail of trodden grasses, bent twigs on bushes, hoofprints. We were sure we were in the place where she was grazing. If you glanced quickly at where you thought she was standing, you might see a flicker. A broken

195

shape. The sunlight and the shade then swallowed her. It was difficult. The more you stared, the less you saw. A change of light. The flash of the undersides of leaves. A flying bird veering to avoid something in its path. A crooked shadow. Like a silver fish in silver waters, she was there and gone. There were the markers you looked for. Occasionally you might catch a gleam of horn or the sheen of damp hair and you thought you might have seen her.

She soon left us, parting the curtains of shimmering leaves at the edge. Somehow her presence, the fact that she was still alive, gave everybody a bit of heart. Despite her enormous size she seemed such a gentle creature and if she could survive the horrors of what was happening on the island then maybe we could too. This was voiced by Rambuta but I think we all agreed with him.

We saw two other scada that day: the unicorn and the senmurv.

The senmurv was the beastie that had puzzled Georgia: the first scadu she ever saw in the forest. Half-dog, half-bird. It was one of the weirdest-looking creatures amongst the scada, with its doggy face elongated to a beak, feathers on its body, and wings. A walking nightmare. But not very big, so not really threatening. I didn't feel menaced. I just felt a bit revolted by it, the way some people do by snakes. It was too peculiar to find amusing or attractive in any way.

The senmurv was nipping fleas on its own butt when we came across it and it stared at us for a moment before dashing off into the undergrowth.

A little later we heard the sound of waves and realised we were near the water's edge.

196

~ Let's get out of here for a while, suggested Grant, ~ and find some fresh air.

Dad agreed.

The brilliance of the light on the lagoon as always made me scrunch up my eyes. I'd forgotten (as usual) to bring my sunglasses. But the smell of the ocean and the booming of the surf out on the reef filled me with a sense of relief. My shoulders relaxed and I shed a sense of foreboding. I hadn't realised that walking in the forest had made me edgy and anxious. Once out here in the sea breezes and where everything seemed normal I knew how uptight I'd been *in there*.

Like the others I looked up and down the shoreline to see if the human we'd heard yesterday was anywhere in sight.

Nothing.

But what surprised me was how high the water was up the sea strand. It had entered the rainforest. There was very little beach left, just a metre or even less. Our tribal log, the one we kids used as our den, where we used to sit and talk when we first came to Krantu — it was gone. Floated away no doubt. That log had been halfway between the rainforest and the water's edge, even at high tide.

The highest ground on the island was not more than a metre above sea level — and the waters were rising fast.

The adults were probably aware of this because they made no comment. They were more interested in the screamer.

~ Whoever that was in distress last night, Lorraine said, ~ is either very quiet or very dead.

~ Mom! cried Georgia. ~ Don't talk like that.

We all sat at the edge of the rainforest. Lorraine had brought a backpack full of mangoes with her, which we peeled and munched our way through. Scouring the horizon I couldn't see any sign of the pirates. They'd been and gone.

Once we'd rested it was time to go back to camp. It was decided to walk along what was left of the beach rather than go back in the forest. We still kept shouting every so often, but without expecting any reply. Maybe Lorraine was right. Maybe the person who'd called was dead. Or maybe the raiders returning to pick him up? We found the place where they had dragged their longboat up – a long deep rut in the mud of the rainforest. It was surrounded by footprints.

I was interested to see that not all the raiders wore shoes. Some of the prints clearly showed bare feet with the marks of the toes. In several ways these raiders were really like old-fashioned pirates.

Back inside the stockade I made friends with Georgia again.

~ I'm sorry I said that about Bradley, I told her when I got her alone. ~ I was just jealous.

~ I know, but girls don't like jealousy you know, Max. It might seem a compliment, but it isn't. It's better you take it on the chin and look as if you don't care. That can make us change our minds.

I stored that one away for the future, not realising at the time that girls don't all think the same way. What works for one doesn't necessarily work for them all. You have to know your girl.

In the meantime dad came to everyone and collected as many drycell batteries as he could find. He'd already double-checked the wetcell batteries used to fence in the Beast, but found they'd lost their charges. No one had bothered to power them up again after the Beast had been set free.

He wired all the drycell batteries together to see if he could get enough power to send a signal to the mainland. One was sent but no one knew if it had been received at the other end or not. We couldn't get the computer going, that was certain. It didn't even boot up.

No emails then, even for a lovesick Californian girl trying to contact her spoiled-brat boyfriend. How sad was that? Not much.

We slept huddled around a campfire that night. I swear we were all half-awake, listening for that scream again. It never came, thank goodness. I think I would have wet myself.

The next day we went out again, but this time we walked up the opposite side of the island. We found the grizzled remains of some scadu close to the beach. It had been caught in one of the forest fires and turned to toast. We also saw a live manticore, which we avoided. No one fancied being stuck with poisoned darts. In the middle of the island we suddenly came across a curious sight: a huge hole in the ground, recently dug.

~ Who or what did that? asked dad, peering down the dark shaft that seemed to slant at a forty-five-degree angle. ~ That's one big rabbit hole!

Grant said, ~ Maybe it was raiders?

~ Why dig a hole that big? Why dig one at all? said Lorraine. ~ It doesn't make sense. A human could crawl down there. I'm not going to, though, she added quickly, with a shudder.

~ Unless they were looking for something, I piped up. ~ Buried treasure?

They all looked at me.

~ I know, I know – they're not storybook pirates.

~ It would be nice if they were, sighed Lorraine. ~ None of this would be real then.

The hole remains a mystery. No one's curious enough to go down it to see what might be inside, if anything at all. We guessed it had been made by one of the scada. Maybe the arrival of the raiders had frightened one or more of the fabulous creatures and one of them had panicked and dug a hidey-hole? That seemed the most logical answer.

~ Dad, I whispered, as we walked home, ~ this hole – it hasn't got anything to do with our secret, has it?

~ Secret? he said.

~ Yes, you know, that – that dead creature I showed you – the one killed by the makara in the forest.

He looked around him quickly, to make sure no one else had heard us.

~ I said not to speak of that again – not until we were away from here, Max. Not till we get home.

~ I know, I know – but do you think . . . ?

~ No – no, I'm sure it has nothing to do with that dead creature we saw. Now, try not to mention it again.

I nodded vigorously. I hadn't wanted to talk about it, but it worried me. It worried me a lot. Not because I thought it was important, but because dad did. I could see it concerned dad a lot.

26 August, Krantu Island

In the middle of the night something rattled the gates.

Rambuta was on guard. He yelled for dad and Grant. All of us heard the noise though. We were all a bit nervy and tense and only sleeping lightly. I think an owl blinking would have woken us.

Everyone leapt to their feet and ran to the gates. Rambuta was trying to peer through the cracks in the bamboo poles.

A loud moan came from the creature outside.

~ Shall I fire through the gates? cried Grant, who had come running up with his gun. He levelled his rifle. We knew it was a powerful weapon. He'd told us it had 'high penetration'. ~ If I space out a few shots one of them is bound to hit.

Rambuta shook his head. ~ We don't know what's out there, Mr Porter. He always avoided calling Georgia's dad Grant.

~ It might be the unicorn, cried a panicky-sounding Georgia. ~ Don't shoot the unicorn, pop.

~ I've got a torch, said dad. ~ Let me through – let me have a look.

Grant stuck the barrel of his rifle between the two gates and eased them open wide enough for dad to shine his light through.

Dad stepped forward.

~ Good God! he cried, as he peered along the beam. ~ There's a man out there.

The gates were opened and a thin man in rags staggered inside the compound. Even in the light of the torch I could see that one of his arms was blackened and hanging uselessly by his side. He was in great pain and he collapsed against Rambuta who caught him in his strong hands. Dad dashed forward and between the pair of them they carried the man into the store hut and laid him on the floor.

~ First aid kit! cried dad.

~ I know where it is, called Hassan.

~ So do I, I said.

~ One of you – Hassan.

I let Hassan go, realising this was no time to compete for dad's respect. I looked at the man. He was very thin. Very thin. His hair was black and wispy, quite short-cropped, and I could see bald bits. There were sores on his neck and probably in other places. His face was sort of skull-like and there was a big mole on the side of his nose. His yellow teeth — with gaps between — stuck out almost like a bird's beak. His eyes were reddish-veined and yellowy round the edges. They looked mad. He looked mad. They kept flicking this way and that. Sometimes it seemed he was trying to look over his shoulder at something which might be creeping up behind him. He had fingers like talons which he kept clenching and unclenching. When he breathed it came out as a hissing sound as if he had trouble with the tubes to his lungs.

Once, he reached out and grabbed Lorraine's wrist, gripping it hard.

~ Ouch! Lorraine exclaimed, and carefully peeled the fingers away to reveal deep red marks where his dirty nails had been. The man had after all been in the rainforest for days, probably clawing away at tree roots to get stuff to eat, or digging in mossy banks for grubs. It was no wonder he looked like he did. Anyone would, sea-raider or not.

Grant looked concerned. ~ Did he break the skin?

Lorraine inspected her wrist. ~ There's no blood.

~ Put some iodine on it anyway. You never know — hepatitis and all that.

Hass came back with the kit, which was not so much first aid as several stages of aid. It was what dad called a Comprehensive Medical Kit, with hypo needles, medicines, dentist stuff and all sorts of weird and shiny instruments of torture. We watched — all of us — while dad fixed up the man's arm. The patient's eyes were wide open and staring but he said nothing the whole time dad was putting ointment on his burn and then winding a bandage round the wound.

Lorraine went to heat up some soup, which was then given to the man, who perked up a little.

~ Is he Chinese? asked Grant, staring at the man in the light of a hurricane lamp. ~ He looks it.

~ Definitely of Asian origin, agreed dad, as the man sat up and stared at us. ~ Chinese, but not necessarily from China itself.

Grant said, ~ Rambuta, you speak Chinese, don't you? Ask him how he got that arm.

~ I'll try, Rambuta said. Then turning to the man he said, ~ Ngaw yau dee see-gon seong toong nay gong.

The man immediately followed this with a stream of words. It sounded like all one word to me, but then when people talk foreign languages it always sounds like that. He kept going on and on and nobody tried to stop him. His voice got higher and higher until he coughed then groaned and fell on his back again.

~ What did he say? Grant asked Rambuta.

Rambuta replied, ~ I've absolutely no idea.

~ What? That wasn't Chinese then?

~ Yes, it probably was. It sounded like Hok Yuen Chinese. He may be originally from Singapore. Most the Chinese there speak Hok Yuen. If he was from Hong Kong he'd probably understand me, even if he was a Hakka. If he comes from mainland China, it could have been anything from Shanghaiese to Mandarin, though I would recognise it if it was Mandarin which is very sibilant, even though I don't speak it myself. I only speak *Gwong-dung wa* – Cantonese to you.

Grant looked at Rambuta as if he were mad.

~ What the hell are you talking about, man? cried a frustrated Grant Porter.

~ I'm saying that there is no one single spoken Chinese language. There's only one *written* language, common to all, but being a picture language you can use different words for the same picture. There are several Chinese dialects and they might as well be different languages — they're nothing like each other. This fellow and me might just as well be talking Russian and Polynesian at each other.

Grant looked baffled. Then his face brightened.

~ Well then, he cried, ~ you can *write* to each other. Get some paper and a pen. You can write your question and he can write the answer.

Rambuta smiled ruefully. ~ That would do it, *if* I knew how to read and write Chinese characters, which I don't. I know a few but to be even semi-literate in Chinese you need to remember some four thousand characters. Look, Mr Porter, I only speak Cantonese. I don't write the language and I don't know what dialect this man is speaking. Like you, I can only make guesses.

Grant shrugged and looked belligerently at the patient, as if it was his fault there was a breakdown in communications. ~ Well, there it is. We'll just have to try to get it out of him with sign language or something . . . but by that time the man had collapsed again, this time into unconsciousness.

Dad and Rambuta gave the man a blanket bath and then put him in a camping cot to sleep.

~ Shall we go out and see if there's any more of them out there? asked Grant.

Lorraine said, ~ I don't think anyone should go out there again.

~ We could go out in pairs, said Grant, reluctant to let go of his argument for a search. ~ If one pair gets into trouble they can signal the other pair for reinforcements.

~ I'm still concerned about all these burned bodies, muttered dad. ~ There could have been some sort of fire, in a remote part of the island, but it doesn't make a lot of sense. I think we should leave well enough alone for now.

~ Okay, okay, grumbled the jeweller. ~ We stay here for now. But we can't stay for ever. Somehow we have to get off the island. We have to make plans. We can't wait for a rescue at some indefinable date. We need to have a back-up plan.

~ Should we make a raft? I interrupted. ~ Hass and me would help.

Hassan nodded in furious agreement.

~ We don't need a raft, pointed out Georgia. ~ We've got the yacht. What we haven't got is a sail for it and navigational instruments. Right, dad?

~ Quite right, princess. I guess we could make a sail out of pandanus leaves, the way the locals once did. I could work out some rigging for it, given a little time.

Rambuta pointed out an obvious flaw. ~ Do you know how to weave pandanus leaves into a sail?

~ Don't you? asked Grant, falling into the typical error of the Westerner who assumes that all Orientals carry the same vast knowledge of primitive skills. ~ You know plants. You're a local.

~ I am a local zoologist. My skills lie in knowing the Latin names and properties of plants, not how to turn them into furniture.

~ You know other stuff as well. I've heard you talking about it to the kids. You have knowledge of the stars and nocturnal navigation.

~ And diurnal navigation, but I can't weave a basket to save my life, said Rambuta, ~ and it follows that I can't weave a sail. We could all try but I don't know how far we'd get.

Lorraine said, ~ I thought we'd all decided that we shouldn't take our chances with the sea.

~ But, sweetheart, things have changed, argued Grant. ~ We've got an arsonist loose on the island.

Dad said, ~ We seem pretty safe in here. He could have run out of fuel. If so, he's no more dangerous than any other man.

~ In which case we can go out and shoot him, Grant said.

~ That's not up to us, dad continued. ~ We are not the law, we shouldn't administer justice — or even revenge for that poor creature lying on that cot over there . . .

~ Poor creature, dad? I cried. ~ He's a pirate. He's probably killed people.

Dad gave me a look, then said, ~ You're right, son. But my argument remains valid. We can't go out there and kill a man in cold blood. I doubt you can do it, Grant, no matter how you feel now. Once you've got a human being I don't care how many men you may have killed before now.

~ None, I hope, admitted Grant. Then he added, ~ Not counting the other night — I don't know if I actually *hit* anyone.

~ Well, there it is. I propose . . .

We never did find out what dad proposed, not at that moment anyway, because our fugitive sat up and spoke.

~ Help me, he said in perfect if croaky English. ~ Please to help me and not let me die, and I will speak the truth.

*

Everyone gaped at the man who had said these words.

~ He speaks English! cried Grant. ~ Why didn't he do so before?

Rambuta supplied the answer to this. ~ He was under great stress – he's had time to rest now.

Dad went over to the man. ~ What is your name? he asked in precise English.

~ I am So Kam, sir, replied the man. ~ I am this poor fisherman you see before you – my vessel was in great storm . . .

~ Enough of that, snapped Grant, his rifle in the crook of his arm, ~ we know you're a damn pirate. We'd be within our rights to hang you now from the nearest tree. What the hell do you mean by attacking us on this island? There's no gold here. No real money. You and your friends stole all my possessions from my yacht. You're going to jail, my friend.

So Kam nursed his bad arm as if it were a baby.

~ No, no, you are mistaken, sir. I know the bad pirates of which you speak. They often attack my village. I myself am just poor fisherman, trying to earn my daily rice.

Dad stepped forward and grabbed So Kam's good arm. He held it up for us to see. ~ A Rolex watch? On a village fisherman? I don't think so. You're a sea-raider and we know it.

Grant swung his rifle down from his shoulder and pointed it at the Asian pirate.

~ Shall I shoot him now, James?

So Kam was on his feet in an instant. ~ No, please – yes, you are right, I was with those men who come here, but I only join them very short time ago, when they invade my village. They carry off three, no, four of my people and force them – yes, sirs, *force* them to join pirate crew. They – they give me this watch, but I not want it. Here, he used his teeth to grip the expanding gold bracelet and ripped the watch off his wrist, letting it fall to the ground, ~ you have it, sirs. It your watch now. There is also some money, lot of money, in my pocket – Hong Kong dollar. You share it. He gave a faint little laugh. ~ You deserve it, after all, since you save my life. You help me now, to go away from this island?

~ Mr Kam . . . began Lorraine, but dad interrupted her with, ~ His family is So. Kam is his familiar name.

~ Oh, that's how it's done, is it? Well then, Mr So, we all want to get off this island. Unfortunately, we don't have a working boat, thanks to your colleagues. And tell me, just what did you do on the pirate ship? I'd like to know that.

~ Do? he almost spat the word back. Clearly it was demeaning for him to talk to a mere woman. ~ I do my job, he said.

Lorraine persisted, despite the man's obvious hostility towards her. ~ And that would be – what?

~ Me? I scrub deck, I cook meal.

Lorraine folded her arms. ~ Oh, I see – you're just the cook. You realise we dressed your arm of course?

~ Only cook. Only scrub, shouted Kam. He gestured with his good arm at the men. ~ What this woman want from me? Why she talk like this? Dress Kam's arm? What that mean, bloody hell?

Grant said, ~ Honey, I don't see . . .

~ I do, Rambuta interrupted him. ~ I can see just what Mrs Porter is getting at. This man has soft hands. He's never scrubbed a deck in his life. What's more, I can add to her suspicions. See that tattoo on his arm? A scorpion? That's a badge of office. It means he belongs to a triad gang. The triads are the Far Eastern equivalent of the Mafia.

~ I just get this when small boy, whined So Kam, his eyes glaring hatred at Rambuta. His tone then turned nasty. ~ You just a Malay kitchen boy. You leave talking to real men. He nodded at dad and Grant. ~ Tell this boy go sweep out hut while we talk.

Rambuta stepped forward smartly and with a loud *crack* he slapped the pirate's face a stinging blow. I think this action shocked everyone. I know it shocked me. So Kam was stunned for a few seconds. The blow must have hurt him quite badly. Then he leapt forward and tried to claw at Rambuta's face, his expression twisted by fury. ~ I kill you, he screamed. ~ You dare to strike *me*?

Rambuta smacked him again, harder this time. So Kam fell to his knees. He hung his head and sobs came from his lips.

~ This man, Rambuta said calmly, ~ also has some characters tattooed under his gang insignia. I told you I don't know many characters, but I know one or two. Those two I do know, since they are common enough amongst criminals of his kind. They read *Big Brother*. It means he was the boss. Gentlemen, Rambuta said, ~ we are looking at the pirate chief, the captain of the junk.

Grant's eyes opened wide. ~ Well I'll be ... he said. He stepped forward and placed the muzzle of the rifle against the forehead of the kneeling man. ~ I really *am* going to shoot him.

~ Daddy, no, cried Georgia, but the pirate was already back on his feet. ~ Yes, yes. I confess. I am chief of pirate vessel. Please don't shoot me. He looked seaward and snarled. ~ My men, they leave me here. They take my junk and sail away. I will kill them all. Have pity on me. I am like you, I have had all my

209

thing stole from me. You must see what wretched fellow I am now. You must feel pity for my plight.

~ He's certainly got a way with words, Grant murmured. ~ Now, you will tell us how you knew there were people on this island.

~ We sail by one day. See white yacht. Is all.

Grant said, ~ So, what do we do with this guy? I still say we shoot him. We can't keep him with us. We'll have to guard him night and day. It'll strain all our resources. When we hand him over to the authorities they're going to hang him anyway. You know that. They're very keen on capital punishment out here.

~ Grant, dad sighed, ~ you know very well you wouldn't be able to shoot him. Neither can I, and I doubt Rambuta can. So that leaves your wife, who is the only member of our party famil- iar enough with firearms to have any history of doing such a thing. Do you want Lorraine to execute this man?

Grant's chest swelled, then he came out with the word we all knew was coming. ~ No.

~ Right then, said dad. ~ Let's be more practical about this. We have no responsibility towards him. Let's patch him up and send him on his way. Let him find his own passage off this island. Dad turned to So Kam. ~ You understand what I'm saying? We are not responsible for you. You are a robber and a thief, and probably a murderer. We have no duty towards you. Go and build yourself a raft or something, or signal to your crew to come and pick you up. We don't want you here.

~ I might die! shrieked So Kam.

~ Not our responsibility, repeated dad, waving his hand. ~ You came here to do mischief and you must suffer the con- sequences of your criminal activities.

So Kam's hysteria continued. ~ I am human being.

Grant said, ~ True, but you're also a thug. Just like all your so-called men — especially the one who started the fires. You brought him here — or them, if it was more than one — and you should bear the responsibility for what has been done.

~ I bring him here? screamed the sea-raider. ~ You bloody liar-man. I no bring him. You bring him. He your damn creature.

~ Now you know that is totally false, Grant riposted. ~ And I might remind you, I am the man with the gun. Call me a liar again and I'll make you sorry.

So Kam went off into a stream of words, spittle flying from his mouth in all directions. He waved his burned arm in the air, careless of the fact that it must have hurt him like heck to throw it around. He seemed incensed by Grant's claim that his men were responsible for setting light to the rainforest. Finally he ceased his tirade of abuse — that's what Grant called it later — and kneeled down, thumping the hard earth with his right fist.

Rambuta was staring at him. He now spoke to So Kam.

~ Are you saying your men *didn't* start the fires?

The pirate looked up quickly. ~ Why you ask me that, you stupid lascar? You know who start fires.

~ Your arm, pointed out Rambuta. ~ How did you get that?

~ This? screeched the pirate. ~ Bloody dragon, of course. Where you think I get it? It kill my men, that bloody creature. It kill us and make us run for boat. Man behind me go up in stinkin' mess of fire. Some of the flame go past him and burn my arm. I fall over. Men leave me — bastard. All go for boat, leave their captain. I get up, run for boat again, screaming at my bastard men. Dragon come again. I hide under tree, quick, quick.

211

He paused and held up the charred stick that used to be his left arm. ~ Dragon do this to me. Bloody dragon, that who.

~ A dragon! said dad. ~ Of course. Why didn't we think of that? That hole we found in the rainforest? That was its lair! I should've guessed. The one mythical creature that outlived the others back in those times when scada roamed the Earth. Probably destroyed them.

~ How do you account for that? asked Grant. ~ I mean, what's your destruction theory?

~ The dragon, explained dad, ~ is present in almost all mythologies, regardless of geography. Almost every culture has a dragon. Welsh dragons, Chinese dragons, Egyptian dragons. From the Mexican Cipactli to the Babylonian Tiamat, dragons span the Earth. And they were the last of the mythological creatures to disappear. Dad warmed to his theme. ~ Look how they figure so prominently in the British culture – St George and the dragon – and in other cultures too. For instance, the dragon is the *only* mythological creature in the Chinese astrological cycle. The Year of the Dragon? All the other eleven are real creatures.

He paused before going on.

~ The dragon is supreme. The dragon reigned over all the other mythological beasts. It possessed an awesome power unique among fabulous creatures. I remember reading once that it seems likely that all dragons are related to each other, whether Chaldean, Norse or Oriental. My guess is the dragon wiped out all the other scada and remained the only one of its kind for many centuries afterwards.

~ Okay, professor, muttered Grant, ~ we get the picture. Thing is, what *do* we do about it?

~ We have to kill it, said dad, ~ before it destroys us. It hasn't yet matured enough to learn to fly. Once it takes to the air we won't stand a chance. We have to hunt it down and kill it now.

Lorraine asked, ~ Are you sure it can't fly yet?

~ Not absolutely, replied dad, ~ but I haven't seen it flying around yet, have you? It'd have the greatest difficulty, even if it did manage to leave the ground. The rainforest is too thick for it to fly through. It would have to soar above the canopy and attack from the tree tops. But I have no doubt its flames will be able to penetrate through the foliage and reach us on the ground, once it is in full command of the air.

~ Ha! cried So Kam. ~ Now you get a taste of same medicine.

~ You be quiet, Rambuta said, ~ or we'll stake you out and leave you as a sacrifice for the dragon.

The pirate chief paled at these words.

~ You not do that. You can not do that. I am a citizen of Malaysia, like you. I born in Kuching. I half-Dyak.

~ Then you're a disgrace to our country, said the Malay professor. ~ And my Chinese and Dyak friends would agree with me. Rambuta turned to Lorraine and explained, ~ For the most part Malays, Chinese and Dyaks live comfortably together in our country. But one or two always turn out like this one – criminal to the core.

~ It happens everywhere, my own country included, agreed Grant. ~ There's always the rotten minority.

~ Seriously, said Lorraine, out of the hearing of So Kam, ~ what are we going to do with him? We can't keep him tied up all the time. His circulation will suffer and he's not in good condition anyway. Yet if we let him wander around he'll find himself a weapon.

213

The children especially are in danger from him. What's to stop him using one of them as a hostage? All he needs is a knife or a club.

~ We'll lock him in the fish-drying shed for now, said dad. ~ Pile sandbags up against the door. That'll hold him.

They did this while we kids were watching. They had to drag the protesting So Kam to the shed and throw him inside. He was obviously weak from several days without food, and from his encounter with the dragon, but still he managed to dredge up reserves of strength to kick, bite and scratch his captors. I shuddered to think what would happen if he got out again. You could see he was someone without any conscience. He wouldn't hesitate to harm a kid like me or Hass or even Georgia. However, I knew we couldn't just shoot him.

~ You kids stay away from the shed, warned Grant. ~ We don't want any further truck with that guy.

~ What's going to happen now? I asked. ~ You going to kill the dragon?

~ We're going to try, dad replied. ~ Lorraine will stay here with you kids, while we three go and hunt for the thing. Do as she tells you, mind. I'm placing you all on trust. No arguing and no talking back.

As if we would at a time like this! Some adults have got no sense.

The three men left the compound armed with rifles. We watched them go, as they entered the rainforest. We had collected a few AK47s from the raiders that had been killed by the dragon, which were now stacked in one of the disused huts. It seemed to us that the best thing to do would be for us kids to be armed as well.

~ Can I have a Kalashnikov? I asked.

Lorraine looked at me with wide eyes. ~ Certainly not.

~ Why not? asked Hass. ~ I've fired one before.

~ I don't care whether you've won an Olympic medal for shooting, you're not going to have a Kalashnikov.

~ Well, I think that's pretty mean-spirited, I said in my best haughty private school tone. ~ We could be under siege.

Georgia rolled her eyes at these antics. ~ Max, pur-lease! You sound like some British geek.

~ I am a British geek, I pointed out. ~ At least, I'm British, and this is the way we talk in England. Anyway, we don't whine through our noses, like you lot.

~ I don't whine, Georgia said hotly.

~ I don't whyyyyynnnne, I copied her, exaggerating her nasal twang.

This, of course, was a big mistake. Completely the wrong thing to do. Georgia got the hump. She glared at me fit to combust. At that moment I was glad we hadn't been given AK47s or I would definitely have been shot to bits. Hassan wisely stayed out of it. I would've too, if I'd been him. I forgot about the Kalashnikovs. I decided to get out of the line of fire and asked Lorraine if I could take the first watch.

~ Yes, she said. ~ Your dad, Grant and Rambuta made a tower out of bamboo this morning, so's to be able to have a clear view of the rainforest on all sides. She pointed to a thing that looked like a machine gun post on the corner of a POW camp. There was a rickety-looking ladder to climb. I went up it, to the cabin at the top. There I spent the rest of the day, looking out over the forest, watching for the dragon.

The dragon never came, but the unicorn did, around early evening.

I yelled down. ~ Georgia!

~ What? she shouted back up at me. ~ What do you want?

~ Your favourite pet's outside, I told her, hoping to get back in her good books. ~ The unicorn.

Her eyes lit up and she went to one of the gun holes in the fence to look out at the scadu. It came to her when she called it with soft words. They seemed to have an affinity, she and this horse-with-a-horn. Georgia reached through with some salt and the unicorn took it from her palm. If I tried that it would have severed my hand at the wrist, I was sure. But Georgia seemed to know that it would be gentle with her. And it was. It licked her forearm while she giggled and waggled her fingers. Then, as the evening turned the sky to a lilac colour, the creature trotted back into the swiftly stretching shadows of the rainforest.

Hass said, ~ The dragon will probably kill it.

He was just talking, but now he was in trouble.

Boy, was he in trouble.

~ You have a nasty vindictive mind, cried Georgia. ~ I don't want to speak to you ever again. Nor you, she yelled up at me. ~ You're both as bad as each other.

~ What did I do? I yelled down. ~ It was me told you the unicorn was outside.

But since she wasn't speaking to me — to either of us — I didn't get an answer.

I came down from the tower a half-hour later. The men still hadn't returned. There hadn't been any gunshots, not that we'd heard.

~ Are they all right, d'you think? I asked Lorraine.

~ Of course, she replied, without much conviction. ~ Here, I've made some soup. You can give it to the prisoner.

Hass and Georgia pulled away the sandbags while Lorraine stood back with a good view of the doors. When they were opened we expected So Kam to rush out, but the doorway was empty. After a short while he strolled to the entrance and looked at us with contempt.

~ What you think I do? he cried. ~ What you think I do with this bad arm? He held up his blackened stump of a limb. ~ You think I attack you and kill you all? Huh. Give me my food.

He snatched the billy out of my hands, spilling some of the soup.

~ Now look what you do! he yelled at me. ~ You clumsy-boy. You no fit to feed man like me. You idiot. Get me rice.

Lorraine said, ~ There's rice in the soup. Get back into the shed. Max, don't get too close to him. Don't let him get within grabbing distance.

I stepped back from the sea-raider.

Just at that moment the men came back, opening the gate and then locking it behind them. Grant called, ~ You having trouble with him?

~ Just a little, replied Lorraine.

~ So Kam, get back into the shed or I'll come and kick your butt for you, Grant told him. ~ I warned you not to make trouble. How about we make a snake pit and put you in that? Will that keep you quiet?

The pirate muttered something ugly and took his plate into the darkness of the hut. We kids closed the door behind him and piled the sandbags up against it again. Then we ran to the men.

~ Did you get it? cried Georgia. ~ We didn't hear any shots.
~ We saw it, said Grant.

~ Briefly, added Rambuta. ~ Very briefly.

~ It came out of its lair, dad explained, ~ and ran into the forest. We didn't even have time to get a shot in. I think it's as I suspected. It's a nocturnal hunter . . .

~ Hunts at night, I explained to Hass.

~ I know that, said Georgia, sniffing, thinking I meant the explanation for her.

~ We've put some bamboo gin traps around the hole, dad said. ~ Grant knew how to make them.

~ Grant? said Lorraine.

~ Honey, explained her husband, ~ I've never done that sort of thing before, but you remember I went to Vietnam on business? I visited the Ku Chi tunnels while I was there and this guy — ex-Vietcong — he was showing us how to make jungle traps with bamboo. You know, grids of spikes that come flying up at you when you tread on the spring? Or the one with a pointed stake on a pole that swings out of nowhere and impales unsuspecting GIs . . . he looked at his astonished wife and daughter before finishing lamely, ~ . . . stuff like that.

~ And you *remembered* how to make them? said Lorraine incredulously.

~ Well, yeah. You know, boys' toys.

~ Toys? *Booby traps?* And, she repeated herself, ~ you remembered how to make them? But you can't even fix a blocked sink.

~ Yeah, I know, honey — but this was really neat.

~ When we get back home, she said, going domestic, ~ I want that shelf you've been promising me for eighteen months!

~ I'll put it up. I really will. I promise.

The matter was dropped while we listened to Rambuta's description of the dragon, though he and dad had only caught a quick look at it.

27 August, Krantu Island

~ Wouldn't this be a good time to tell us just how all this came about? asked Grant of dad. ~ We know there's a mother Beast in the rainforest, who gives birth to mythological creatures. What we don't know is how she came to be there. It's time you told us.

With the pirate safely locked up, we were all gathered around the camp table. It was a solemn party. For some reason the Porters had dressed up a bit. Grant was wearing a Hawaiian shirt and white slacks, with white yachting pumps on his feet. He had on his aviator shades. Lorraine had a bow in her hair, some sort of flowered dress, and silver sandals. Georgia had yellow slacks and shirt, with white trainers. They all looked immaculate.

~ I'm afraid we can't match you for style, dad said, when they had entered the camp. ~ You'll have to take us as you find us.

The Porters looked at each other as if they were seeing one another for the first time that evening. I don't think they dressed up deliberately for any reason. I think it was a sort of subconscious thing.

Grant muttered something about 'ceremony' and it being 'an occasion' and then Hass and I went to get the drinks.

Once we were all seated with fruit juices in our mitts, dad, at the head of the table, began his speech.

~ What I'm going to tell you is very strange, very strange indeed. No doubt it will shock you. If I were to hear it from someone else's lips, I am certain I would be shocked too. It will sound incredible, but believe me every word is true. Rambuta will vouch for that . . .

The sun was going down swiftly behind the rainforest and the faces before us began to change as shadows filled the hollows: the eyes, the corners of mouths, the furrows in brows. It was as if someone were painting darkness into the crevices of the skin. Those faces became disturbingly unreal: the faces of primitive statues coming to life.

Rambuta lit a hurricane lamp. The sallow faces lit up. Black clouds of insects swarmed in around the glass.

~ . . . every word is true. Dad paused before continuing. ~ I'll start at the beginning, in Jordan. He cleared his throat. I could see Grant Porter leaning forward on the table, big hands knitted, looking intently into dad's eyes even though he already knew a lot of what dad was going to tell us. ~ Hassan, who is now my adopted son, he nodded towards Hass, ~ brought me a jar he'd found in a cave. That jar contained scrolls, similar to the Dead Sea Scrolls. They had writings on them in Aramaic script, which I and an Arab colleague began to translate. They turned out to be war scrolls, with lists of warriors, armies, weapons, supplies. Interesting enough, but not earth-shattering. Yet, his voice took on a faraway quality, ~ there was something there I couldn't quite get hold of. Something that needed *deciphering* rather than translating.

~ It evaded me, for a long time. I was frustrated and angry with myself, but I realised I needed a key, a code if you like, to unlock the secrets of the scrolls. He looked at Hass and me. ~ I would never have found it, if those two boys had not taken it into their heads to explore the cave of the scrolls one last time. They found it, they found the one scroll which unlocked the secrets of all the others.

~ I found it, I said. Then shut up.

~ In short, dad said, ~ such scrolls are not made of paper, or papyrus, or any kind of parchment that would deteriorate — but of animal skin. Often it is goatskin. These particular scrolls however came from a mammal previously unknown. The deciphered writings told of a Fabulous Beast, the Mother of All Mythical Creatures, who wandered the Earth before man was on two legs. It was a stunning revelation. Dad laughed harshly. ~ Oh, I took the bit about being the mother of myths with a pinch of salt of course. Some shaman's imagination gone wild. But the hide itself did seem unusual. There were indigo camouflage symbols and patterns on it, which were not dye. They were natural markings.

~ There was also an account of how renegades who had been thrown out of various tribes banded together to form a separate group of their own. They lived on the fringes and terrorised the peaceful tribes of that era.

~ Outlaws? asked Grant.

Dad was a stickler for exactness. ~ Well, not quite outlaws. To have someone outside the law you need laws in the first place, but certainly the tribes would have *rules* — rules which probably changed with each new chieftain, but nevertheless there would have been an unwritten code of conduct which the renegades would flout. Quite naturally I suppose the Mother of All Mythical Creatures was a venerated creature, a deity to these primitive peoples, and the scrolls say that the renegades hunted her down and killed her to spite their enemies.

The shadows on dad's face were deep as he leaned forward in the lamplight.

~ Imagine this – a group of painted hunters, strong muscled men and perhaps women too, surrounding a forest, driving out the wild animals within. They would not be able to see the Beast because of her camouflage but they would have watched for signs of her: trampled undergrowth, fresh footprints in the riverbank mud, things like that. In those days too, man's sense of smell would be almost as good as that of the game he hunted. They would scent her presence.

~ They would enter a forest knowing she was somewhere within, to flush her out on to the grassy plains of some great valley, where her camouflage was not quite so effective. Perhaps they might drive her into a fast-flowing river, where she would be hampered by the currents and visible by her thrashings. Chosen spearmen would hurl their weapons at her, pinning her, until those with clubs and axes could go in to finish her off. Finally they would skin her and cut up the hide, sharing it amongst themselves to use as magic battle shirts or enchanted shields.

I glanced at Georgia and saw that this picture had upset her.

~ Why would they do that? she asked in a tight voice. ~ Just out of jealous hate?

Dad said, ~ Well, there is a practical reason. In order to thwart your enemies you do everything you can to hurt them, psychologically. You knock away their supports. If they rely on a god or goddess to bring them good fortune, you destroy that deity so they feel vulnerable. The renegades wouldn't have thought in the terms I'm using of course, but they would know exactly what they were doing in killing the Beast. Destroying the Beast was like breaking down a wall which protected the tribes.

Grant took a sip of his drink, but his eyes never left dad's animated face. Dad was having to raise his voice now above the noise the crickets were making.

~ Anyway, continued dad, ~ I am coming to the point of my talk. You must listen carefully. One night the two boys, he nodded at us, ~ came to me and told they'd seen something unusual. I was tired and frankly a little ill, but my mind was still quite sharp. Dad paused, probably for effect, before saying, ~ They showed me something that made the hairs on the back of my neck stand on end — so bizarre I found it difficult to catch my breath . . .

~ What? asked Georgia, looking scared. ~ What was it?

Dad laid a gentle hand on her arm. ~ Don't be afraid, Georgia — I'm not trying to frighten you. I just want you to get an idea of the impact this phenomenon had on me. Despite the fact that I deal in lost dreams — the vague histories of our past — I'm a fairly practical man. I don't believe in the super-natural. Yet, though the light was poor and I was fatigued I witnessed the unassisted movement of two inanimate objects.

~ Say what you mean, Lorraine said. ~ Georgia doesn't understand you.

~ I saw one piece of scroll move towards the other one — in fact they both moved — towards each other.

Georgia said, ~ They moved?

~ They crept towards each other as if they were alive — and they joined. They were like two pieces of a jigsaw, perfectly

233

matched. They melted into one another. I was left with one piece of skin where before I had had two. They had been one piece before of course, when they formed part of the beast's coat. Now they were one again. Not whole, because there were more pieces. I took the other hides and placed them next to their counterparts. They too melded. At the end of an hour I had only one large piece of hide.

There was a thick silence amongst us as Georgia and Lorraine came to terms with this weird story.

~ There must be some answer to this, said Lorraine. ~ Some rational reason which can be explained. I don't believe in magic.

~ Nor I, stated dad. He picked up a large black notebook from in front of him on the table.

~ I'll read the notes I made at the time:

It is my belief that the individual cells that make up the hide of the Beast have remained live but dormant all these millennia, each possibly protected by its own personal armoured casing, similar to a nutshell. Something has caused them to become active, to shed these cases and seek their brothers and sisters, to join together as a family once more. What is more, I also believe that each of these cells has its own memory, which it exercises in its efforts to recreate the whole, the complete creature. Certainly it lives and its natural chemistry is producing secretions which encourage growth . . .

Georgia said, ~ This is pretty scary stuff, Professor Sanders.

Dad looked at her from under his black eyebrows. ~ Yes it is, Georgia. He seemed to see the need to apologise. ~ I'm sorry about that.

At that very moment a deep vibrating fog horn note came from the heart of the rainforest. Creepy? I think we all turned crusty grey at once. All except dad, who simply frowned. We'd heard that sound before of course, but only lately.

~ Well, there you are, he said quietly. ~ Let me continue, said dad, appearing not to notice his audience was in a state of shock. ~ The writings on the scrolls told of other pieces of the creature's coat, scattered about the world. I determined to track them all down and fit them together to make a complete hide. Dad's eyes shone in the light of the lamp. ~ Just think of that! A whole creature the like of which has never been seen before by mankind. We could even, he licked his lips, ~ we could even make a framework, suggested by the shape of the complete hide, and fit it over that framework to make the Beast itself.

~ That's what you were doing in the fish-drying shed, said Georgia, the revelation hitting her. ~ That was the big secret of the shed!

~ Correct, replied dad, ~ that's the secret your father was seeking, having been employed by the Krenshaw Institute to spy on me.

He held up a hand. ~ For which I no longer blame him. But let me take this slowly, so you can take it in piece by piece, because it's an unbelievable tale and you need to absorb it by degrees.

There were nods around the table.

~ Let's start with the pieces of hide. I was helped in my search by the writings on the scrolls themselves, which pointed me in various directions. There was an ancient and sacred Pawnee drumskin from your own country, Grant. I purchased that. And a Tibetan religious banner carried by those priests guarding the Dalai Lama when he was taken to India after the Chinese invasion. Also three khana or sections of a Mongol-Kulmuck ceremonial yurt. A Zulu war shield – that's when I got you those Zulu spears, boys – and a tapestry hanging in a temple dedicated to the god of fisher folk in a village in Vietnam . . .

Grant interrupted with, ~ All these artefacts – they sound precious to the owners. Did they just hand them over?

~ In some cases I paid a lot of money for them. Like you, Grant, I'm fairly wealthy – well, to be honest, very wealthy. There were book covers for a uniform edition of the works of Aleister Crowley, including his writings on Thelema and the Hermetic Order of the Golden Dawn – I bought those from the university which owned them. But for the most part, especially with the religious artefacts, I persuaded the owners to part with them for nothing. I showed them the scrolls. I demonstrated the ability of the hides to melt into one another. They learned from the writings where their banner or yurt came from in the beginning and where it fitted into the grand design. Once they were aware that their particular sacred object was part of a whole they recognised the higher purpose.

Dad cleared his throat, before continuing.

~ I was not going to desecrate the monks' tapestry or the Pushtun cloak used in Afghan tribal rituals, I was merely the instrument who would fulfil a destiny written thousands of years ago. Re-forming the Beast was the reason for the hides being holy in the first place – their sacredness was a device, if you like, to protect them from destruction and loss over the millennia. Now their ultimate purpose had been revealed, the owners were for the most part willing to allow me the use of these relics.

~ For the most part? queried Lorraine.

Dad looked only slightly shame-faced. ~ I had to take at least one by force – and steal two more – but I believe there is justification for my actions, in the purpose to which I intended to put the objects.

Grant frowned. ~ Well, we won't go into that – could be a hell of a long argument – anyway, you and Rambuta, you sewed – no, wait a minute, you didn't sew anything – you put this Beast thing together?

Rambuta said, ~ Over a light framework – bamboo.

Another mooning note drifted over, from somewhere deep in the rainforest, sending a chill through me. I looked at Georgia's face: it was as white as nan's bone china. Hass too, was pale. We were all pretty scared I guess, by the tone of dad's voice rather than what he was actually saying. It had that spooky quality which comes when an adult is trying to sound calm and matter of fact, but knows someone might become un-hinged at any moment, by what they have to say. A sort of desperate attempt to quell any underlying panic that might be in the air.

~ And once the Beast was whole, said dad, his voice becoming terrifyingly croaky, ~ it came alive.

Grant sat bolt upright.

Lorraine, however, let out a loud gasp and I saw Georgia shoot an anxious glance at her mother.

Rambuta took over from dad. ~ Like everyone here, I would never have believed this six months ago. But it is true. This creature is not like any we have known before. Not just in looks, but in its natural make-up. It has the ability to build itself, re-form cell by cell, until it is once again whole. If you think about cloning, Mr Porter – this is not that, of course, not cloning – but with such science you only need one tiny cell of a creature to reproduce it . . .

~ But this creature was dead, scattered to the four corners of the Earth, cried Lorraine.

~ But still, the DNA was there. The pattern was there. Once one cell had revived itself – who knows how? – it copied and copied, multiplied and multiplied – until once again it was a creature with senses, with a heartbeat, with blood pulsing through its veins, with a brain, lungs, liver, all the organs that it needed to call itself alive.

We went silent for a few minutes. I swallowed to clear my ears which were bunged-up like they get on an aircraft flight. My head was buzzing as if it was full of bees. I glanced nervously towards the rainforest and noticed others were doing the same. Was it out there, watching us, waiting to – to do what?

I asked quietly, ~ Is it dangerous, dad?

Rambuta answered with, ~ We don't think so. It hasn't shown any inclination to hurt anyone yet. It appears to be quite docile – as gentle as a domesticated cow. It is a herbivore.

~ So are hippos, said Georgia, ~ but they're supposed to be quite ferocious if you bother them.

~ True, replied Rambuta, but didn't add anything.

~ Why did you let it go? asked Georgia.

Dad looked towards me. ~ I didn't. Max frightened it one night, by accident, of course. He felt sick and went into the shed with a bright torch. The Beast was alarmed and broke through the back wall, disappearing into the forest. We haven't seen her since. She was so well camouflaged, once out in the sunlight and shadows. You look, you look hard, but she is impossible to see whole. Perhaps a fluttering leaf, or a shifting shade might tell you where she is, but you don't see her.

~ I thought it was a rhino, I blurted. ~ It wasn't my fault.

~ No, it wasn't, Max. It was our fault. Your father's and mine, Rambuta said quickly, without looking at dad. ~ We haven't been honest with everyone and we've only ourselves to blame.

I took a quick glance at Georgia, who was staring at me. She looked away when our eyes met. Then I felt Hassan's hand on my arm and I knew my brother was supporting me.

Hassan said, ~ We could catch this monster. We could cage it, father.

Dad replied, ~ Firstly, it isn't a monster, Hassan — not in the way you think, and secondly — you explain, Ram.

Rambuta nodded and turned to the others. ~ As James has said, you can't see it. A fleeting look, continued Ram, in an even voice, ~ a change of light, here and there, is all that you do see. Once within the surrounding trees, inside the rainforest it's insubstantial, like a ghost. It's solid enough — evidence the crushed bushes and tracks it leaves — but its camouflage is perfect. It has these indigo markings on its hide — almost like tattoos — symbols, shapes, patterns. They form a dizzying design which breaks up the Beast's shape and melts it into the background. In the sunlight and shadow, especially in the rain-forest where there's flickering light, laceworks of sun and shade, it simply can't be seen. Oh, you can see tracks and broken paths, and places where it's been grazing, but not the creature itself. Not in that environment.

Dad added, ~ And it's surprisingly fast on its feet for such a large creature; it doesn't amble or trundle along, as you'd expect. It's there and gone. It has these ancient survival techniques. Of course, at one time it must have been hunted down and killed — probably by the first men — but catching it would not be an easy task for us.

~ You could shoot it, muttered Grant.

~ Dad! cried Georgia. ~ Don't!

Lorraine gave her husband a hard stare and he looked down at his feet.

~ You can't shoot what you can't see, pointed out my dad, ~ but I know what you mean. If you fire at changing shadows you might hit it eventually. However, I repeat, this fabulous Beast means us no harm. It could have trampled us a dozen times before now. It could have destroyed our camp and speared us with those great horns.

Grant suddenly looked terribly weary. His face was grey and lined. He said, ~ It's my bunk for me. I need some sleep. I shall have to cope with my daughter's nightmares tonight, no doubt, so we might as well hit the sack early.

Hassan spoke up. ~ But what about the mythical creatures?

Dad replied, ~ Simple, Hassan — the Beast gave birth to them. They're her children. One of each, no more. They cannot reproduce themselves: they haven't the means. But there they are, unnatural wonders. And they're ours. They will make us all rich and famous, those absurdities of hers. Just you wait and see . . .

And I could see him savouring the word 'famous' for dad was already rich and didn't care much for money anyway.

My mind was in a great whirl. All I knew was my dad wouldn't lie, not about such stuff. And nor would Rambuta. If they said the Beast was out there, munching grass and trumpeting, I believed them. But it was hard. Very hard. It was like having to believe in magic. Yet, when you thought about it, some science is like magic. Magnetism and compass needles pointing north, and that sort of thing. Electricity. Even biology. Babies growing inside mothers. That's a kind of magic too. I felt kind of weird, like I wasn't in the real world anymore. It was as if I'd stepped through some portal and was in another place altogether.

~ You feel weird? I whispered in Georgia's ear, as she left.

~ Totally, she murmured in reply.

1 September, Krantu Island

There was a night when the crickets were making a racket, mozzies were whining inside the tent and the tree frogs were trying to outdo the bull toads. On top of all this din the wild pigs were restless. Bearded hogs had gathered around the compound. I think they'd been shifted out of the forest by the threat of the dragon. Anyway, what with one creature and another there was a hullabaloo going on, which Hassan slept through as soundly as if he was on a feather bed in Slumberland.

I got up, wringing with sweat. My vest was hanging on my shoulders limp and moist. (I am a pretty thin kid and getting thinner by the day.) I wear these flimsy Arabian 'pyjamas' in bed, which normally billow nicely and allow my skin to breathe. But tonight they stuck to my legs and made me feel like a drenched kitten.

Once outside the tent I found a little breeze and felt better. The night sky was absolutely chockablock with stars. You could see clusters of them in every corner of the sky. I wandered around for a bit, looking up at what Georgia called the 'spangled velvet', then realised I wasn't alone. Dad was up too, sitting on a stump, smoking a cigarette.

Dad? Smoking?

~ Hi, pop, I said, trying not to make him jump. ~ What's this? You promised mum, you know.

He looked up, looked at the cigarette, then stubbed it out against the stump below him.

~ There, he said. ~ Happy?

~ Mum will be.

He nodded slowly. ~ You're right, I shouldn't go back to it, even though I'm stressed to hell at the moment.

~ Where'd you get 'em?

~ The pirate. He had them in his pocket. Dad made a face and stuck out his tongue. ~ They're actually quite foul – I think they're made from something out of the mangrove swamp. They taste like wild pig dung.

I laughed. ~ That'll teach you.

We were quiet for a while after that, then I asked him, ~ Why're you stressed, dad? We're all okay at the moment.

~ For the moment, but I won't relax until we're all safe. Dad put an arm around my shoulders. ~ Thanks for supporting me, anyway, son. I appreciate it. We need to get off this island. I

232

must put my mind to that little problem. The sea is rising fast. And then there's the reef weakened by the tsunami. It just needs one storm, one good shove off that reef, and we're going to be swamped.

~ I think I'll get back to bed.

~ Yes, yes — you go and get some sleep. And don't worry about me. I'll be fine. I've got to relieve Rambuta in thirty minutes, anyway. Poor chap's been on guard since midnight.

I went back to the tent. I'd managed to cool off a bit now. The night chorus was still in full flood, but if nothing else is bothering me, like the heat, then I could usually tune them out.

Next day I breakfasted on yams with Georgia and Hass.

~ How'd you sleep last night? I asked Georgia. ~ I slept really badly.

~ Not too good. I was thinking about the dragon. I hope he stays away from my unicorn.

~ I slept terrible, said Hass. ~ Bad dreams. He munched on yam.

~ How can you say that? I argued. ~ You were away with the fairies!

~ So much you know, brother. I heard you get up. You went to our father.

~ Yes I did. He — he was a bit worried about things.

~ That's good, Hass said, nodding. ~ You should help our father. You are his son. He needs you to help him.

~ He needs you too.

~ But not as bad as he needs you, Max, Georgia added.

I guessed they were right. I was glad I'd spoken with him then.

Later in the day they let So Kam out of the fish-drying

shed for some fresh air and exercise. Dad had given him back his cigarettes and he was sitting on the same stump Dad had used the night before, puffing away on his weeds. He looked a bit forlorn today and wasn't as cheeky as he had been when he'd first come into the camp. After he'd finished smoking he took a tin flute out of his pocket and put it to his lips. He began a jigging sort of tune. It was pretty good. He could really play. I wondered where murderers like him learned to play good music.

After a while he stopped and put the tin flute into his shirt pocket.

~ Hey, boy, he called to me, ~ you like football?

~ Football?

~ Yeah. You and that other kid. You play football?

Grant came over, his rifle slung under his right arm. ~ I don't want you hurting those boys – you'd best leave them alone.

~ What, just kicking a ball? cried So Kam. ~ How that hurt them, eh?

~ Oh, Grant said, ~ you mean soccer. I thought you meant American football. I still don't know . . .

But dad said it would be okay, if we wanted to. He could see how bored we were all getting. I said yes. So did Hass. And Georgia and her mum joined in too. And Rambuta. We had a really good kick-around. So Kam was flashy on the ball – he'd watched a lot of the South Americans, obviously – but he had no big kick. Hass had that. Hass could drive the ball like a bullet from twenty yards out. No one could head the ball like me, though. And Georgia and Lorraine did their best but they weren't much cop, not because they were girls, but because they'd never played the game before. Grant said Georgia was

234

great at basketball and when he got a moment he'd fix a hoop up, on one of the trees.

~ Then we'll see who's a dodo, Max!

~ I didn't mean to call her that. It just came out.

Georgia said, ~ Well my fist is just going to come out, if you call me names again, Max Sanders.

~ What you yabber for, you kids? cried So Kam, flicking the ball from toe, to knee, to head. ~ You play football, or what?

We played football.

After an hour of kicking around Rambuta gave a yell from the observation post.

~ The dragon's in those trees! I can see the dragon.

Everyone rushed to find an eyehole in the compound wall, which was pretty silly when you think about it. The dragon would only have to huff towards us once and everyone would be blind. But people don't think. Me especially. I never think in situations like that. I rush in like those fools in the saying, where angels won't go at any price.

At first I couldn't see anything.

~ Where is it? I can't see it, I said.

~ Over there, Georgia whispered, ~ in the shade of the trees. By that mango. You can just make out its shape.

I looked at the place she was indicating and yes, there was a vague dark shape of something there. Like with all these scada, it was well camouflaged, and one minute you could see a misty sort of outline, the next it had melted into the shadows. Then I saw its tail flicking — a wicked-looking tail — stripping the bushes of leaves every time it swished through foliage. There was a killer barb on the end.

~ Can you get in a shot, Rambuta? called dad.

235

Rambuta was in the best position to see the creature. He replied that he could.

A shot then rang out which made me jump three metres in the air.

~ Missed! cried dad, a few seconds later.

Rambuta said, ~ I didn't miss.

Dad got himself into a better shooting position, as did Grant. They both opened up with their weapons. After five minutes of shots echoing in the forest, they stopped. So far as I could see, the dark shape of the dragon was still standing there, mocking us.

~ It's magic, Hass whispered. ~ It is a magical beast. We cannot kill it. It is immortal.

~ Then how come all the other dragons died? Georgia said. ~ There's got to be a way.

I agreed with her.

~ What's happening? asked Lorraine, who was in a poor position to see. ~ Is it dead?

~ No, dad replied in a quiet voice. ~ It's not.

Grant added, ~ The bullets are going right through it. They don't seem to affect it at all. Hey look, guys, it's leaving . . . it's gone. Slipped away into the jungle, dammit. What the heck do we have to do to kill that thing? Rambuta, do you know?

Rambuta was down from his firing position.

~ Only tales I was told as a child — about dragons.

~ And?

~ You can't kill them with a bullet. It goes right through. A dragon's flesh isn't as solid as ours. Under that hide, which is almost a carapace — a shell — the flesh is soft, like that of a crab or a turtle. It's not as substantial as ours.

~ But, argued dad, ~ it must have a heart.

~ Oh, it has a heart, but like the rest of its flesh, it allows a missile to pass right through it, then the hole seals itself immediately. From what I remember you have to kill it with a spear or a sword and leave the weapon in there, to keep the wound open so that it bleeds to death.

~ A spear, sword or lance, mused dad. ~ That would make sense. St George and the dragon. All those old pictures of men killing dragons. They always have the warrior with a piercing weapon.

There was silence for a little while. I was sure all the others, like me, were thinking about the practicality of sticking a pointed weapon into the dragon. The images that danced in my head were terrifying. That was one fierce creature out there. Big. Powerful. I bet there wasn't one of us, dad included, who relished the idea of going up against such a fearsome beast with just a spear. Hand-to-hide combat? No way. No way José. Not me, anyway.

Georgia said, ~ Maybe an arrow would do it?

~ If we had a powerful enough bow, said Rambuta, ~ which we don't, the trees here don't produce the right kind of wood for bows. They're mostly all hardwood timber, or without any spring. What about your yacht, Mr Porter? Is there anything on there which would serve as a bow? Maybe a *steel* spring of some kind? Or a thick plastic strip?

~ My yacht, why . . . there was a clatter as the wind blew back the gate against the inside of the bamboo wall.

Grant swung round.

We all did.

The gate was wide open.

237

Hass cried, ~ Hey, where's So Kam?

We all stared.

Nowhere here, that was certain.

Clearly So Kam had done a bunk.

We all ran down to the shoreline together. There was no beach at all now. The sea had encroached on the rainforest. It had claimed at least twenty metres of new territory. But So Kam had swum out to the yacht. He had stolen a tent to use as a sail. Clever So Kam.

~ Why didn't we think of that? asked Lorraine.

~ We did, my dear, replied her husband, ~ but rejected it. That material won't last more than a day before it's ripped to shreds by the wind. It's too thin.

So Kam waved to us and grinned.

~ It'll get him to his island hideout and his crew, said Rambuta. ~ That's only just over a day's sail away. It wouldn't have been any good for us, just exchanging one island for another, but he's got his junk there.

~ He hopes, growled Grant. ~ Maybe they've upped sticks and gone? Anyway, I think I can get him from here . . . He raised his rifle to his shoulder. So Kam ducked down behind the boat's cabin. A fist came up, waving in the air.

Grant lowered his rifle again.

~ Can't do it. Can't kill a man in cold blood.

~ No, sighed dad. ~ I don't think any of us could.

Lorraine said, ~ He might be back – with his crew.

~ We've got to get off before then, dad argued. ~ Time to build a raft and make some sort of sail out of local produce. I know we've talked about it before, but now it's imperative. He squished around in the salt water on the forest floor. ~ This island is going under fast.

2 September, Krantu Island

My dad is a scholar. He scholarises everything, even dragons. I found this assessment in one of his notebooks:

Legend tells us that dragons are the most terrible creatures ever imagined. Their strength and fortitude is phenomenal. They don't fly very often but when they do they sweep the countryside at night, searing all below with their fiery breath, turning whole cities to charred, smoking ruins.

They're especially dangerous when they're threatened by men, who are the dragon's mortal enemy. They hate us with every drop of their cold, emerald blood. Their fear and loathing for humankind is so deep and lasting they can be venomously cruel, even with children and babies. They have no mercy in them whatsoever, so don't expect it.

This was certainly our dragon, which would take life without a second thought, without a qualm.

*

We began to collect bamboo for our raft almost immediately, but the next morning we had to abandon the task. The wind which had blown the open gate back against the compound wall picked up in strength and grew very cold for this region. During the night it began to rain: a fine slanting rain that came down as hard as needles. By the morning we knew we were in for a storm: a big one.

~ Typhoon coming in, said Rambuta, matter-of-factly.

~ That's like a hurricane, right? asked Georgia.

~ Yep, dad replied. ~ Not a lot of difference.

~ Why don't they call it a hurricane then? persisted Georgia, tossing her blonde hair in irritation. ~ Why fancy it up with another name?

~ Because this is the South China Sea, not California, replied her mother. ~ I believe it's Chinese for *Big Wind*, isn't it, James?

Dad said, ~ Yes and no. It does come from the Chinese, but also stems from several other sources. From the Greek *typhon*, meaning whirlwind and also, interestingly enough, from a Hindi word, *tüfän*, itself a corruption from the Greek – oh, and I recall something about the Port of Tufäo – Aramaic and Persian . . .

By this time eyes had glazed over, but then I did warn you about my dad – you mustn't ever give him something like that to chew on, or he'll be spouting stuff like that all day.

The typhoon came. We didn't know its name, though it had probably been given one by the met. people. Grant said it was without doubt a female typhoon, since the last one he remembered being told about on the yacht was called Typhoon Frederic.

~ They go in alphabetical order, he said.

~ Oh, I said wickedly, as the wind howled and screamed through the rainforest, ~ so this one is probably called Georgia?

~ How would you like a big wind knock your head off?' muttered my lovely girlfriend from California. ~ Or to feel my foot in your mouth?

The typhoon tore through the trees, ripping many of them down, throwing others as giant javelins, this way and that.

240

Shredded leaves filled the air like green snowflakes. Branches and boughs tore away from their trunks and spiralled through space like boomerangs. Creepers and vines turned to whips, lashing the rainforest foliage.

The sky was heaving with dark clouds that rolled in on themselves. They shed rain like nails which drove into wide waxy leaves. A drummer-boy rattled his way across the land from end to end.

This, and other noises, were terrifying. They were not so much deafening as menacing. Lorraine said the cacophony reminded her of squadrons of war planes coming in. Grant said it was more like the sound of Armageddon, though I wondered how he knew.

The wind grew in strength and we became more and more afraid. I did, anyway. My one hope was that the dragon was in a worse state than we were, though it was doubtful. It had that lair it had dug to hide in and the typhoon would pass right over it. Maybe, just maybe, some tree as big as a cathedral spire would fall over and block its exit.

That would be a miracle, I think.

It was more likely the dragon — and of course some of the other scada — might drown because the water on the windward side of the island was whipped into a fury. Waves came rushing across, dragging all sorts of debris with them. They bulldozed their way through. Coral broke away from the reef in chunks and its claw-like branches tore avenues through the undergrowth. I've never been in a storm like that typhoon before or since. It thundered around us with winds that could strip a tree of its bark, let alone its leaves. All we could do was hunker down behind our earth-filled oil drums and wait.

White-water spray filled the atmosphere like a fine mist, blown from the windward side of the island. No one could take a breath without swallowing salt water. We were drowning in our own air. Above the noise of the tearing wind in the trees we could hear waves crashing into the rainforest. Birds and fruit bats were flung from their perches and sent hurtling into the heavens, lost for ever. Our tents were torn to shreds and scattered amongst the branches of the forest. The contents were whisked away: clothes, cameras, luggage, camping beds, everything. We would be left with nothing once it was all over.

We tried talking to each other, over the tremendous noise.

~ When I was a boy, shouted Rambuta, ~ they used to tell me a typhoon could blow the stars away.

~ That's comforting, cried Lorraine.

~ In the desert, yelled Hassan, ~ we hated the hot wind – it would send a man mad.

~ Equally comforting, cried Georgia.

~ Where I come from, Grant shouted, ~ we called the wind Maria.

~ Very funny, yelled dad, but we kids didn't see the joke until they told us it was a song from their era. The two men started to sing it until we yelled at them to stop. Listening to their efforts at entertaining was worse than suffering the sound of the typhoon.

At the storm's height the earth-filled oil drums rocked, but thankfully held steady. I thought my ears were going to explode with the pressure and the drumming noise. It was like standing on the central verge of a motorway with giant trucks thundering by and jumbo jets flying low over our heads. We all lay hugging the ground, arms around each other, making us one large lump. In this way we managed to stop from being tossed away like the other creatures of the island.

The typhoon lasted twenty-four hours.

At the end of it we were drenched and cold, battered and bruised. Everything was wet, both from rain and spume. Coral sand was plastered on every damp surface. Seashells, lumps of coral, fish and crabs littered the ground amongst the broken branches and other loose bits from the forest. Lifeless snakes draped bushes like ribbons. Lizards and other reptiles covered the earth. Dead birds, wild pigs. The typhoon was not just a big wind, it was a big killer, which destroyed life.

And then the sun came out again as if nothing had happened!

We rose to inspect the damage.

Jammed in a narrow gap in the bamboo wall we found a dead scadu, the ahuizotl, half-human, half-monkey. Its eyes and mouth were open. It looked at us as if the typhoon had been our fault. Georgia used the word *chilling* to describe the broken ahuizotl. She said it was one thing seeing a dead animal, but when it was part human it was really weird. Rambuta went off to bury the ahuizotl outside the wall, in a proper grave, just as if it had been a real person.

Not far from the compound were several more dead scada. Those the dragon hadn't killed, the typhoon had.

Perhaps they'd tried to reach safety behind our wall?

Dad said he only recognised the features of two of them, the rest he didn't know. One of those he did know was called a rompo. It was just bits of lots of other creatures: the head of a hare, the ears of a man, a long body and tail, the fore feet

243

of a badger and the hind feet of a bear. Really weird. Then there was a gulon, a lion-hyena with the tail of a fox. But the rest were just as strange, though as I said, we didn't know the names of them.

Hass and I then looked around the compound at the havoc the big wind had caused.

The camp was in ruins. The wall had not protected it. In fact, one big section of the bamboo stockade had blown down. Virtually everything we owned had been lifted and thrown away, smashed against trees, torn to shreds, or had simply disappeared up into the sky. Chaos.

There were bits of unidentifiable rags hanging from branches. I found a parang stuck in a tree, buried a third of the way up its blade. Equipment like computers and cameras, aerials and radios, were all smashed — those we could find — and the parts scattered. We were left with the clothes we stood up in. Hass and I had our assegais because they had been kept in the weapons box along with the rifles. The weapons box had been with us all the time, inside the ring of drums.

We gathered together what we could, piling it in a heap in the middle of the compound.

At Georgia's insistence, Grant went out with his daughter to look for the unicorn. Georgia was afraid it might be hurt and needing help. Of course going out was dangerous — we didn't know if the dragon had survived — but after going through the experience of the typhoon we'd all reached a point where we sneered at danger.

I didn't hold out much hope for the unicorn though, considering what had happened to the rest of the scada.

I helped Lorraine and dad to start clearing up the mess,

while Hass went down to the shoreline to see if our raft was still there.

Hass came running back, excited.

~ Father, father, the yacht!

Dad looked up from what he was doing. ~ What is it?

~ It has come back, cried a breathless Hassan. ~ It is on the reef.

We all ran down to the shore.

There on the outer reef, shattered hull and broken mast, was the Porter yacht. Ocean waves washed over the sunken wreck. So Kam was nowhere in sight. If he was still on the boat he had surely drowned, because most of the wreck was below water. If lost at sea, definitely gone to the bottom of the ocean. It made me feel to sick to think of it, even though he'd been a rotten bugger in life. I kept remembering him kicking that football around, only a short while ago, and now he was probably covered in crabs and being nibbled by the fishes.

Lorraine went back to the camp, leaving us to stare at the remains of her husband's once beautiful vessel.

I thought about it for a long while. So Kam's last hours must have been pretty awful in that blast. You could say he got what he deserved, but a typhoon at sea lets you live for quite a long time while you're stuffed to the gullet with absolute terror. If you can imagine, the only solid thing within a thousand miles is a flimsy little boat which is being chucked about like a toy on giant raging waves. You try this, you try that, but you're thrown, shaken, spun, turned upside-down, and everything you do is useless. You know you're going to die and you panic and panic and panic until you go out of your mind with fear. Then what happens is you finally get crushed, or hung on a wayward rope, or you're filled with water.

~ Well, that's that, said dad. ~ Grant? Shall we salvage what we can from the wreck? There're some ropes and steel cables which might be useful.

~ Sheets and stays, corrected Grant. ~ Right. Rambuta? Can you help too?

We kids left them there.

Lorraine came running up to the three of us as we approached the stockade.

~ The unicorn! she cried. ~ I've found it.

It was a miracle.

The unicorn was down on all four legs. It rested in a sheltered ring of bushes that had been protected partly by our oil drum refuge, partly by the bamboo stockade. When we approached the fabulous beast, it looked nervous, but didn't get up and run. Lorraine managed to reach out and touch it and it looked up at her with liquid eyes.

It was much smaller than I'd first thought. When you saw it dashing about the forest you didn't get a good idea of its size. It was more like a pony than a horse.

Georgia was over the moon of course. Here was the animal she adored, sitting right at her feet. The tall slim horn on its forehead appeared deadly to me, but when you looked into the unicorn's face you could see there wasn't any menace there. They seemed to have a special relationship, this girl and this strange animal.

~ Can I stroke him? Georgia asked her mother.

~ Ain't no hims or hers with scada, I muttered.

Without waiting to hear Lorraine's reply Georgia reached out and ran her fingers through the silken mane. A sort of tremor rippled through the unicorn which then trickled up Georgia's arm and into her body. Then something tremendous happened, right before my eyes. I don't know what it was exactly, but it was as if they had changed places for a moment. Well, it sounds stupid even while I write it, but it seemed like Georgia had become the unicorn, and the unicorn her.

But it must have been — what is it? — an illusion. I don't know. I'm just writing what I thought I saw. Maybe it was a spell, or an enchantment, if you believe in those things. I'm not saying I do. I'm just saying what it felt like. It was obvious there was a knowing between them. You could see that they trusted each other, like a Border collie and a shepherd trust one another, completely and utterly. Yet they hadn't got close to each other before today, had they? What happened was strange. It was strange to be there. I didn't like it. It was weird.

I didn't understand then. It seemed to me that something unnatural was going on. A horrible shiver went through me.

~ What's happening? I asked, stepping quickly away from the pair, as if they were charged with electricity. ~ What's going on?

~ Don't be frightened, Max, murmured Lorraine, as if she was fascinated by it all. ~ Mystical things aren't always bad.

I didn't like any of this. I thought Georgia had been bewitched by something. Maybe the unicorn. I almost kicked out at it, in my fright, to get it to run away into the forest. But I didn't, thank goodness, or Georgia would surely never have spoken to me again. She remained in raptures stroking this beast. Finally Georgia did an amazing thing: she climbed on the back of the unicorn as if it had been a horse.

Now even her mother was worried.

~ Careful, sweetheart, whispered Lorraine, her voice going a little tight. ~ Don't do anything silly.

But it was as if this act was completely natural. It was how things should be. A girl riding a unicorn. I'd seen pictures like this in books. They went together. Georgia ignored her mother and gently prodded the unicorn's flanks with her heels, the way one would a pony. The unicorn rose now, shimmering with dew, from the mossy ground. Its eyes grew very wide, no longer blue, but grey. Its nostrils dilated, flaring sharply. Light zig-zagged up that single slim horn to the dazzling red point. Muscles in the flanks, the back, the neck and the legs of the creature turned to iron knots. It seemed it was going to fly like an arrow from a bow.

Oh my God, I thought, she's going to die.

But the white beast didn't bolt, or try to throw her, or anything like that. It simply trotted forwards into the compound, then round the packed-earth square. Georgia rode high and proud on the creature's back, just as if she were doing dressage in a gymkhana back in her home town.

I breathed a sigh of relief. I thought I heard one or two others beside me. We were all pretty relieved.

Hassan said, ~ She rides well. I have ridden in the sheikh's races and I know what it is to ride well.

~ We know you've ridden in the flippin' sheikh's races — you've told everyone a hundred times, I said.

~ Not a hundred times, Max — perhaps once or twice.

We watched and admired the beautiful girl on her wonderful mount for quite a long time, until finally Lorraine said, ~ That's enough now, Georgia, and Georgia took hold of the silken mane

248

and gently drew her fantastic charger to a halt. She slipped from the unicorn's back to the ground and patted its neck. Only then did it go flying off, hooves kicking up divots of moss, crossing into the rainforest to its depths.

~ There'll be no talking to her now, I warned Hass, as Georgia joined her mother. ~ Look at her. She's shining like an angel. We won't be able to match up to that creature. She won't want to know us.

Georgia did indeed seem to have an aura at that moment. Serenity, I suppose it was. I've looked it up and that's what I think. An aura of serenity. But I was wrong about her not wanting our company. What's more, she didn't crow. She didn't lord it over us (I suppose that should be lady it over us) and she didn't stuff it down our throats. We asked her what it had been like and she simply said, 'Fantastic,' and left it at that. I thought that was pretty big of her, not to get puffed up. I'm not so sure I wouldn't have. In fact I'm certain I would have.

I did hear her telling her mum that it would have been one in the eye for 'The Triple-one'.

~ Who's that? Triple one? I asked her later.

~ Girl at my school, she replied, with a smile. ~ Irene Imogen Ingatestone. Three I's? Triple one?

~ Oh, I get it.

~ I don't, Hass said.

So we had to explain it to him, him coming from a different culture. Even when he got it he thought it was a strange sort of joke.

But jokes aren't what Hass is about. Hass has other things about him which interested Georgia. He's a deep one, my adopted brother. Dad once told me that Hass has a lot of spirituality,

249

which made me want to get a bit of it. I tried. I tried very hard to get some, but when I later asked Georgia if I'd got any of that stuff they called spirituality, she said, ~ Keep looking, Max, but I love you just the same. I was a bit hurt by that. I wanted to be admired like Hass was admired, for the same things, but I see now I've got things he hasn't got (I'm not going to tell you what — that would be bragging) and I have to be satisfied with them.

Now that our log had gone from the beach, floated away on the rising waters, we kids had to find another meeting place. Since we weren't allowed to wander, it had to be near the stockade. There was a flame tree on the edge of the rainforest. It seemed to be always in bloom, bearing blossoms the bright scarlet of blood. The flame tree is to the tropics what the oak is to England. Flame trees are thick-trunked, dependable-looking blokes who might have stood on the same spot for ever.

It was in the raised roots of one of these trees that we kids met to put the world to rights.

Both me and Hass were curious about Georgia's experience.

~ What was it like, sitting on a scadu? I asked. ~ Did it feel different to a pony or a horse?

~ Much different, Georgia answered, hugging her knees.

Hass asked, ~ How did you feel?

~ Wicked, she said.

Then, looking into our faces she obviously realised we weren't going to take the usual offhand one-word reply to such questions.

~ Oh, I don't know, it was kinda how you would react to meeting an e.t. I suppose. I was so excited I could hardly breathe — yet I was as calm and relaxed as if I'd just woken from a beautiful dream. It didn't feel real. It felt like we could fly off, up into the sky somewhere. I could feel its heart beating under my knees. Fast, faster, faster still. I knew the unicorn felt just as weird having me climb on its back, as I did sitting there. Yet both of us knew it was right. It felt right. It seemed like I had been born to ride a unicorn – and the unicorn was created for me to ride it. We knew it was right. Does that make any sense? I don't know. You have to do it to feel what's it's like, I can't *really* explain it.

~ Would you do it again? Hass asked.

~ Just give me a chance, replied Georgia, picking up a twig and placing it in the path of a line of marching ants. ~ I will, too.

I said, ~ I wouldn't want to – would you, Hass?

~ I think I would be afraid, was his reply.

This was some admission from Hassan. He had supposedly fought with poisonous snakes and wolves. He had spent black nights alone in isolated caves without sensing fear. He walked the desert without a map or compass and only goats for company. And – hey, oh yes – he'd ridden in Sheikh Othman's horse races. Hass wasn't slow to inform me of these accomplishments either. I hadn't been left in any doubt that he was brave and fearless in the face of wilderness horrors. Yet here he was admitting he would be too scared to climb on the back of a unicorn.

~ I dunno that I would be *frightened*, I said, but they both saw through me and let me know with their eyes I was lying. I turned away but to my relief no one said any more about it.

~ Them ants will get washed away soon, I said after a period of silence. ~ They don't know it, but they will.

Each of the black ants was about a centimetre long. Georgia's twig hadn't turned them from their path. They simply hiked over it. Hill and dale. Barrier or fence. Nothing changed the course of a caravan of ants. They were so determined to go from one place to another you could put Mount Everest in their way and they'd tromp over it, I bet.

~ Perhaps they'll sail away on broad leaves? said Georgia, who my dad called 'the optimistic maid'.

~ Coconuts travel for miles on the sea, Hass added. ~ They could travel by coconut.

~ Sounds a bit like a comedy sketch to me, I muttered. ~ An ant voyage on a coconut.

No one argued with me. We went back to the compound. The adults were working hard on the raft.

3 September, Krantu Island

Dad said there wasn't a lot we could do for the scada. We had our raft but they had nothing. We were taking our chances with the sea, while they had to stay on the island. This upset Georgia a lot, of course. She said we had to take the unicorn with us.

~ Impossible, Grant told his daughter, taking the heat off dad. ~ I know you and that creature have some kind of bond, Georgia, but it wouldn't work.

~ We could make it work, she said tearfully. ~ We could have another raft, tow it behind us.

We could all see how daft that was. You only needed a big swell or a choppy ocean, let alone a storm. And the thing wouldn't stay sitting all the time. It would stand and upset the balance. You couldn't tie it down. And who was going to feed it, and how? It was all daft stuff.

But I knew better than to try to reason with Georgia over such a thing. I kept quiet. So did Hass, and Ram and dad. We left it to Lorraine and Grant to make her see sense.

Lorraine said, ~ It's not practical, Georgia. Just think about it for a second. It's not fair to us and it's not fair to that poor creature.

Georgia stormed off.

~ I guess, Grant said, stroking his big black moustache, a sure sign he was unsettled himself, ~ we could herd all the scada that are left on to the highest ground. It wouldn't be there for a great deal longer than the rest of the island, but if we got picked up early by a ship or something, we could tell the authorities to get a craft to call by.

~ Two metres, three metres, it's all going to be gone pretty soon, said dad.

~ But we could try, couldn't we? pleaded Grant. ~ Georgia . . .

~ What about the damn dragon? asked Rambuta, using a swearword for the first time since we'd met him. ~ It's killed most of them anyway. It'll probably get us too, if we go out there.

~ There's a good chance that thing died in the typhoon, Grant said. ~ I say we go out there, with caution as our watchword, of course, and just see what the heck is going on. You said yourself, James, that the dragon hunts at night. We'll go during the day, when it's safe.

So the men went out. They talked a lot about shooting the dragon's eyes out, if they *did* happen to confront it, but I knew that was just waffle. None of them were *that* good a shot. They spent half a day roaming the island, and returned long before sunset. They hadn't found one single scadu. Not even signs of the mother Beast herself.

They had found several carcasses of other scada, killed either by the dragon, or by the typhoon, but no trace of the mother Beast. Dad was inclined to think she had slipped into the sea. Perhaps she could evolve swiftly, he said, into an aquatic creature? She had shown her skill at survival, even over several millennia. Why not? If she could regenerate, as she had done, from an empty hide to an airbreathing scadu, then she could transmogrify, develop gills, change into an undersea creature.

~ It's true she has the ability to camouflage herself, but we didn't smell her or see any signs of recent spoor. When was the last time we heard her? That mooning note that used to drift over the forest? I would say the Beast is at the bottom of the ocean, waiting for the right era to rise again and start producing her fabulous young, dad said. ~ But I don't think it'll be for a very long time. I imagine this current experience has been enough to keep her hidden for several ages to come. He paused before adding, ~ The saddest thing is we have no proof of the existence of her or any of her creatures. The cameras, the recording equipment, all gone — destroyed in the typhoon. We have only our word and no one's going to accept that.

~ We'll know, Grant said, ~ but I guess you're right — even if we all swear the story about the scada is the truth, they'll think it's a conspiracy. No one will ever believe us.

~ We'll have the Beast's hide, I pointed out. ~ Isn't that proof? And we can make her again, once we get back.

There was a funny look on dad's face and I knew at that

moment he was thinking about the secret that only he and I knew. The secret I wasn't supposed to tell anyone – no one at all.

~ Perhaps, he said.

Georgia said hotly, ~ And what about my unicorn?

Your unicorn? I thought. How possessive.

Grant said softly, ~ Well – things happen, sweetheart.

Georgia looked sharply at her father. ~ You saw it? When you went out?

All three men averted their eyes. Grant opened his mouth as if to say something, but closed it again.

~ You saw it, didn't you? demanded his daughter.

Dad sighed. ~ Yes, we saw it, Georgia. It – it had slipped away.

~ Slipped away like the mother Beast?

~ No, he continued gently. ~ The dragon . . .

Georgia went pale and stared at him. Then she cried out, as if she was in terrible pain. ~ No! No!

Grant put his arms around his daughter.

~ I'm sorry, princess, he said. ~ I'm very, very sorry.

Georgia pulled away from him. She was now white with anger.

~ That – that *thing* is still alive.

Rambuta nodded. ~ We think so – was – there were tracks.

~ Where? Georgia whirled around, as if she was prepared to run into the rainforest and seek out the murderer of her beloved unicorn.

Grant said, ~ The tracks led up to its lair. We could hear it sleeping inside. Georgia, we piled rocks and timber at the entrance, then filled it with earth. The dragon will suffocate.

Justice has been done. We did it at great risk to our lives, princess, so don't look at me like that. The dragon has paid for its crimes. The scada are gone, the whole blamed lot of them. It's over. It's all over. Now we have to leave.

~ Are you telling me the truth?

~ I wouldn't lie to you – you're my daughter.

Georgia searched the faces of the men. Then she burst into tears and her mother led her off. Grant shrugged unhappily.

~ What can you do? he said.

No one could answer such a question.

The work to get off the island began in earnest now. Rambuta and Grant between them had designed the raft in the style of the old Polynesian seagoing canoes. There were two outriggers made of bamboo poles lashed together to form cylinders. Thinner poles were placed at right angles to the outriggers for the decking, making a square platform between the cylinders. A hut was built in the middle of this platform with a mast in front of it. Lorraine had abandoned the idea of making a sail from coconut fibre or palm leaves. We had realised we still had the hide from the mother Beast, which was cut and shaped to make the sail. It was a fine craft. Rambuta and Grant were to share their knowledge of navigation by the stars, waves, sea birds and other practical signs. There was every indication, dad said, that we would reach land again.

Now everyone except Georgia was carrying coconuts and gourds full of water to the raft, along with local produce: yams, breadfruit, taro, sweet potatoes and bananas. Fishing lines were made and some meat which had earlier been smoked or dried was put on board. The adults were down on the raft putting the finishing touches to everything. Once the fetching and carrying had finished, we kids were finally left to our own devices in the stockade.

Hass and I were gathering our own personal things together when Georgia suddenly appeared out of the shack. Her tear-streaked face had a sort of determined look to it. We guessed trouble was coming. She marched off in the opposite direction to where the adults were working on the raft. Hass and I looked at each other and panicked.

We ran after her just as she was about to enter the rainforest.

~ Where do you think you're going? I said, grabbing her arm and swinging her round. ~ We're just about to leave.

Georgia shrugged off my hand and looked towards the raft.

~ They'll be a couple of hours yet. You know how they fuss over everything. Especially a trip like this.

~ And? I said.

She looked at me defiantly. ~ I'm going to make sure that dragon is good and buried.

~ That is not a good idea, Hassan told her. ~ Perhaps the dragon was not in its hole, after all?

~ I think it is, she said, ~ and I'm going, whatever you wimps say. Scared of your own shadows, you two.

I said, ~ No, just scared of a bloody great dragon, that's what. And before you say anything, Bradley would be too. Anyone would.

~ I'm not.

~ That's because you don't know any better, I said.

~ Please, said Hassan, ~ please come back with us to the camp.

~ No, she replied shortly. ~ I'm going to make sure that dragon stays trapped underground.

Her eyes flashed like steel knives. ~ It killed my unicorn. It has to pay for what it's done.

~ It'll die soon anyway, I argued. ~ The flood?

She shook her head. ~ Who's to say it won't fly to neighbouring islands, or even to the mainland? You remember what that book said which your father found? A dragon will fly great distances when its life is threatened. It might even attack our raft on the way.

~ But, I pleaded, ~ the men have already done the job — you heard them.

~ In which case I shall be in no danger, said Georgia. ~ Now, are you coming with me, or not?

Here was a new turn! We were to go with her. I suddenly saw a way of stalling her.

~ We'll come, but we need to get our weapons — our assegais.

~ What for?

~ In case we have to fight the dragon, Hassan explained, having caught my eye. He was always quick on the uptake when it came to knowing looks. ~ If the dragon is there, we may have to kill it.

Georgia frowned. ~ You'd do that for me?

~ Like a shot, I told her. ~ Come on, Hass.

She waited there while we walked back to the ramshackle huts.

~ We might as well wear some camouflage, I called to her, hoping to gain more time.

I stripped to my shorts and began to smear mud on my body. Hass did the same. Then using a hunting knife we cut wide strips from the remnants of the mother Beast's skin. These we made into

258

shifts by shaping a hole for our heads. We tied them at the waist with another strip of hide. More mud was plastered in our hair and on our faces. Then we took up our assegais. Funnily enough, as we dressed and armed ourselves, I began to feel different. I began to feel – I dunno – invincible. Suddenly I *wanted* to fight the dragon. It seemed right.

I felt strong and full of energy.

Before the arming I had hoped the adults would appear to stop things from going too far, but they didn't: they were still down by the shore messing about with the raft. Now – now it was different

~ Where is she? asked Hass, looking up. ~ She's gone.

~ Gone? I cried.

Georgia was nowhere to be seen.

~ Oh flippin' heck, I said. ~ She's gone in.

~ Shall we tell her father, Max?

~ No, by the time we get to him she'll be deep inside the rainforest. Come on. I started running. ~ We'll have to fetch her back ourselves.

I ran past the spot where I had once found that limp pale body – the secret carcass which only dad and I knew about – and I shuddered as if stepping on my own grave.

4 September, Krantu Island

The horn was beautiful.

And it came away in my hand, just like that. No fuss. The rest of the body was charred black, but the horn wasn't marked.

I could give this to Georgia. A gift. Maybe it was her birthday soon? It'd have to be from the both of us, of course. But I bet myself Hass would say yes, give it to her. We'd have to hide it from dad though, because he wanted everything like this. He would just add it to his collection of bits and pieces. Waste of a good find.

~ What have you got there? asked Hass. I sensed him moving up beside me. ~ Oh, wow.

~ Yeah, and it's ours, this one. We'll give it to her.

~ Good idea.

Funny thing, the carcass of the unicorn didn't smell. You'd have thought it would, being burned to a frazzle like that. But it didn't. It didn't smell of anything at all. It could've been made of glass. The leaves around it did. And the grasses and bamboo. But not the corpse.

I got off my knees and stuck the horn in my belt like a sword.

~ Right, said Hass. ~ Are we going to do this thing, or what? Are we going to make the kill?

Hassan was naked to the waist. His upper body and legs had been painted with river clay. Symbols. There were white rings around his eyes. Fishbone chevrons down his nose. Swirls and maze-squares on his chest and stomach, down his arms, his shoulders, his back. Patterns copied from the beast's markings. And his loincloth had been cut from her sloughed hide. I wore a similar one. We were both painted, covered in her designs. There was white clay in our hair too, which stuck out in stiffened points.

In our right hands were our assegais, the Zulu spears dad had brought back from Africa.

When we stood still, in the mottled shades thrown down

260

by the canopy, you couldn't see us. We were the invisible people. Our camouflage was perfect. It had been perfected by the Beast over thousands of years. The zebra's stripes, the tiger's bars, the leopard's blotches. Those were simple camouflage markings. Our markings were much better, much more complicated. The Beast had got her own dizzying patterns. Her skin was her hiding place. She needed no more. When she stood in the dappled shade she became part of the shadow, completely lost in the stippled flickering light.

We too now had her power.

~ Let's go, I said.

We ran on soft feet through the undergrowth. Our passage was silent. Not only did we need to remain unseen, we had to be unheard. We had to melt into the rainforest, our breathing no louder than the sound of overhead breezes. There was a determination in us. You could see it in the way Hass gripped his spear. You could see it in his eyes. No fear. No terror at the thought of losing life, or even of taking life. Only a strong desire for the spear to find its target. The piercing of a heart, if there was such. The stabbing of a brain, if there was one. A task to be done.

Hass asked, ~ Where will we find the prey?

~ The cave. You remember. The hole it made?

Finally, the washing of the spears. ~ We will become men today.

A flicker of fear went through me. ~ Yes.

But that feeling only lasted for a split second. Then I was strong again.

~ Will it be there?

~ It has to be, sometime.

When we reached the cave, it looked empty. There was dirt, stones and lumps of old wood scattered round the entrance. Of course! Dad and Grant had filled the hole in earlier, when they found it occupied. But the creature had dug its way out. It was in the forest again.

~ Is it in there?

~ I don't think so.

~ Then we must wait, said Hassan. ~ Wait and watch.

~ And listen, I added.

We waited, watching the dark avenues worn through the rainforest. The smell was of salt and rotting plants. The ocean was invading the island now. We had splashed through pools of seawater deep in the forest on our way to the cave-hole. The sea was coming, rising up, covering the world of green plants. Soon this island would be not much more than a line of coral on the surface of the ocean.

We listened for the rustle of wings, the thrashing of a tail. Our prey was cunning. Vicious and cunning. Our only hope was surprise.

But we were determined. We would prevail. We had to prevail.

Hassan went to one side of the cave, I to the other.

Actually it was not so much a cave as a hole in the ground, about two metres by two metres. A burrow in the dead coral floor of the island. It was flanked by two giant trees. Water-pines. The bark from these trees littered the ground where it had cracked and peeled. Pine needles made a soft mat beneath and in the doorway of the cave. The branches of the water-pines danced in the wind, creating moving shadows. We lost ourselves within these pools of shadow, becoming the same.

It was difficult not to drown. It seemed my heart had stopped. We were mesmerised by our own invisibility. I kept wanting to call out, 'Are you there?' but knew I couldn't. Silence was our protection too. Unseen. Unheard. Our scent was that of river clay and forest gunk. We had rolled in leaf mould and rotten vegetation. We smelled of forest.

I fell asleep, standing up.

How long I dozed, I do not know.

I woke, leaning on my spear, my hand clasping the shaft.

What? What was that?

Something was coming.

A wave of stinking breath enveloped me. There was a cautious shuffling. Something was coming down one of the avenues flattened through the rainforest. A rasping of skin against bark. A short cough. Then a more positive movement. The drumming of feet.

I looked across in alarm. Hassan had slept too. He was still asleep. I could hear by the sound of his breathing.

What was I to do? I couldn't call. I couldn't move.

A hornbill landed on a tree nearby. I prayed for it to cry out. I silently begged it to screech. But it didn't. It heard that which was coming down the dark lane and it flew off without a sound. I didn't blame it. I wished for wings at that moment. I wanted to take to the sky.

I stared hard at Hassan. Wake up! Wake up, you fool!

Suddenly I could see two white orbs, which almost instantly became hooded again. He was awake! His eyes had sprung open. I felt relief wash through me. I wouldn't have to do it alone. I wouldn't have to kill without help.

At that moment a figure emerged from the rainforest.

Georgia!

Now she was in trouble. She wore no body paint or tattoos. Nor was she camouflaged in any way. Unlike Hass and me, she was plainly visible to the eye. In fact, she was as easy to pick out as a delicate tropic bird among a flock of raggle-taggle frigate birds.

She looked hot and bothered, but more than that, she looked absolutely terrified. With a quick look over her shoulder she made straight for the cave. I wanted to shout a warning to her: *not in there.* But I was too late. She had dropped to her knees and crawled inside.

Something was in pursuit. We knew what it was.

It crashed through the pale of the forest now and stood there, red-eyed and snorting. It sniffed the air in the glade, satisfying itself that its prey was within reach. Its quarry had not escaped but was merely hidden. Its eyes settled on the entrance to the cave. It knew where she was. With a slow, swaying walk it made its way towards the dark hole.

Georgia was inside the dragon's lair.

The dragon stood at the entrance, staring, knowing he had prey trapped inside his hole. None of Grant's jungle gin-traps had been sprung. The dragon had been too canny. It had stepped carefully round those obvious patches where the foliage had been disturbed.

No fool, this dragon.

What was going through its mind? I had no idea. Did it have a mind that could think? Or was it some cold-brained creature guided only by instinct?

Hass stood unmoving on the other side of the beast. I couldn't see him. Even if the dragon's body wasn't in the way we were both too well camouflaged. The dragon hadn't seen us either. Our markings, the tattoos on the mother Beast's skin, broke up our shapes perfectly, hid them amongst the mottled shadows of the leaves.

Could the dragon scent us?

It seemed he couldn't. With a furnace in his throat he could probably only smell fire-ash and smoke, which would surely overwhelm every other odour. And there was stinking swamp mud on our bodies, which covered the scent of man. So long as we didn't move, we would be safe. We had to remain perfectly still though, like the hunters of old, like the bushmen of today, waiting for the right moment to strike.

To strike?

Were we going to attack this fearsome beast then?

I knew then that we were. We had to. This vile monster was staring at that black earthen cave. Our friend was trapped inside that hole. Georgia was down there. Our Georgia. There was no way on Earth we could leave her to die. Even if this vicious creature from out of the past took all three of us, we had to try to save her.

I don't know why I felt so calm. I should have been shaking with terror. Yet I was as steady as stone. I was completely focused. There was something deep inside me, a primitive feeling that had been dormant for thousands of years, now needed again. It had been given birth and nurtured by my many-greats stone age grandfathers. Now it had reawoken inside this youth. It was necessary again, after all these millennia, aeons of time, to own the unswerving confidence of the hunter. Everything narrowed down to one task: that of killing the dragon. Every fibre of my body, every cell of my brain, was working to this end.

265

Somehow I knew Hassan felt the same.

We had both reached down into our ancestral memories and brought back the ancient determination of the hunter.

Courage bubbled up from my abdomen. Nerves were taut but controlled. Thoughts were focused on a single action.

The energy was stirred from below. When you see a cat coiling itself inside, ready to release itself at its unsuspecting prey — that's what was happening to me. I was as still as stone, but a terrible unstoppable force was rapidly growing deep down, somewhere at the base of my spine, spreading through my whole body, filling me with contained strength. I was like a steel spring readying itself for release.

I was the hunter. I was the dragon's bane. I was the scourge of all things evil. I was Death with a spear in its hand.

~ Now! I yelled.

The swift leap forward.

I plunged the assegai into the dragon's left side. Green blood gushed up the bright metal. Hot steaming blood, boiling and spitting on the cold broad blade. The keen weapon went down through the leathery drumskin wing, deep into the dragon's flank. Then further downward, downward, downward. With all my newly found strength behind it, the point of the assegai struck the ground beneath. It lodged. I held it there, sinews starting from my arms, youthful muscles knotted. Darkness swirled from the gaping wound, hissing, spiralling up my arms. I still held. Gobbets of a blacker blood now, oozing after the green.

~ Got you! Hey, I've got it!

My own words startled me.

The terrible beast was pinned.

The dragon screamed in shock. It whipped its head round. The mouth opened.

Hassan sprang.

Hassan.

Hassan saved my life.

A spirited yell of triumph. His spear pierced the right flank. Through the dragon's wing, through its lower belly, point travelling down into the earth, pinning the foul creature on the other side.

We had it trapped between us.

The dragon reared, roaring. The tail thrashed back and forth, shredding bushes, severing saplings from their roots. Claws raked the leaf mould on the forest floor. It kicked, it fought, it clashed its jaws. It struggled mightily, whipping its body back and forth, trying to break loose. A long neck arched. Cavernous nostrils flared and hissed damp scalding breath. Legs jerked. The back hunched. Teeth crashed together. Eyes burned with utter hate and fury.

It was strong. Oh yes, was it was strong. It screamed its rage at us, trying to wrench itself free. Turning its head, it tried to snap our bodies in two with its elongated jaws. But we were too far round, even for its sinewy serpentine neck. It snapped at air. And it couldn't use its fire, or it would have burned its own wings, its own body.

Yet we could do no more.

We too were trapped.

My arms began to ache with the strain. I could hold on only a little longer. My spear was loosening in the wound. We could not kill the monster, yet if we withdrew the assegais for a desperate thrust, we would be crushed or mauled to death

267

before we could make the plunge. If nothing else happened soon we hunters were doomed.

At that moment Georgia came running out of the cave.

~ In my belt! I yelled to her. ~ Quickly.

I twisted my spear in the wound, causing the dragon to lift its head and bellow in pain.

She ran under the great jaws to my side, snatched the unicorn's horn from my waist, and back underneath the throat of the beast. As it reared up and bent its head underneath itself to get at her, its chest lifted. The vulnerable core of its being was exposed. Georgia drove the unicorn's spike like a sword, into the dragon's breast, deep, deep into its heart. Green blood flowed down the horn, flowed bright emerald. The dragon let out a scream of terrible agony. A ripple went down its ridged back.

~ Come on, cried Georgia. ~ Let's go.

Hass and I withdrew our assegais and ran back.

As we tried to slip away fire suddenly belched from the dragon's nostrils. Its furnace breath burned a swathe through the undergrowth. Long fiery tongues of yellow, red and white licked out, frizzing the leaves, torching twigs. Even as it fell over, crashing on to its side, the hot searing flames spurted forth through the funnel of its mouth. Vines withered in the heat, bushes blazed, tree bark turned to charcoal, leaves to ashes.

~ It's huffing! cried Hass unnecessarily. ~ Get back. Get back.

We three withdrew, scattered, watched from a safer distance.

The beast was not trying to burn us. It was simply letting

its frustration out. If it was a human it would have cried out, or prayed to some god or other, or cursed its enemies. Because it was a dragon it coughed fire. The foliage didn't stay alight for long. Inside the rainforest the plants were too moist and spongy. On its side now, the dragon seemed to be fighting for breath. Its throat rattled.

The dragon let out a mournful cry. It squirmed and thrashed, a creature suffering a deadly hurt. Just as a wounded snake will coil round itself in its agony, tying itself in knots, so the dragon did with its tail, its long reptilian body. It heaved and flopped and spread its wings. Its eyes first grew wide and angry, then closed to despairing slits. Finally, after many minutes its body collapsed on the forest floor. With a groan its head lolled and followed its torso. The tongue came out, long and limp. The eyes finally closed. Its breath ceased to hiss.

~ Take that, you murderer, said Georgia with satisfaction in her voice. ~ My unicorn got its own back, after all.

At that moment the dragon opened one eye.

All zest for fighting had gone out of me.

~ It's still alive! I yelled. ~ Run!

The three of us dashed along a rainforest pathway to the sea. The dragon, wheezing and snorting, lumbered after us. When we reached the water's edge, which was now well inside the rainforest, we splashed on, running as if through a mangrove swamp.

The dragon continued to chase us.

Once in the sea proper, we feared for our lives.

But when the dragon left the trees it suddenly and miraculously took to the air. There was a tremendous flapping of its damaged wings as it rose upwards, one metre, five metres, ten metres from the surface of the lagoon. The effort it put in was nothing short of remarkable. In that moment I felt sorry for the creature. Its desire for life burned like a forge within it. I don't think it had ever flown before, but now its life was draining from it, threatened to be extinguished, it forced its ungainly body off the ground and into the blue. Its wings moved like those of a swan, with such grace and strength, but ripping apart with every flap. Where Hass and I had punctured them, the taut wing-skin tore in the wind.

The dragon rose up and up, higher and higher, leaving a trail of green blood which drained from its wounded heart.

~ It's getting away, said Georgia in despair. ~ I told you it would.

But just when we thought it might do that, its wings folded in mid-flight. The dragon dropped like a stone out of the sky. It hurtled earthwards and came down with a great splash in the sea. There was a brief struggle as it tried to stay afloat, but it had been sorely wounded by Georgia's sword. Clearly its strength had gone. Still thrashing the surface of the water, it sank. The ocean boiled over the terrible beast.

~ Yeeeeahhhhh! I yelled in triumph. ~ Got you!

My elation was shortlived. Only minutes later there was a cracking, grinding sound. A large chunk of the coral reef suddenly gave way. It had been threatening to do so for days now and in its poor state had finally collapsed under the weight and pounding of the Pacific waters, weakened beyond recovery by the typhoon.

There was a gap in the reef.

~ Wave! cried Hass. ~ Run!

The jaw of the island had broken. And having been damaged, more broke away with the sudden rush of floodwater.
Ocean gushed through the breach. It formed a huge white-
green wave that rushed towards us. We turned around and
raced along our path back through the trees. The ocean
washed after us, racing us through the undergrowth. By the
time we reached the camp, where the anxious adults were
calling and searching for us, we were up to our thighs in seawater. Now our camp was part of the lagoon, and the lagoon
covered our camp.

~ Here we are, cried Georgia, her eyes alight with victory.
~ I killed the dragon.

Adults grabbed our arms and we fought our way through
the surge towards the place where the raft was moored. It
was like battling against a tidal flood. There was no time to
tell us off. No time to ask why we boys were covered in indigo
dye. No time to question the incredible Georgia statement, 'I killed the dragon'. Time was precious. We reached
the raft, were dragged on board, and then everyone grabbed
a paddle.

In a short while we were out on the ocean proper.

Grant raised the sail: the hide of the mother Beast.

When we were a long way off we all took a last longing
look back at Krantu Island. It was a strangely moving sight,
very eerie. There was no land to be seen. Just the tops of
trees standing in the water like the spines of a drowned
porcupine. Over this a cloud of birds, hundreds, of many
different types. Some were gliding around in a confused way.
Others were flying out in a desperate bid to cross the ocean.

271

A few remained perched on the tops of the trees, doomed to starvation.

A shiver went through me. Just a short while ago we had been living, playing and working on that island. We had run through a rainforest teeming with life. Now it was gone, below the waves. It was like watching the drowning of an old friend. No one would ever again walk on those forest paths, or beaches, or coral strand.

Krantu Island was gone for ever.

Georgia said in a choked voice, ~ All those poor animals . . .

Hass and I nodded gravely. Some of the birds could fly away to safety, but not all of them – there were many who wouldn't make it. The rainforest had been alive with creatures of all kinds: insects, mammals, reptiles, amphibians, even shore creatures like crabs. Thousands probably. Not to mention the mythical beasts, those that the dragon hadn't killed.

~ The trees, murmured Lorraine. ~ A whole island rainforest – my beautiful flowers . . .

They weren't actually Lorraine's of course, but she'd adopted them all, the magnificent blooms of shoreline and forest.

~ It's time someone took climate change more seriously, Grant was saying to dad. ~ Damn global warming! If Western politicians could see beautiful islands like this disappearing beneath the waves, they'd wake up to what's really important to this planet of ours.

Georgia had killed the dragon. We had helped her, but Georgia was the dragon-killer. It had to be her: no one else could have done it. She was special. She was the unicorn rider. She was the avenger of the unicorn's savage death. Hers was the victory, not ours.

But something had changed between us. Now that the island had been left behind, Georgia seemed more remote: somehow almost out of reach. Out of my reach, certainly. And Hassan's. It would not be long before she would become the distant jewel of a memory. She could never be mine, though I knew she would never forget me. How could she? We had shared so much together. All three of us. But Georgia was the unicorn rider, the dragon-killer. In those acts she had become a great heroine and had put herself beyond the reach of boys like me.

There were two people, I knew, who would always be close to me. Hass and Rambuta. Rambuta was like an uncle to both of us boys now and he would always be in touch. Hass, well, he was my adopted brother and brothers are very important. Brothers go their separate ways when adult life puts them apart, but they are always there for each other. Hass and I would be like that, always pleased to see one another, always ready to help when problems arose, always tightly bound.

And I was beginning to understand dad, too. I hoped it was mutual. He was a man with a cluttered mind, but somewhere in that mind, and in his heart, I was important. I knew now that though he might go dashing off all over the world at a moment's notice, he was aware of my needs and welfare. He loved me, in his dotty way, my dad.

Between them, Rambuta and Grant got us into the shipping lanes, and we were picked up by a passing cargo vessel bound for Singapore. We were taken aboard in a bosun's chair. When the raft was empty the captain of the ship asked dad if he wanted the raft winched up and strapped to the deck. To our surprise, dad said no. We didn't tell the whole story to the captain, of course – just enough to satisfy him.

Later I heard Grant say to dad, ~ The Beast's hide was still fixed to the mast – you let it go.

~ Yes, replied dad, ~ enough's enough. I've no desire to repeat the experiment. Let someone else find the skin. I'll stick to archaeology in future. I know what I'm doing with bits of pot and old weapons.

~ Like the axe of the apostles, I said, making dad grin and leaving Grant looking puzzled.

One starry night dad and I were standing at the rail in the stern of the ship staring at the wake. Since we were alone I decided to try to talk to him about our deadly secret. I think he knew, or was expecting me to come out with it.

~ That scadu we found, I said. ~ The dead one you said not to tell anyone about?

~ Have you talked about it, Max?

~ No, but I want to be sure – it was a scadu, wasn't it?

~ I think so. I'm certain of it. One of the mother Beast's mythical children, yes.

~ Okay, I said. Nothing more.

Dad's voice had been calm, but I knew that inside he must have been in turmoil. He knew how enormous this was, this secret we held between us. He must have been tempted to tell the world, but the risk was tremendous. In doing so he might have become one of the world's greatest scientists, as big as Darwin or Einstein. Or he might have come to be regarded as the world's biggest fool. I think it was the last that he feared most, so he would never divulge our secret himself. That's been left up to me. I don't care what the world thinks of me.

The fact is, that pale delicate creature, that corpse we found in the forest, broken by violence and running with stormwater — it was a man. Or a woman. Either-or. You couldn't tell by looking at it whether it was one or the other. What we were sure of, even without talking about it with each other, was that it was one of the mother Beast's children. All the signs were there, of the recent birth, and other marks too. We had seen enough scada births to know one when we came across it.

So — think of it! — the human was originally a fabulous animal, a mythical creature, a fantastical monster. One of nature's unnaturals. Not like the dog, or the horse, or even the lowliest slug. Some of us must have guessed it, those brainy Greek philosophers, people like that? I mean, we build cities, spaceships, write books, compose music, think up great new inventions like the iPod. Dogs don't do that. Monkeys who look like us and have hands don't do it. Slugs might've done it, if they had dolphins' brains and monkeys' paws, but I think not.

Somehow the first mythical man-woman survived where all other scada were killed. It survived and developed ordinary ways, became capable of remaking itself — the only one of the mother Beast's unique offspring to do so. Maybe we lost uniqueness, then became rare, and finally became common as toads and worms and sparrows, but still kept that sense of being special? Of being only one of one? Maybe that's why we still *feel* so all alone, even amongst our teeming millions?

Knowing I'm a fabulous beast should make me feel special, but it doesn't. It makes me feel like a stranger in my own skin. I wonder about our own animals. How do they see us? As one of them, or as weird creatures?

Yesterday, I caught the ship's cat staring at me very suspiciously . . .

Garry Kilworth was born in York in 1941 but has travelled widely around the globe ever since, being fascinated by the folklore, myths and legends of the places he has visited. He has been attracted to various forms of fantasy and supernatural writing but has more recently written a number of acclaimed and much-loved stories for children. Garry has been twice short-listed for the Carnegie medal. For more information visit www.garry-kilworth.com

Find out more about Garry and other Atom authors at
www.atombooks.co.uk